RANDOM STORIES

D1531089

for John Jermain Slocum

who first read many of these stories

R A N D O M

STORIES

by James Laughlin

Foreword by Octavio Paz

MOYER BELL LIMITED

MOUNT KISCO, NEW YORK & LONDON

Published by Moyer Bell Limited

The stories were originally published as follows: "Melody With Fugue", *Story*,
October, 1934; "The River", *New Directions Pamphlet*, #3, 1938; "Forty Days and
Forty Nights", *Harvard Advocate*, April, 1933; "Shadows of the Evening", *Harvard
Advocate*, May, 1938; "What the Butler Heard", *Fantasy*, #3, 1939; "Night Winds
Rising", *Harkness Hoot*, February, 1934; "A Natural History", *Harvard Advocate*,
September 1935; "Salle d'étude", *Choate Literary Magazine*, 1932 and *The Atlantic
Monthly*; "Partial Eclipse", *Story*, October, 1936; "Looking Across at the Sil-
vretta", *Harvard Advocate*, March, 1936; "A Visit", *William Carlos Williams News-
letter*, Spring, 1978; "This Is My Blood", *Story*, May-June, 1939. Some of these
stories appeared in a limited edition published by the Yolla Bolly Press, entitled
This Is My Blood, 1989. "A Visit" was first published in the William Carlos
Williams Newsletter 4, No. 1 (Spring, 1978), and is here reprinted from
WILLIAM CARLOS WILLIAMS AND JAMES LAUGHLIN, SELECTED LET-
TERS, edited by Hugh Witemeyer, with the permission of the publisher, W. W.
Norton & Company, Inc. Copyright © 1989 by James Laughlin. Copyright ©
1989 by the Estate of William Carlos Williams.

First Edition

**LIBRARY OF CONGRESS
CATALOGING-IN-PUBLICATION DATA**

Laughlin, James, 1914-
[Short stories. Selections]
Random stories / James Laughlin : introduction by Octavio Paz.—
1st ed.
p. cm.
Contents: The river—Melody with fugue—Forty days and forty nights—
Shadows of the evening—What the butler heard—Night winds rising—A
natural history—Salle d'étude—Partial eclipse—Looking across at the
Silvretta—A visit—This is my blood.
ISBN 1-55921-029-X (cloth)
I. Title
PS3523.A8245R37 1990
813'.54—dc20   90-6297
                                                                CIP

Printed in the United States of America
Distributed by Rizzoli

CONTENTS

Skis and a Typewriter

W hen I first met James Laughlin over thirty years ago in New York, he was already well known to me. New Directions books had begun to arrive in Mexico City around 1940 at the Misrachi Bookshop, the only place in the city where one could find the latest literary works in English. A small group of us—apprentice writers and enthusiasts of foreign literature—used to haunt the stacks at the Misrachi. We were particularly fascinated by the New Directions annuals: for us, each volume was a map, not of discovered and colonized lands, but of the unknown territories that were being explored (or invented) by the new writers. Rather than limiting themselves to the United States, the New Directions anthologies were closely following the movements and individual writers that were appearing in the four corners of the earth.

Our fascination with New Directions was understandable: We felt hemmed-in by Mexico, a country that at times has been suffocated by the richness of its traditions and the complexities of its past. We were cut off from the world not only by the mountains and volcanoes that surrounded us, but also by the invisible wall of the centuries—a wall constructed by the passivity of those within and the indifference of those outside. To read the New Directions publications was to open a window and to glimpse a landscape that both attracted and terrified us: modern literature.

A few years later I too became an object of Laughlin's international curiosity. One auspicious day I received a letter from a young professor and critic named Lloyd Mallan who was interested in Latin American writing. Along with his letter, asking for information about the state of Mexican poetry and particularly for news of the young poets, Mallan sent a few translations of my own poems. Thus began a feverish correspondence that resulted in a small project: The enthusiastic Mallan would make a selection of five Mexican poets, translate the poems, write an introduction and send the manuscript to Laughlin. We all anxiously waited—and not without fear—for the verdict from that remote and severe reader. Laughlin read the manuscript and, with some hesitation (was this really modern poetry?) decided to publish it under the title "A Little Anthology of Mexican Poetry" (*New Directions #9*, 1947). Some years later another generous friend, Muriel Rukeyser, also became interested in my poems. She translated some of them, published them in various magazines, and, predictably, ended up proposing a small book to New Directions, which once again, was accepted.

The preparation of that book put me in correspondence with James. In 1957 or 1958—I don't recall the exact date—I took advantage of a short stay in New York to phone him and set up a meeting. The next day we met at his offices in the Village. Austerity, little furniture, but many books. In every room were tall metal filing cabinets—were they grey or green?—which no doubt guarded the manuscripts and letters of Pound, Williams, Neruda, Michaux and so many others. A secretary took me to his office; the door opened and there, rising from a table filled with papers and books, was this tall athletic man—later I found out he was an ardent skier. An open face, close-cropped hair, wide forehead, energetic chin, questioning eyes, large hands, slow gestures, and, above all, a simple courtliness, made of both cordiality and reserve.

Accustomed to the circumlocutions of Mexicans, the effusiveness and abruptness of the Spanish, and to the rituals of *politesse française*, Laughlin's affable, open manner was, for me, especially delightful. The meeting was quickly followed, a few days later, by an invitation to eat at a little Italian restaurant nearby. There, warmed by a bottle of Chianti, we discovered that we had friends in common and shared certain enthusiasms and dislikes. Among them were an affinity with India, the poetry of Apollinaire and the Greek Anthology. He told me he had been a student of Dudley Fitts, whom I had admired for his transformations of the ancient epigrams of Meleager and Paulus Silentarius into living poems. Saying goodbye to Laughlin that night, I told him that meeting an editor I had discovered a poet. We've been friends ever since.

James often talks about poetry but never or rarely about his own. The modesty of the lover who keeps secret the name of his beloved. For poetry has been his great passion; the other has been skiing. His life has been divided between poems—the ones he writes and the ones he publishes—and the figures that skis trace in the snow. Passions that are quite different and yet connected: They are neither lucrative, nor do they bring power. Neither authority nor gain. Rather they are the opposite: They are risky aesthetic games, arts that require nimbleness and whose great danger is a fall. Laughlin, the skier, has written poems since his youth. He writes them like one who glides down a hill between tall trees.

His greatest affection has been and is for Ezra Pound and William Carlos Williams. Two antennas of poetry: one devoted to recapturing the international tradition, the other to inventing the American tradition. But neither of these two appear in his poems. James assimilated his lessons so deeply and completely that, rather than stifling him, they allowed him to find himself. His poetic voice is unmistakable.

His short poems offer the eyes a series of couplets, a luminous typographical format in harmony with his syntactical structure: concision and clarity, humor and melancholy. James laughs at the world and at himself, but ends by accepting, with a shrug more ironical than resigned, the universal madness and his own. He is closer to Epicurus than to Calvino, because of his Protestant background. A poetry that is intelligent, sensitive, and, in a word, civilized. An urbane poetry like the Greek epigrams, immersed in our everyday passions and deceptions, in the comedy and ridiculous tragedy of our lives. Despite his literary allusions and his deliberate use of various techniques from the world's poetic traditions, Laughlin's best poems do *not* make us think of Martial or the Provençal poets. They are strangely modern and—I'm tempted to say—might have been written by that great melancholic master who never wrote a word: Buster Keaton. Not a literary similarity: a spiritual kinship.

The poet Laughlin has, in recent years, also been revealed to be a notable critic and chronicler of modern North American poetry. His books of essays combine critical insight and a lively memory and add to these the veracity of the portraitist. They are simultaneously literary studies and memoirs that help us to understand both the works and their authors. Written in a fluid and precise language, they are free of the pedantic academic jargon that is the verbal disease of our times. A prose that is frequently ironic but not impious: Laughlin knows his heroes, laughs a little at their frailties, ends by forgiving them. The admiration he feels toward Pound is entirely lucid: He has not closed his eyes to the terrible mistakes of the man and the lapses and the arbitrariness of the poet. In his love inspired by the work and the figure of Williams there is also a tender irony toward the doctor's puerilities. It is not enough to end with this aspect of Laughlin's work: His contribution has been essential, as the witness to an era and as a critical reflection of some of its greatest protagonists. His essays are indispensible for those who wish to know the inside story of the fertile and powerful movements of North American poetry in this century.

Laughlin's literary essays depend on psychological acumen and the art of the chronicler. Qualities that are also apparent in the narrative writer. It is natural to collect in one volume both his fictional and non-fictional stories. The texts that form *Random Stories* were written in his youth, with the exception of "A Visit" (1978), and published in magazines at the time. All of them retain their initial freshness and power. The primary virtue of these stories is, as in the case of his poems and essays, their sobriety. The story may be tragic but the language is never pathetic; Laughlin does not indulge in the rhetoric of tears nor in the pirouettes of a clown. Economy and concision; irony and, once again, its complement: the understanding of the other, the only way one can understand oneself. Sobriety but also a naturalness: His prose unwinds without forcing, it runs like water, and like water is transparent: We can see the bottom.

Some of the stories that Laughlin tells us move us, others make us laugh (almost always with a sad smile) but all of them entertain, in the best sense of the word: They awake our interest and hold us until the end. At times the narration is linear, at others it employs the methods of modern poetry: juxtaposition and the simultaneity of times and situations. Yet whatever his subject or technique, all of the stories have one note in common: human sympathy. It is the center, the nucleus of Laughlin's poetic and ethical vision. Sympathy was the supreme virtue for the Stoics: The world was, for them, a totality held together by the universal flow of friendship. Its other name—its Christian and modern name—is brotherhood.

Epicurus corrected—or more exactly, completed—by Seneca. Between these two extremes is the poetry and prose of James Laughlin: They are not separate worlds, they are in constant communication. His work is an example, not only of the conjunction, but of the cohabitation of contraries. Writing this phrase I suddenly thought of a circle. Or more precisely: I saw a circle. It is a perfect geometric form, an emblem of the reconciliation of opposites and of contradictions. Laughlin's work can be represented as a circle around a fixed point: poetry. A form that is no different than the one drawn by skis on the snow.

Octavio Paz
Mexico City, 21 August 1990

(trans. Eliot Weinberger)

Some Fictive Autobiography

It nearly broke my father's heart when I didn't go to Princeton. Like so many in Pittsburgh ours was a Princeton family. My grandfather had been a trustee and gave the University a dormitory, Laughlin Hall—it's still there—one of those pseudo-Gothic creations which symbolized learning. He also gave the farmlands east of campus to which the University has now expanded, happily not in the old architectural style.

As soon as my brother and I were able to behave ourselves we were taken, along with many cousins, to Princeton class reunions in June. We loved the parades with the college band going on before. We were given little straw boaters with my father's class numerals, 1900, or "oughty-ought" as that year was called, on the hatbands and orange and black pennants to wave. Usually we were housed at the Nassau Inn where there was the attraction of an outdoor swimming pool. Some years there was a tiger in the parade, not a real tiger, of course, but a student cavorting in a tiger skin.

My brother was five years older than I and most of the time quite horrid to "the spoiled brat." But he did not disappoint father. He sailed through Princeton, making Tiger Inn, one of the most important clubs, and he was second All-American fullback on the soccer team. There was only one blot on his record; he wrote his senior paper on Proust, a degenerate, no-no author in Pittsburgh.

It was Harvard for me, not Princeton. No question about that once I had come under the spell of a great master at Choate. That was Dudley Fitts, a poet and translator of the classics, who later went on to teach at Andover. Fitts's courses were in the English department, but in Sixth Form Honors there was a bit of everything from the *Oresteia* and Aristotle's *Poetics* through Chaucer in the original to the French Symbolists and Eliot. Fitts made it clear that Harvard was the only place for someone with pretensions to literature. And Carey Briggs, whom I had in Fifth Form, had extolled the wonders of the stacks in Widener Library. "Hup" Arnold, my Latin master, told us stories about the legendary E. K. Rand, the Virgil scholar. Finally, there was the Boston Symphony and skiing in New Hampshire and Vermont.

My father took Harvard bravely though I know it wrenched him. He had indulged me all my life and he didn't stop then. But the day he drove me up to Cambridge to help me get settled he was quiet and looked downcast. He bought some furniture for the ugly rooms in Weld Hall in Harvard Yard which had been assigned to Larry Angel, my classmate from Choate with whom I was rooming, and myself. He paid my term bill at Lehmann Hall. He even took me in to Boston to his own tailor, the venerable Mr. Lucas, to have me measured for some proper Harvard garb, tweed jackets and charcoal gray flannels. (White shoes, which were then the fashion, were too much for him. If I had to have white shoes I could get those for myself in Harvard Square.)

Father's only mistake was one which someone from Pittsburgh and Princeton could not have foreseen. He invited the two young men in the next suite for supper. They were polite but extremely cool. They were two boys who had been to Groton, swells from old New York families, Anthony Bliss and Peter Jay. Between Choate and Groton, between the Middle

West and old New York, there was an uncrossable social barrier at Harvard in those days. Larry Angel and I tried to be friendly with our neighbors, but there was no response. They never invited us into their rooms or greeted us with more than a nod in the hall. It was awkward because we shared a shower. As it worked out, we took our showers in the morning and they theirs in the evening. The dormitories in Harvard Yard are used only by freshmen. Sophomores go into one of the houses (mine was Eliot House) or to digs if they are destined to join a club. Our chummy neighbors moved on, I think, to the "Porc," the Porcellian Club, the apogee of those circles. Apart from the amenities, the "Porc" is good insurance. It is said that if a member of the "Porc" is too stupid to get a job one will be found for him by an older member of the club. Bliss, let me report, went on to a life of great distinction, first as a lawyer and then as an executive and patron of the Metropolitan Opera. I hope Jay did as well; I haven't kept track of him. Aristotle writes somewhere about the "natural pride of man"; it depends, I guess, what you do with it. I'm sure that Harvard is more friendly now. The ostracism didn't bother me much because I soon made friends with other pariahs and later in literary circles.

In a recent article in *The Harvard Magazine*, Dean Henry Rosovsky states that "today the average size of [Harvard] classes is smaller than it was twenty years ago" and that "90 percent of our senior faculty teach at least one undergraduate course a year." To be sure, I was in college fifty not twenty years ago and the enlargement of Harvard took place between those two points. What the Dean doesn't point out, I think, is that there is a difference between teaching a course and a star professor's readiness to spend some time with a student. How different it was in the smaller Harvard of my day. I was on an almost family basis with some professors and could call on others if I gave them warning. It was a special and so rewarding kind of education, such as I had had from Ezra Pound the year I studied with him in Rapallo. Such as I would later have from

Kenneth Rexroth when I stayed with him on Potrero Hill in San Francisco in the 1940s, and from Tom Merton on my visits to him at his Trappist monastery in Kentucky. There is no substitute for an intimate relationship with a learned mentor.

Perhaps, before I confuse the reader more, I should explain that I am hopelessly anachronistic. Webster says that I practice "chronological misplacing of persons, events, objects or customs in regard to each other." I'm sure of only three dates: 1066, 1776, and 1914, the year I was born. I entered Harvard in 1933, but soon after that I began to move around. The records from University Hall are not too clear. I may have taken as many as three leaves of absence; the first to study with Pound in Rapallo, another the card says "for further language study abroad," though it might better have read "to study at the Hannes Schneider Ski School in St. Anton-am-Arlberg" (well, I did learn some Tyroler Deutsch there), and the last, who knows, perhaps they stopped trying to keep track of me. I did finally get a diploma in 1939. Harvard was easygoing in those days, and the Dean indulgent. "Just let me know a few months ahead if you want to come back." I wish I could be more synchronic, like Pound, rather than anachronistic. It would be so much more distinguished. In the *Cantos* we find Odysseus, the Chinese emperors, John Adams, and Uncle Willie Yeats all in the same "time warp." I remember many events, most of them good ones, but seem unable to keep them in sequence.

E. K. Rand was on the Harvard faculty when I was there, and one of the eminent Latinists of his day. *The Magical Art of Virgil* was his most admired book but he wrote on other Latin authors as well. The Rands lived in a fine old 19th-century house on one of the side streets that lead off Brattle Street. I suppose I was invited there for tea or dinner, usually with a couple of other students, a dozen times. Rand's discourse was superb, but he wanted us to talk, too, and knew how to draw us out. Mrs. Rand was dutifully tacit, beaming when E. K. was in particularly good form. One of my pleasures was looking through his old editions of the classics, which he encouraged as long as I got the jam off my fingers and didn't pull the books off the shelves by their tops. He had Aldines and Elzevirs and Plantins and Didots among his treasures. I was excited by the grace of those printings, the immense amount of labor on hand presses that had gone into them. He showed me how the ligatures of early Greek italic types derived from the scripts of the monastery copyists. And explained how multiple copies were made in the monasteries before the days of printing; a lector would read from one manuscript and a dozen monks would copy down what they heard. This accounted for the variations which have kept textual scholars busy over the centuries. I shall never have a collection like Rand's, but the books I do have are a tribute to his taste and knowledge.

I had read some Virgil with Rand before I went to study with Pound. With Rand's encouragement I had done a free-verse translation of the Fourth Eclogue, which I sent out as a Christmas card. This is the poem that Christian commentators later interpreted as a prophecy of the birth of Christ.

> The great circle of the centuries begins again . . .
> A new line is sent down to us from the skies
> And thou, Lucina, must smile
> Smile for the birth of the boy, the blessed boy
> For whom they will beat their swords into ploughshares
> For whom the golden race will rise, the whole world
>   new . . .
> For thee, little boy, will the earth pour forth gifts
> All untilled, give thee gifts . . .

On my return to Harvard from Rapallo I had to tread warily with Rand because Pound had stuffed me with heresies. Pound thought Virgil was a pompous blowhard. His men were Catullus and especially Propertius. In fact, Pound imagined that he was a revenant of Propertius as we know from his suite, *Homage to Sextus Propertius* of 1918-1919. Therein he took Propertius as his *persona* and rewrote him according to his own interests. Propertius became a twentieth-century figure who, Pound told me, who had he "rip-vanwinkled today would *not* be an editor of the *New Republic*." Pound made fun of Augustus (i.e., the British imperial establishment) and mixed classical allusions with satiric anachronisms, all written in a flowing free verse which scandalized academic classicists. The poem has a tone of supreme irony. Its method is dissonance and dislocation of sequence. Everything boring is omitted. It's an attack on the "Babu" translatorese of the scholars: it is glorious fun. Such lines as:

> *the devirginated young ladies*
> *and if she plays with me with her shirt off, we shall construct many*
> *Iliads . . .*
> *It is noble to die of love, and honorable to remain uncuckolded for*
> *a season.*
> *You are a very early inspector of mistresses.*
> *Zeus' clever rapes in the old days*
> *Of all these young women / not one has enquired the cause of the*
> *world . . .*

Rand was a strict scholar. Pound's recreation of Propertius was hardly his dish. So in doing my paper on the rescription I had to be two-faced. I began with a list of Pound's literal "boners" in the text, most of which were intentional, for irony, then edged into the virtues of his interpretation and the beauty of the English lines. Rand had the humor to enjoy the charade. His comment on my paper was "A most original evaluation. But a little more care with your syntax, please." And below that "Cur tua præscripto sevecta est pagina gyro?" (Why has your page swerved from the course prescribed for it?)

Ted Spencer was my favorite professor at Harvard. He was also the favorite of the Radcliffe students, including my wife Ann, who was his student ten years later; she raved about his manly charm. He was tall, blond, and very handsome, a self-deprecating aristocrat. He had been to varsity in England; there was a pleasant tinge of "U" in his accent. A knight from the field of Agincourt but his weapon was humor. The seminar that I took with him in Joyce, Mann, and Proust was enthralling. He never really expected us to read those long texts. Scene after scene we received all the high spots and best passages in his witty and elegant utterance. Ted had written his first books on Shakespeare, which led to his job at Harvard; then he turned to the moderns. His interest in me clearly came from what I could tell him about Pound. Soon he was inviting me to play tennis and to meals at his house. Finding that his wife was much concerned about the state of the world, I converted her—much to Ted's amusement—to Pound's doctrine of Social Credit. She even joined the Boston Social Credit party, which was headed by an equally high-minded lady on Beacon Hill, Mrs. E. Sohier Welch. There were tea parties of intense indignation in a Jamesian setting. But I was one of very few converts. Too many of Mrs. Welch's friends were the wives of plutocrats. It was wind in a bucket. Boston was firmly in the grip of bankers and lawyers whose management of the economy was acknowledged to be perfect. I was a bit more militant; one day I was ejected from the Boston Mass Transit for distributing handbills to the downtrodden.

When Pound returned from Italy to the States in 1939 he headed first for Boston. He had been corresponding about monetary crime with Congressman George Holden Tinkham with whom he wanted to consult on strategy for ridding the country of usurious banks. Ezra had great hopes for the legendary Tinkham, a Brahmin who once while campaigning had made headlines by riding his horse into a bar in Roxbury. Such a man obviously had a flair to publicize Social Credit to the electorate.

When I told Spencer that Pound was coming to Boston, Ted invited him to be his house guest. The week of Pound's visit in

Oxford Street was certainly the most colorful that the Spencer household ever experienced. Wyndham Lewis had christened Ezra the "Pantechnikon" for his entrepreneurial energy. Joyce described him as a "bundle of unpredictable electricity." Add Pound's ever-darting lively eyes and his foxy charm. Harry Levin, in his book *Memories of the Moderns*, recalls Ezra's visit in Cambridge. Harry was then Ted's student and was delegated to help Pound meet some Harvard professors.

> Delighted as I was by this prospect of casual association, it ended by baffling us all. Politely but shortly and wearily, he would reply to my literary and aesthetic questions. What he really wanted to talk about, it became clear, was Social Credit and the corporate state. It was as if Dr. Johnson had insisted that Boswell limit their conversations to the stamp tax. Pound expressed particular eagerness for an evening's discussion with some of Harvard's foremost economists. Never had Ted or I, who made the arrangements, been more keenly embarrassed by a nonmeeting of minds. It may be that this anticlimax prepared Pound for the greater one he was next to experience as a self-appointed lobbyist in Washington, and consequently for his return to wartime Italy, where he would soon be caught up in his tragic errors.

There was another regrettable event, at least for Ted. Ted fancied his artistry on the tennis court, but Ezra trounced him in doubles. Ezra's game was based on force not speed. He would position himself at half-court, scowling fiercely at his opponents, and wait to unleash a powerful full-body-pivot forehand which was quite unreturnable.

My friendship with Spencer continued well past Harvard days. Eventually, I published a book of his small poems, *The Paradox in the Circle*. Delmore Schwartz, who could be affectionately malicious about his friends, described the work as "tasty Yeatsies," but I admired their succinctness.

A CIRCLE

Adam and Eve like us
Stood up to watch the sun;
Like us, Eve and Adam
Lay down under the moon.

Like Adam and Eve we ask
Our questions of the sun;
And lie, like Eve and Adam,
Unanswered under the moon.

Later Ted persuaded the Harvard Library to purchase from Joyce's agreeable brother Stanislas, the manuscript of James Jhesus's (Pound's name for him) *Stephen Hero*, the first version of *A Portrait of the Artist as a Young Man*, and insisted that New Directions should be the publisher of it. An important book; I designed the cover myself and have always been proud of it: lines of Joyce's handwriting superimposed on the shape of a very green Erin.

One of the most endearing Harvard professors was "Matty" Matthiessen who did so much to contemporize our thinking about American literature. His seminal books were *American Renaissance* (1941) and *Henry James: The Major Phase* (1944). I never took a class with him, but he became a friend through my acquaintance with Ted Spencer. A kindly, quiet, deliberative man with a wit that he didn't push, all his students adored him because he gave them so much intuitive support. Perhaps his empathy was so great because he had a problem in his life which was insoluble in those days. Nobody came out of their closets then.

Although Pound wrote and talked about Henry James, it was "Matty" who started me reading James systematically. It's hard to believe today but in the thirties and forties James was little read. There were the similar cases of great writers who had dropped out of fashion after their deaths. Scribners had not kept Scott Fitzgerald in print. For a few years I was able to lease the rights to *The Great Gatsby* from them for my "New Classics" series. When Fitzgerald's literary executor Edmund Wilson put together the *Crack-Up* collection it was turned down by all the big New York publishers. It fell to me in 1945 and quickly went through several printings. There was a similar situation with E. M. Forster. When I began doing revivals only *A Passage to India*, a Harcourt Brace book, was in print. Alfred Knopf had been his original and regular publisher. There was gossip that Alfred had lost interest because Forster had forgotten a lunch date in London. Goodness knows, good old Alfred, my idol in publishing and later a close friend, was touchy, offended by and offending to many people, but I think this anecdote is apocryphal. Be that as it may, I was able to lease *The Longest Journey* and *A Room with a View* for a number of years. These leases were cancelled, of course, when the original publishers took note of the sales figures on the New Directions royalty reports. Other revivals that came my way were Evelyn Waugh's *A Handful of Dust* and Céline's two great classics *Death on the Installment Plan* and *Journey to the End of the Night*, the two Célines both happily still on our list in revised translations.

But it was Matthiessen who put me on the road of revivals, abetted by Malcolm Cowley, one of the poets in our "Poets of the Year" series. In 1944 Matthiessen edited for New Directions a collection of James's *Stories of Writers & Artists*, which quickly found its way into college classrooms all over the country. Matty was somewhat "left," but he never tried to put me on that track. He understood that all I needed to save the world was Social Credit. His friend for years had been a distinguished painter with whom he shared a vacation house in Maine. Not so long after his friend's death he went into a deep depression and shortly after committed suicide. The note that he left was, I'm sure, intended for the press: "As a Christian and a socialist believing in international peace, I find myself terribly oppressed by the present tensions." Certainly that was the only part of the sad story that he wanted to record. More of it, in fictional form, may be found in May Sarton's novel *Faithful Are the Wounds*. A lovable man, a brilliant writer, a great teacher. We know that the gods play cruel games.

I can't recall that I ever encountered a woman professor on the Harvard faculty and only one Jew. Harvard and Radcliffe were separate then, each with its own campus. Harvard professors repeated their lectures over at Radcliffe. There was no lack of social contact with the "Cliffies"—for that I can vouch—but the attitude in the clubs around Mt. Auburn Street was that "Cliffies" were a rung below the society girls of Beacon Hill and the North Shore. Another caste system. Nobody had heard of feminism then. Women had the vote; what more did they want? Harvard and Radcliffe classes were consolidated in 1943. Then it became apparent that the "Cliffies" were more serious students, and frequently smarter, than most of the Harvard boys.

Some of my best faculty friends were only instructors, men who never finished their dissertations to get on the tenure track or who simply didn't want to get involved in the politics of academia. There was Ted Morison, the great friend of Robert Frost, who taught composition, though we would now call it "creative writing." Most of the stories in this collection which I first published in *The Advocate* passed under his eye and were greatly improved by his caustic exhortations to concision. "You're not Proust," he noted on one of them, "keep your sentences down to five lines at most." And: "One hanging clause per sentence is enough." And on one which I thought was a masterpiece: "Much too long . . . far too much detail . . . too much walking from room to room . . . reduce by 15 pages and you may have a living scene."

Harry Levin, over the years the closest of my Harvard faculty friends, was still a non-teaching junior Fellow when I was in college. Harry could "get up" an author in a few weeks. When I was preparing for New Directions the reissue of William Carlos Williams's *wanderjahr* novel *A Voyage to Pagany*, I casually asked Harry if he would care to do a foreword for the book, although he was not a Williams specialist. What came to me in six weeks was not a foreword but a full-scale introduction covering every aspect of Williams's work. This piece is now in Harry's *Memories of the Moderns*, published in 1988, which began with a ten-page letter dedicated to my efforts at New Directions. The letter is anything but a puff from a friend. Speaking of my publishing Stein and Cocteau, Harry asked: "Were you not constructing, so to speak, an old actors' home?" And of Hermann Hesse's *Siddhartha*, the biggest seller New Directions ever had: "Hesse's mystical vogue must have done wonders for your treasury." (It did; and it was Henry Miller who recommended the book to me.) The letter is important because it is a concise history of Modernism, covering the major figures and touching incidentally on seventeen whom New Directions had published. "In spite of its vanguard title," Harry wrote,

> New Directions has been primarily engaged in fighting rearguard action. I don't mean to question the things you stood for or your wholehearted commitment to them, but simply to note that they were receding, temporarily superseded or sea-changed. . . . What was innovation for the precursors has become convention for the aftercomers. The ironic fate that wafted the books of the *avant-garde* from Bohemia to Academe has installed them within the curriculum, where they are imitated as well as explicated.

Harry was so right. New Directions only became profitable when professors began to assign the books of Pound, Williams, and others to their classes. And perhaps no single book was more influential in bringing Joyce into respectable classrooms than Harry's pioneering study of his work which appeared in my "Makers of Modern Literature Series" in 1941.

I must have begun to "heel" *The Harvard Advocate* toward the end of my freshman year. That meant doing all kinds of dirty work connected with getting out the magazine and running for coffee for the higher echelons. The *Advocate* office was then located in a squalid little frame house that somehow had gotten stranded in a courtyard back of Claverly Hall on Mt. Auburn Street. Later, through the generosity of Frank Vanderlip and the *Advocate's* graduate trustees, wealthy men who had fond memories of literary parties, it was moved to spacious quarters over the Dunster House Bookshop opposite the *Lampoon* building. By mischance I contributed to the interior decoration of the new premises. For the opening party someone had thought it would be amusing to spike the punchbowl. As the party progressed, I became very contentious and, espying a carton of ink bottles, began smashing them against the walls, hurling them at my tormentors and other members of the *Advocate* staff who resented my arrogance. It was a costly lesson in temperance. And dear little Professor Cross, the Russian historian, never again attended an *Advocate* party.

James Agee was the president of *The Advocate* during my freshman year. He stood head and shoulders above the rest of us. He was writing and publishing the poems of *Permit Me Voyage*, which would soon win the Yale Younger Poets prize. In whatever he did he was already a mature writer. We could sense the greatness coming that would be embodied in *The Morning Watch*; and in his book about the Southern sharecroppers, *Let Us Now Praise Famous Men*, one of the classics of the century; and in his film criticism which raised writing on film to a new level. I published a section of *Let Us Now Praise Famous Men*, with the Walker Evans photographs, in the *New Directions* 1940 annual. There had not been social writing of that kind before.

Jim loved his likker—it may have helped kill him in the end, though the strain of working for *Life* certainly contributed—and he didn't discourage some strenuous drinking parties (male only) in the *Advocate* hovel. The problem was that Prohibition was still on. What the bootleggers provided was rotten stuff. Sickening hangovers. Once we drank something that put us over the edge. We roared out into Harvard Square and in some form of protest not clearly defined, laid down our bodies across the streetcar tracks. "No paseran!" shouted Frankie Sweetser, a man of considerable bulk. We had half a dozen trolleys backed up before the Cambridge cops arrived, bored as usual by more Harvard nonsense. They sent for "Colonel" Apted, head of the Harvard security force. A parley ensued. Because we were trespassing on city property we should have been taken to the lockup. But the Colonel's view that "the young gentlemen have only been a bit intemperate and will be severely dealt with by the college, probably expelled" prevailed. He conveyed us to the Harvard Infirmary, had the nurse lock the doors . . . and the Dean's office never heard about it. Dear old Colonel Apted. I readily forgave him for the many tickets he had put on my car over the years for parking infractions in the precincts of the university.

Another brush with the law, some years later, had also to do with *The Advocate*. The previous summer, John Slocum, a friend from old days at a summer camp in the Adirondacks and then president of the magazine, had joined me for a week's visit with Pound in Europe. Ezra took a great shine to John. He saw him as a possible recruit for his "network," a band of young literary Myrmidons all over the world with whom he corresponded, inciting them to spread his economic doctrines. *The Advocate*, reasoned Pound, would give him a foothold in Boston. We told him that it published only students and had a minuscule circulation. But in earlier days it had published Eliot and Cummings and so there was a "base." He would write for us and urge his friends to do so. *The Advocate* could become another *Dial* or *Little Review*. He would make it a "vortex."

Pound sent us his Canto XXXVIII, a lively one which made quite a stir:

> "An' that year Metevsky [Sir Basil Zaharoff] went over to
>   America del Sud
> (and the Pope's manners were so like Mr. Joyce's,
> got that way in the Vatican, weren't like that before)
> Marconi knelt in the ancient manner
>   like Johnny Walker sayin' his prayers.
> His Holiness expressed a polite curiosity
>   as to how His Excellency had chased those
> electric shakes through the a'mosphere. . . ."

Next came a piece from Pound's old friend William Carlos Williams, "Advice to a Young Writer":

> I'd go so far as to say that everything a man can be taught in his youth has only this value, that unless he is a man it will kill him. Whatever he sees, whatever is brilliant to him, closest, most significant, no matter what anyone else says about it, that is the thing he's got to work with till he disproves it or makes it into a satisfying whole. And for this, there is an ocean of time.

This proved to be one of the themes which Williams elaborated in the book he wrote for his two sons when they were setting out to college, *The Embodiment of Knowledge*, which we found among his papers and published posthumously in 1974. His ideas were quite a contrast with "The Problem of Education," which Ezra extracted for us from Eliot:

> But I am certain that the theological background—however far back it may be is the only one that can provide the idea of order and unity needed for education. And I believe that if education is not rearranged by people with some definite social philosophy and some notion of the true vocation of man, the only education to be had will be in seminaries and colleges run by Jesuits.

There is no evidence that Eliot and Williams ever agreed about anything except in their affection for Pound. They were poles apart. The publication of *The Waste Land* and its instant success was a kick in the stomach for Williams, who was beginning to formulate his theories of a strictly American poetry, an "American idiom," of our language as it is spoken. Eliot, he felt, was a traitor to his American origin, contaminated by European traditions. In 1939 Williams wrote me: "I'm glad you like his verse, but I'm warning you, the only reason it doesn't smell is that it's synthetic. Maybe I'm wrong, but I distrust that bastard more than any writer I know in the world today. He can write, granted, but it's like walking into a church to me." Apparently, similar sentiments were reported to Russell Square; Faber & Faber did not publish Williams in England, and it took some fifteen years to find a publisher who would risk the ecclesiastical wrath. Pound's ideas on education were more vitriolic; these are from "Ignite! Ignite!," which also appeared in *The Advocate*:

> There is, if not a time-spirit, at any rate a TIME-FOETOR that reeks through the whole of an infected period, stinking from each prominent vent-hole. No man who lived in power through the Harding-to-Hoover epoch smirking and unprotesting, is fit to instruct the next generation. . . . The college presidents of America dare not read either HOW TO READ or my ABC OF ECONOMICS. The cretinism of their era has left them no shred of decency.

Ezra had no use for what he called the "beaneries." They enshrined too many authors whom he considered second-rate, and most of the professors of economics were stooges for the banking system. Nicholas Murray Butler of Columbia was the archfiend. As Pound's contributions became more polemical the other *Advocate* editors cooled on him.

The bubble really burst when Henry Miller gave us a delicious burlesque called "Glittering Pie." Apart from his other gifts Henry was a wonderful comic writer. His motto was "always merry and bright." Through it all—years of constant poverty, censorship, and critical neglect—he was "merry and bright." "Glittering Pie" is in the form of a letter to his pal Alfie Perles (the Mr. Corles of Pound's Canto XXXV) in Paris, in which he satirized the culture of California where he was then living:

At the burlesk Sunday afternoon I heard Gypsy Rose Lee sing "Give Me a Lei." She had a Hawaiian lei in her hand and she was telling how it felt to get a good lei, how even her mother would be grateful for a lei once in a while. She said she'd take a lei on the piano, or on the floor. An old-fashioned lei, too, if needs be. The funny part of it was the house was almost empty. After the first half-hour everyone gets up nonchalantly and moves down front to the good seats. The strippers talk to their customers as they do their stunt. The *coup de grace* comes when, after having divested themselves of every stitch of clothing, there is left only a spangled girdle with a fig leaf dangling in front—sometimes a little monkey beard which is quite ravishing. As they draw towards the wings they stick their bottoms out and slip the girdle off. Sometimes they darken the stage and give a belly dance in radium paint. It's good to see the belly button glowing like a glow worm, or like a bright half-dollar. It's better still to see them [eleven words deleted by the cautious *Advocate* editors]. Then there is the loudspeaker into which some idiotic jake roars: "Give the little ladies a hand please." Or else—"Now ladies and gentlemen, we are going to present to you that most charming personality fresh from Hollywood—Miss Chlorine Duval of the Casino de Paris." Said Chlorine Duval is generally streamlined, with the face of an angel and a thin squeaky voice that barely carries across the footlights. When she opens her trap you see that she is a halfwit; when she dances you see that she is a nymphomaniac; when you go to bed with her you see that she is syphilitic.

By present standards that is pretty tame stuff; it might even run in *The Atlantic*. But in 1935 it was too much for Boston. In the Square *The Advocate* was selling as it never had before. Then we were raided by the Cambridge constabulary who carried off all our copies. Next day a young district attorney, who was running for re-election, went on the radio to denounce sex and sin at Harvard. There followed such headlines in the Boston papers as DECADENCE AT HARVARD and SEX IN MT. AUBURN STREET. University Hall was blessedly tranquil as ever; "It is not our policy to supervise or censor student publications," the Dean told the reporters. In the end the district attorney was pacified with two tickets on the 50-yard line for the Yale game and there was no indictment. But *The Advocate's* graduate trustees were upset and requested that there be no more outside contributions.

I had my own little part in the general decadence with a story called "A Natural History." It was a naturalistic account, colloquially styled, about a night party on a Florida beach, of a search for turtle eggs buried in the sand, of much beer, of mixed skinny-dipping, and a bit of concubitas in the palmettoes. Poor stuff. My poems were, as Pound once described them, "all mush and slither." My stories had some content but never any plot. They told what happened in some situation from dawn to midnight and then stopped. But, after all, Aristotle prescribed that "tragedy endeavors as far as possible to keep within one revolution of the sun." (Poetics, 5)

My worst *Advocate* poem was a commencement ode. It is so bad I tried to blot it from memory. It is signed with a pseudonym, "Oliver Howe Childs." Yet it might have a minute historical interest because it was the first writing for which I was paid. The class of 1909 was having its twenty-fifth reunion and requested some poetical tribute. The job fell to me though I suspect that I may have had help from Frankie Sweetser—and a good deal of beer. "Lines for a Twenty-fifth Reunion" runs to eight stanzas, like these:

We hymn a past we know not yet revere
Hymn days unlived and yet remembered well;
We tell your names, as we our own shall hear
From lips unformed that here will one day sing.

. . .

Think not that only carven stone remembers,
Or dusty words upon the faded page;
Because these walls hold what you gave them,
We promise you a love transcending age.

I would like to think that this poem might find its way to oblivion, but I know that the pseudonym will give me away eventually. Any biographer with pretensions to scholarship will know that great-great-uncle Henry Oliver made his fortune mining ore in the Mesabi Range; that great-grandfather Howe distinguished himself by surviving the War Between the States; but that great-grandfather James Childs did not. He had his head shot off by a cannonball leading a cavalry charge at the battle of Antietam. Both parts were sent back to Pittsburgh in a basket. Fortunately, he had impregnated my great-grandmother before going off to the war.

First after midnight it was the watchmen who went by. They came slowly up the road from the center of the village and paused by the house at the corner and went slowly down the other road back toward the village. They flashed their lamps on garden gates and house doors; they went along slowly and steadily in the darkness and did not speak to each other at all. They did not wake the watchdog of the house at the corner, but a little further down the road a dog howled as they passed. Then another dog woke and howled furiously; even a dog far out in the country howled just once very faintly and was quiet. Soon one dog and then another was quiet until none were howling at all. When the watchmen passed the house of the Herr Dr. Tienus, they saw a light glowing in the corner window. There were no other lights along the whole length of the road.

Then it was the carts going by in the first dawn when all the light was still soft and the trees of the forest were still close. They went by slowly with their heavy wheels thumping and jolting on the hard road. The drivers sat quite still on their perches as though they had not yet awakened, and the slow movement of the oxen was full of sleep. There were no flies around their heads this early; they went along with their necks low and sleep in their eyes.

Later when the dawnlight was hard and bright, it was the

forest-workers who went by dragging their little trailers. The wire wheels of the trailers rattled and jerked; some of the forest-workers walked quickly, throwing their shoulders against the weight of the trailer-harness, swinging their arms briskly; these were the young ones, the young men and the girls. Others walked slowly with their eyes on the road before them, not even looking up when the young quick ones went past; those were the old ones, the old women, and the old, small-headed men. Only old ones and young ones work in the forest. Few of the old ones think about when they were young in the forest; mostly they think of what happened between their leaving it and returning to it. The young ones seldom greet the old ones when they pass them in the road.

The old lady in the high corner room in the house at the corner of the roads woke up with the rattle of the first trailers going by. She had been dreaming again, that night, and though she couldn't remember her dream, she was sorry that she had wakened. She did not lie abed for a moment. Slippers and dressing-gown. Washing and combing. (She wiped the wash-bowl with the used part of her towel.) Dressing and prayers, kneeling at bedside, eyes quite shut. But as she walked briskly downstairs to knock at the serving-girl's door beside the kitchen, she was still trying to remember what had been her dream.

Ernst on the third floor and his mother below woke at the same moment, for the old lady's little sausage-dog began barking below in the garden. She barked at a fat farmer riding past the garden gate on his bicycle. The farmer had a big mustache and a necktie and a black hat; his belly was so big that his knees stuck out akimbo, as he rode. The old lady in the garden stared blindly after him where he went; she could not remember even the last part of her dream.

Ernst lay on his back and looked up; the plaster was cracked in odd lines all across the celling. When he was small it had been people and things; he had used to see crooked faces and twisted men there; an army marching with spears and a horseman at the head; a great eyeless mouth crying out, "*It is a war, you must all come.*" That was in the years when columns of soldiers marched along the road past the gate; when there had not been enough to eat; when his mother had made him drink water before going to bed to fill his stomach for sleep, and they had had to kill the dogs. Afterward, he had not seen the things in the ceiling so clearly. Now, it was just another of the broken things for which there was not enough money for repairs.

The old lady was stooping in turn beside each rosebush in the garden to take up the little flower pots hanging upside down on the low stakes beside them. She lifted the damp straw out of each and then picked out the beetles between two thin fingers. She dropped the beetles on the gravel of the path and crushed them sharply under the toe of her right shoe. (Later, when she went back into the house, she would wipe her shoe carefully on the doormat.) After she had taken up all the pots and put them back again, she knew that there had been more beetles than usual that morning, though she had not counted.

When Elsa, the serving-girl, pulled open the second bureau drawer to take out clean stockings, she saw the new pink silk slip lying folded and neat in the corner. She looked long at it and touched it; she took it up in her hands and felt it flow over them. She held it against her cheek, pressing it into her cheek with the palm of her hand. Then she put it back without closing the drawer. When she had drawn on one stocking, she sat still and her eyes went back to the drawer, though she knew, somewhere in the back of her mind, that she must hurry to start the stove for their breakfast tea. Suddenly, she jumped up viciously, tore off the plain cotton shirt, and slipped into the new soft silk. She stood before the bureau mirror, quite far back in the room so that she could see all of herself in the little square mirror, and all of her body was content all over. She passed her hands over her soft silken belly and up over her tense, quivering breasts. She held her two hands close under her breasts, as she rubbed the insides of her thighs together, feeling them soft and smooth in silk. Then she saw her face in the mirror, her face above the lush body, her face with its purplish blotch on the cheek. All her body sagged; arms fell to the sides, fingers drooping; her knees bent and she fell sobbing and choking on her bed.

In the small bare closet off the studio that was his washing room, the Herr Professor was shaving. Thin-armed in undershirt and braces, thin chin up, tilted, he shaved the cheeks above his pointed beard. He shaved slowly and earnestly, holding the razor between thumb and two fingers, the little finger upraised, while the left hand pulled taut the skin beneath the blade. He did not see well without his glasses, so that the small thin eyes strained toward the reflection in the glass. When he cut himself under one sharp cheekbone and a spot of blood gouted up, face muscles twitched sharply, but he put down the razor carefully, washed the suds from his cheeks, and dried his face thoroughly, taking care that no blood should touch the towel.

When Ernst was still at the university and took an early train to the city each morning, he had always made his bed before going downstairs to breakfast. And he was making it now, even though he knew that a whole empty morning lay before him. As he took off the top sheet to tuck in the foot of the one beneath, he wondered whether there would be another of those insignificant little announcements in the paper that morning: "Professor So & So has been obliged by 'ill-health' or 'pressure of affairs' to give up his post at the university." Sometimes they even had the colossal cheek to add: "The Herr Professor has been active in the affairs of the university for over a quarter-century and his loss will be widely felt." Why in hell didn't the bastards have the courage to tell the truth, since they knew well enough that no one would dare strike back at them? Why didn't they come right out and say: (he squared the top of the sheet with the edge of the bed before tucking it in) "We have disposed of Professor Reinald, a Jew, and replaced him with a Nazi with no experience or research degree." Or "We have asked and accepted the resignation of Professor Schneider, (good old 'Tunnelears' who would tear your head off in seminar and then ask you to his house for dinner) a member of the Socialist Party. Professor Schneider's courses in Marxist ideology have been abandoned." How long, he wondered, would intelligence let itself be terrorized? Smoothing out pillow and puff, he heard his father's steps on the stair, and, glancing in the mirror to be sure that he had brushed his hair, he followed him downstairs to breakfast.

They sat at the four sides of the square table and no one spoke. The old lady sat stiff and small in her chair with her eyes staring at something above her brother's head. One wrist rested on the table, the fingers still closed over the handle of her empty teacup; the high, tight collar of her dress, fastened up close under her wrinkled chin, might have been a climbing, choking vine. Her brother's thin little eyes seemed, as they always did, to be laughing at some joke of their own, as he sponged up the last streaks of jam from his plate with a morsel of bread. Ernst sat with both elbows on the table, resting his chin in his cupped hands, waiting for someone to talk about something and not thinking of anything at all. His mother was finishing the last of her slices of teacake; always she would first eat bread with the others; then, having poured her second cup of tea, she would go out to the pantry to cut slices from the teacake. These she ate very quickly, putting butter and jam and sometimes even cheese on them all together. Then she would pluck up all the crumbs from the tablecloth with her fingernails, popping them into her still hungry mouth.

Pulling aside the long curtains of the great north window, the Herr Professor let bright new light surge into his cluttered studio. It flashed on gilt frames of exhibition pictures along the south wall and filtered away into shadows in far shallow corners under the eaves. He stood for a moment looking straight up into it, wide-eyed, bright-faced; he watched delicate poplar tops quivering ever so gently in no wind with a great full-breasted cloud squatting behind them. When he could see them no longer for the strength of the light against his eyes, he turned from the window and prepared for the morning's work, buttoning on his faded smock, fresh water in dipping-bowl, choosing brushes. And thus, just at half past eight, as the baker's boy was starting out from his master's shop on the morning round, Herr Professor Roebels climbed up on the high three-legged stool before his drawing desk, as he had done day in, day out for more years than he cared to remember. In all that time he had never let a day go by without practice, "keeping his hand in," as he called it; Sundays and fête days were no exception, and even the day of Ernst's birth, when he had stumbled home from the hospital sweating and weak with relief, something inside him had forced him to light a lamp and sketch out the scene as he had lived it there in the lying-in ward, before dropping, only half-undressed, into bed. So again this morning, as it had been each morning for several weeks, he would "keep his hand in," though there were no orders or even the possibility of one forthcoming. And as he worked along, slowly, painstakingly, sketching in the familiar lines of a wayside Christus, such as he had put in so many postcards (not because he felt religiously for them, but because they lent themselves so easily to the sentiments that meant large sales: a wayfarer in prayer; little peasant children standing in awe; an old woman with faggots on her back pausing to make the sign; a limpid-eyed shepherd boy watching his flock), as he blocked in the background greens, careful and sure, his thoughts moved back from his work into memory; near memories of Ernst, his house, his wife, and then more distant ones of the time before they had come to him; back and further back, till he stood once more, cap in hand, in old Professor Hartbach's studio in Leipzig. A few trivialities, the old man wiping his hands on his apron, coming close to him to look down into his face; then the words he had waited so long to hear without knowing what they would be, that had so branded themselves into him that he could hear them now, even to the finest intonation, words that were now as much a part of his life as the parts of his body: *"No, I am afraid there is no sign of genius, only facility, an aptitude."* He had rushed away without speaking in the numbness of his shock. Then, later, he had returned again to falter weakly, hardly with any hope: "And is there then no chance, no possibility . . . ?" The old man stood looking at him for perhaps a quarter-minute before he said, quite quietly: "Yes, there is always one thing for all of us; there is always work."

Ernst stared at the rusty elbow of the washbasin drain, while he wondered what he would do until it was time to eat again. The joint in the elbow pipe leaked, and there was a yellow stain on the floor beneath it where the drops had been falling year after year; if he hurried he would be able to catch the 9:21 into the city. That was a schnellzug that made the run in nineteen minutes; then ten minutes walk out the Luisen Strasse (he had stopped taking the trolley the winter his overcoat was stolen; it meant a saving of two marks a week if he walked) and he would have two whole hours in the library stacks before he need come home for lunch. He wondered who might be using his stack-desk now and had the new owner found out about the hole in the back of the drawer where his notes had been always dropping out and being lost. Perhaps, some of the books would be gone from the stack, his stack, as he had come to think of it; but surely, in their haste, they couldn't have gotten down so far that night when they blundered through, plundering for their barbarous bonfire. If they'd gotten Tripke, the only Tripke in Munich, whose pages he knew almost by heart. . . . He shifted his weight, letting his eyes drift along the opposite wall; they might not even recognize him any more at the stack gate. How long was it? Five months? Six months? And just a year and a half before he had been going in nearly every day, plodding on hour after hour as his thesis took shape, his work on social stratification that he had hoped, and often believed, too would bring him more than merely his doctorate. (More paint was peeling off the far side of the bathtub; if he could just paint over the old coat without having to sandpaper it all off.) At first, he had gone in quite as often, after he had had to drop his regular courses, then that part-time job had kept him away, and when he had lost that, the incentive seemed somehow to be less strong. Once a week he had made himself go for a little while; then those weeks with the flu, and after that only once a fortnight and finally. . . . The door handle rattled viciously; his mother's voice on the other side: "Come along, Ernst, are you going to be all morning?"

Elsa drew her arms from the dishwater in the kitchen sink, when she heard the bell on the garden gate jingling. It would be that lazy baker's boy again, who would never take the trouble to walk up the path to the kitchen door. She dried her arms and walked out and down to the gate, where the baker's boy was slouching comfortably over the fence, picking currants off a ripe bush. He neither moved nor spoke when she reached the gate, but continued his meal, examining each currant before mouthing it, flicking bad ones away. She studied his insolence with mounting irritation; finally, she angrily demanded her loaf of bread. The baker's boy slowly chose one more currant with special care, lingering over the choice, and then drew a fat loaf from his basket, as he drawled, "What's your hurry, old girl? Don't guess any fellow's coming after you right away." For a second she couldn't move; her face drained white, she trembled. Then she struck him over the mouth with all her strength, turned, and fled up the path, tears welling up in her eyes.

The old lady raked smooth a gravel path in the garden with slow even strokes of her wicker brush. She kept an eye on her little sausage-dog where she squirmed about under bushes and in flower beds; occasionally she spoke to her, when she would look up at her out of one eye before continuing her aimless progress. At last, after the gravel had been made all smooth and she had set about tending the plants, the little dog wearied of her wanderings and lay down with nose snuggled between paws. Her eyes were closed in the warm sunlight, but every now and again they would blink open, roll about till they caught sight of her at her work, and then drop shut again. The old lady went from plant to plant, from bed to bed, plucking off dead leaves which she crammed into one apron pocket, while seeds from ripe pods were slipped into the other. As she worked she was warm in the sunlight, not thinking of anything at all; her mind was in those quick thin fingers that darted here and there, like a hovering hummingbird, over the green plants. Pulling away withered leaves from their stems, she did not consider that she was an old woman, was touching things older than herself, dead things; nor did she remember, as she culled the young fecund seeds, a certain summer night by the lakeshore at Potsdam many years before. But her back was growing stiff, aching a little, from bending over; the sun seemed stronger than usual, tiring her, making her just the least bit lightheaded. Reluctantly, because she had not finished all her plants, she went into the beech tree's shade to rest on the round bench that circled its trunk. She sat quite still and discovered she was short of breath, that her legs were a little heavy, her arms, too. Fear flashed through her mind, but she forced it away with an effort, calling to her dog: "Here, Vaqui, come here!" But the little dog only blinked open one eye for an instant and then dozed off again without budging. Yet, a few moments later, when something stirred along the hedge by the house next door, she was very much awake, scrambling to her feet and waddling off full speed toward the commotion in the hedge. The old lady rose in one movement, forgetting her fatigue, and dashed for the hedge, brush in hand; something white and alive scurried away on the far side and was hidden by the corner of the house next door. The old lady leaned panting on her brush; the little dog wheeled around, dejected, nosed about in a pile of rubbish, and then lay down once more in the bright sun.

Ve . . . di che bella sta . . . sera . . . Ernst's voice faded off into blur, and his mother looked up wearily from the keyboard. "Let's try it just once more; then the scales," she said. Ernst scowled out the window; said nothing. His mother struck the banal opening chords again; he took a breath, concentrated, let out his voice to its full strength till it grated metallically off the back of his throat, and went through the song once more, loudly and lifelessly. He had been working at singing now for over a month; it had been his mother's suggestion and she who had led him on to practicing. First she had succeeded in making him partially believe that he had "a voice," and then convinced him he might as well develop it as not. Though he never said so, or even hinted he guessed it, Ernst understood well enough the real motive behind her urgings; just something more to keep him busy, to give him something to think about and plan for, to keep him from brooding. If he were still studying at the university, or if there were the slightest possibility of his finding another job, she would never have thought of training his voice, let alone given time and effort to it. But his idleness about the house and constant brooding had forced her to it; first she had been merely annoyed, saying curtly, when she saw him sitting slumped in a chair or shuffling aimlessly up and down the garden, "Come along, Ernst, can't you find something to do with yourself?" But as time went on and he fell into these moods of hopelessness more frequently, she grew really worried and tried to fill his time with little odd jobs about the house and garden, tasks which he performed obediently enough, but which left him quite as listless as before. Finally, she realized that mending a chair-seat or weeding cabbage rows meant nothing at all to him because it had no part in his own life, his inner life; it did not help in the least to solve for him the problem of his future. So she had urged him again, as she had so often before, to work with his father in the studio in the hope of bringing out a talent that must surely lie latent in his blood. But, as usual, this appeal was vain; painting had never interested him at all, though he was proud enough of his father's work,

enough so, indeed, to start a fight once with a schoolfellow who
had spoken derisively of "postcard art." And thus in the end it
was his voice that she exploited, though he never really came to
believe wholeheartedly in the scheme. Yet it did give him
something to cling to and was an outlet of sorts for the energy
of his ego. So daily he would practice with his mother's help,
singing over the familiar lieder of bourgeois culture, doing
scales to draw out his range, purifying tone and expression.
Once in a fortnight a young friend of his mother's, "a profes-
sional," came out from the city to criticize his progress. She had
a rather good, clear soprano, but was frail, not "built for
volume," as she ruefully would explain. In nearly ten years of
singing she had only once had a role in a first-class house;
one performance as a benefit Rheintöchter in Dresden, when
she had sung with her two "sisters" behind a canvas rock, while
dummies swung back and forth on invisible ropes behind gauze
drops. The rest of her career had been the dreary winter round
of second-rate provincial houses, where she sang Carmen or a
piping Cherubino to boxes filled with dozing fat burghers and
their fat over-dressed wives. But to Ernst, who hadn't been able
to afford opera since his student-card had been called in, she
was a godsend, and after his lesson was finished, he would
make her sing and go on singing until she was breathless.

He was doing the scales now, dropping a halfnote between
each, until he could go no lower. As he sang, he glanced
occasionally at the little pocket mirror held in his outstretched
hand to see whether he was opening his mouth in the right way.

Elsa heard the music first where she worked by the open
kitchen window. She ran to the gate to watch. Ernst and his
mother heard it coming and went out onto the porch. The Herr
Professor heard it coming but did not leave his work; he had
seen too much marching in the cruel years. The old lady,
stretched resting on her bed, heard it too, but all her body
seemed so tired, so comfortable in rest. A Stalheim band was
leading the way, blaring out the Horst-Wessel-Lied with thump-

ing drums, while the storm-troopers stalked behind, swinging their arms in rhythm with their swinging stride. Bright uniforms were glossy in the morning sun, and the swastika banners, one at the head of each troop, drooped wilting in the heat. But as they reached the corner of the roads, on a signal from their leader, the hoarse strong voices took up the strong, slow cadence of the march, roaring it out defiant against the forest barrier. Ernst's mother trembled as she heard it, and he, for all his hatred and disgust, could not resist the swelling surge of the chant. It seemed to carry him up and on and along, to seize every nerve in his body and set them vibrating in time with the marchers. It was the deep sure song of blood and bone, sweeping mind before it in the surgence of its rhythm, carrying marching men to destiny.

He stood quite still after the column had passed, hearing the endless strophe growing fainter and fainter out the forest road till it died away entirely in the heart of the forest. At last, he turned to enter the house, but checked himself as motion again caught his eye in the road. But now it was a slower tread, coming from the direction where the marchers had gone. A white-cassocked priest, bare-headed and holding the crucifix, flanked by two small acolytes in choir robes, trudged slowly back toward the village; behind them came two mourners, black-clad, heads bent, an old man, limping, and a young girl who held his arm as they walked. Behind them trotted a little white terrier with no spots and his tail in the air.

The Herr Professor put down his brushes and closed his eyes to rest them; he took off his glasses and rubbed his forehead with the palms of his hands. Putting on his glasses again, he stared smiling up at the brown cow and the brown-and-white cow on the wall opposite. He had done them for practice one day out in one of the little backland farmyards and then liked them so much that he hung them there where they now were. The bodies were blocked in roughly in brusque, angular lines, but the heads were really fine; it was the heads which pleased him as often as he might look up at them. They were human somehow, and still quite cowlike; there was stupidity in their eyes, such as all cows have, and yet something more, too: renunciation, he had finally decided, melancholy but contented acceptance of the lot of cowness. His eyes twinkled up at them; then he slipped down from his high stool, took a few limbering turns up and down the studio, and sat down before his little out-of-tune upright. He must have played for over half an hour: Bach, quite accurately, never breaking the time or touching a false note, but quite without personality; Schumann, played rather wistfully, while his body swayed with the melodies and his eyes blurred a little from time to time.

Annamaria, the big blond girl from the house diagonally across the road, leaned over the garden gate and shouted Ernst's name. When his head appeared at a window, she called up to him boisterously, "Come along, you little weasel, we're going swimming!"

At the baths-gate they hung up their bicycles on the rack and bought two tickets at the window. As he followed her big hips down the boardwalk in front of the dressing cabins, Ernst wondered if the time would now ever come when they would share one together. From their childhood it had always been understood that they should marry, big cheerful Annamaria and "her" clever little Ernst. As small children they had played wedding together, been lost in the forest together, discovered sex together, gone to school together, and known each other's house as their own. Older, they had taken the same trains in and out of the city, when Ernst was an undergraduate in the university and Annamaria studying home economics, taken bicycle trips in the Oberland, and planned how they would marry and have an apartment near the English Gardens in the city after Ernst had taken his doctorate. But now, with hope of the doctorate fading and no chance of a job since he wasn't a party member, Ernst wondered how long it would be before

Annamaria would begin going about with someone else, with one of those fellows down at the training camp maybe. Undressing, Ernst speculated for a moment on a large knothole in the wall between Annamaria and himself, as memories from his boyhood welled up and were dispelled; taking off his shirt, he hung it on the hook just above the hole.

They lay side by side *ventre à terre* on the sunning boards; the sun was hot on their bodies, and already the drops of water on her arms were dried up. Ernst moved one leg so that it pressed lightly against hers, watching her face as he did so. Eyes and mouth smiled; he was content, warm all over. He had done a back-flip off the high board without mishap, and she had seemed pleased and surprised. He moved a little closer, looked into her empty eyes, closed his own, was warm all over, warm with the sun all over him.

The old lady wiped pursed lips with a corner of her napkin, folded and rolled it, slipped it into a wooden ring, and called her little sausage-dog to her. The little dog had been lying quietly on her cushion on the big armchair, but all during the meal her eyes had been on the old lady. Now at her call, she waddled joyfully to her, was taken up in her arms, held against her breast. The old lady smiled down into the dog's eyes that stared up at her a few inches beneath her own; she talked to her, stroking her coat and feeding her little scraps of meat and bread saved from her own plate. The dog gobbled down these morsels and was quiet, slowly letting eyes drift shut, breathing slowly in short breaths; the old lady no longer looked at her, but sat with a little halfsmile on her lips and in her eyes, stroking the smooth flank downward from the shoulder, a withered white hand on the rich glowing flank.

Ernst's mother sat down with a Tauchnitz novel and her third cup of tea in the big armchair. The Herr Professor took off his glasses and laid them on the mantle, resting on the rims; he took off his coat and put it over the back of a chair. Sitting down on the couch, he took off his shoes and socks, stuffing socks into shoes, which he squared side by side to the couch's edge. Then he lay back on the couch with his feet toward his wife. His eyes closed, and the hands folded over his belly relaxed; as he fell into a wheezing sleep, his white toes naked and erect, were quite quiet.

Ernst, stretched out on his bed, could not fall asleep; he would have liked to sleep, for then the afternoon would be shorter when he woke. His windows were wide open, but all the countryside was still; only now and again the sound of a train's passing drifted across the fields from the tracks. He remembered that he had not bought a new monthly ticket yet; he lay on his back with his eyes closed, then with his eyes open. He tried lying first on one side, then the other. It was most comfortable to lie belly-down, but the bed springs sagged so much that he was arched till his windpipe was choked. He sat up and surveyed his bookshelf; mostly things he had read a number of times already, except the *Zauberberg* with the mark still sticking up in it where he had stopped months before. He really ought to finish that book sometime, a real classic; then his eyes were caught by the bright cover of an old copy of Uhu. One after another he turned over the pages, pausing to study each, not smiling once.

Before she even slit the envelope of her own letter, Elsa took the others the postman had given her upstairs; there was one for Ernst; there was one for the Herr Professor, which she slipped under the studio door, since it was forbidden to disturb him at his work; there was one for the old lady which she left on the little table outside her door. Then she went downstairs to her own room, closed the door, and tore open the envelope, like a starved dog tearing at a scrap of meat. Her hands trembled as she read, then fell to her lap, as the letter slipped from them and fluttered to the floor. Mid-afternoon sun, slanting obliquely through the window, fell on:

Dear Madam

    We are in receipt of your remittance, but we regret to inform you that according to the rules of our society it will be impossible to place you in touch with another of our members until a photograph (snapshot or passport size) is supplied.

Yours very truly,

. . .

    Lifting his eyes from his work, the Herr Professor caught sight of the letter on the floor by the door and went to pick it up. Hans' handwriting, his old schoolmate; pleased, he settled down in the room's one soft chair to read it in comfort. He turned the page up into the light and drifted contentedly through his old friend's rambling affection: a vacation in the Black Forest; a new car, though business really hadn't improved much in spite of the chancellor's big words; Hans Jr., entering the university: and then . . . He read it over a second time to make sure he had not imagined it: "I know how busy you are . . . but for Sophie's present this Christmas . . . a nice big one that would go well over the dining-room fireplace. . . ." He leaned back in his chair and chuckled for sheer joy; a commission, and a fat one, from Hans of all people, Hans who had probably never been in a gallery in his life. Well, he'd do him a fine one with lots of "things" in it, something in the panorama line with sheep on one side of the foreground and haymaking on the other with a town and mountains behind. Taking up the letter again, he went on through Hans' twinges of gout and complaints over Nazi interference in his office, still smiling.

    Ernst knew before he opened his letter what it would say; if they were even going to consider his application, they wouldn't have answered so quickly. He opened it deliberately and read the neatly typed words above an illegible signature:

"I regret very sincerely that it will be impossible to grant your petition for a general scholarship at the University. Investigation of your record reveals that your work has failed to merit this recognition."

He read it over again dispassionately; then tore it slowly into small fragments that slipped from his fingers one by one to the floor. He couldn't even feel anger; somehow it was all too inevitable, too far outside the mere sphere of justice and injustice, too utterly hopeless. He knew that the same sort of thing was happening all over Germany and that there was no help for it. He sat for a long time without thinking of anything at all, staring in pure despair into nothingness.

The old lady woke late from her siesta; she had slept longer than was usual, but even so she was content to lie resting on after sleep had gone. And when she did at last rise from bed, it was only to sink almost at once into the security of a soft chair. Thus it was not until the tea-bell roused her that she left her room and found her letter outside her door. She paused on the stair-landing to open it; beneath a formal typed salutation it began: "Have you seen our new form-fitting foundation garment for stylish young figures?"

Ernst's mother called to him to come in for his tea as she saw him leading his bicycle out onto the road; but he did not answer. Getting on his cycle, he started out along the forest road, pedaling with all his strength to get up speed. It was semi-dark along the forest road except where sunlight broke through the arch of boughs above to splash lightly on brown trunks and bright-patched moss. He went along at a steady speed watching the tall pines flash past him, trying to filter away that hopeless despair from his thoughts, trying to lose it in the forest depths that stretched away on either hand. It was cool in the forest, though no wind murmured; it was calm in the forest's shade beneath tall straight pillars of living rock. He grew content under its spell, as he always did, and his self glided lightly ahead of him in the long straight track where sunlight fell gaily in odd patterns on the forest's floor. After a time he stopped pedaling, left his bicycle, and walked in a little distance under the trees. There he lay down on his back in the soft lush moss, pillowing head on hands, as he stared up into the sky-flecked green above. Near him a shaft of brilliant sunlight, dustgrains dancing in its beam, rose like a ladder of Jacob up through the dark vault of boughs. He picked up a pine needle from the ground beside him and set to chewing it between two front teeth, tasting its bitter twang on the tip of his tongue. He was content in the heart of the forest.

At the dinner table one place was empty; the old lady had gone early up to bed, saying she was tired, and the room was silent and oppressed by her empty chair. Ernst, prodding tentatively into his soup dumpling, wondered if his nerves could stand the long tedium of another evening in the sitting room. Each night they sat reading in four chairs grouped close under the light until it was late enough to go to bed. After the clank of dishes ceased in the kitchen, there would be no sound in the room beyond the breathing, the slow turning of pages, and two clicking clocks racing out of time. Sometimes the old lady would sneeze unexpectedly and mutter about draughts; finally Ernst's mother would slide off into a doze, head sunk on one shoulder, her book slipping to the floor. No! He would not go through another such evening of restless boredom. He'd take the train in town to visit some of his friends, if it took the last frugal pfennig of his week's allowance.

The Herr Professor stood by the porch railing, puffing at his after dinner cigar, as evening melted into night before his eyes. The forest wall had turned from green to deep distant blue, and low-hovering mists were grey over the flat fields. Far from the forest came the sharp sting of a shot; farmers, at this time of evening, were in the deer blinds above forest clearings. Later, as the haze of fields darkened to blend with the line of trees beyond, a last belated forest-worker came trundling his trailer down the road, slow pacing with the weight of his load. Night was on the land, and the dark silence of night.

Running to catch his train, Ernst bumped into her from behind as she stopped to open a carriage door. The quick look that she gave him was more of fear than irritation; her frightened eyes seemed to look beyond him, as though not he, but some force beyond him had jolted her. The station-master's whistle squealed, and he followed her hastily up into the carriage, slamming the door after him. Though she looked up at him again from beneath her black hood before seating herself, he could think of no fit word of apology. Somehow it was more than just carelessness, it seemed somehow wrong, to have hurt her, who was obviously so helpless and so dependent on her robes for security. Troubled, he sat down and dared not look in her direction; she put umbrella and bundle on the rack above her seat, sat down primly, arranging robes and veil as she did so, and was quite still looking straight ahead of her at nothing. When his eyes finally turned to her, he noticed that her face had the same frightened expression, that now appeared natural to it because of the way that her wide round eyes protruded from the lids. They darted about in fright as he watched them, without ever seeming to see anything at all. He noticed too, that something about her lips and mouth, seemed, though it hardly twitched, to be wiggling and wrinkling like the nervous nose of a rabbit.

It was at the second station after Planegg that the two little peasants got into the carriage; his attention was drawn to them at once because of their presence on a city-bound night train. Obviously it was an occasion, a great one, for their dress was elaborate and they themselves in a state of lively excitement. The eyes of the cropped-headed, wrinkled little peasant darted with flashing interest about the carriage, while his bronze-skinned little wife sat stiff on the edge of her seat, hands folded stiffly in her lap. They were too excited to speak; they sat tense and alert taking in the bare wonder of the carriage. Perhaps they were sixty, so worn, so wrinkled were their faces, so browned their skin with many summers' suns; yet they had the eyes of children, the laughing curious eyes of small children. Their eyes were not still or dull for an instant; there was so much to be seen in one moment, and then to be seen at once again, since its novelty lay beyond any understanding.

The tired frightened eyes of the nun in the opposite corner of the carriage were drawn to the little peasants again and again; each time she seemed to wince, each time looked back once more. Her eyes feared their bright curious eyes, yet could not keep away from them. And they turned to stare at her and laughed in curious wonder at her fear; then as her lips began to flutter in muttered prayer, while her eyes were kept lowered in sheer strength of will, they smiled at her, laughed at her. At first they smiled softly, curiously, and laughed to themselves in wondering mirth. But when her mumbling grew audible in its fervor, while her fingers clutched the beads at her waist, and her eyes, for all the exertion of her will, flew fearfully back to them again in pure terror, they could not help themselves; they fairly choked with laughter. The little old man gave himself up to it altogether and rocked on his seat in helpless agony, while the old woman cackled and shook till tears rolled down from her eyes over her laughing cheeks.

Elsa trudged along the road to the village, her day's work done. She had on her Sunday clothes and a big hat with a broad brim that would hide her face in shadow. She was going to a house in the village, where one of her old schoolmates worked in the kitchen. They often spent their lonely evenings together following the path along the river, where they could watch lovers who came there to be alone together. She walked faster, when she reached the village, keeping her eyes on the road at her feet, avoiding the glances of the people whom she passed. As she was going by the beer-garden on the far side of the street, a man loafing at one of the sidewalk tables called out something to her. Startled, she looked fearfully across the street, and seeing she did not know him she hurried on hoping he would not call after her again.

When she reached her destination, she found not her friend, but a hasty note pinned on the outside of the kitchen door with her name printed on it. Taking it across the street to the glare of a streetlamp, she read: "Sorry to desert you. Out with Willie." Leaning limply against the lightpost, she crushed the note in her fingers; misery surged over her. She was miserable and alone for a long time in the blue glare of the streetlight. No one to see; no place to go; nothing to do but go home to bed. Wearily she turned homeward, bitterness swelling within her till tears of self-pity blurred her eyes. When suddenly, abruptly, as though she had felt a sharp pain deep in her, she stopped; slowly her head came up, her shoulders straightened, and all her bearing changed to a strange new manner it had never shown before. The weak lines of her mouth seemed to harden, her eyes to grow hard and bright. Self-possessed now, with a studied carelessness in her walk, she swung down the street to the beer-garden, where the loafer who had called to her still sat slumped in his chair. Poised and deliberate, she stopped before him, one arm to her hip, giving him a long smile. As he grinned back to her, she slouched down into the chair beside his. "That's the girl", he said, "what'll it be?"

The four young men were playing cards about a low table and they all talked at once. They talked loudly and gaily, paying scant attention to their game that progressed only spasmodically between long bursts of conversation. Now the differing accents contrasted in the general exuberance, Ernst's slurred Bavarian, Pogner's precise clipped Prussian, and the rolling tones of the two Rhinelanders. They had been classmates of Ernst's in his undergraduate days; now they were studying in the graduate schools, Pogner in medicine, the two Rhinelanders in education; none of the four was a party member. They held their cards out before them in the weak lamplight (the shade was a folded newspaper), and the corners of the room were dark behind them. They were warm in the warmth of close companionship, as their laughter grew louder and more frequent. One of the Rhinelanders was raucously quizzing Pogner about monkey-glands, while Ernst impersonated to his own great satisfaction an American tourist trying to order a meal. The room grew hot, and Pogner opened a window onto the vibrant city night. Tea came on a tray brought in by a flowsy landlady; the cards were forgotten and elbowed to the floor. They went over once more the story of their classmate Leschinsky, who had been caught trying to cross into Switzerland in a hay wagon and imprisoned as a communist in the concentration camp at Dachau. Their teacups drained, they lit cigarettes and blew smoke across the lamplight. Pogner, keen with recalled excitement, told of an emergency operation in which a torn heart had been deftly and perilously sewn; his eyes were bright in the light as he talked, his fine thin hands dancing in the air as he described each delicate life-and-death step. Ernst's thoughts ran on while he listened: Pogner's father was head surgeon of a huge clinic in Berlin; he would have a job as soon as he wished it after graduation; his father's influence would easily overcome the fact that he was not a party member; there would be no trouble for him; with his position and skill Pogner would be a success, perhaps even famous, before he, Ernst, might even have a chance to get started at something. Through this despondency that had swept over him after the earlier gaiety like sudden summer rain, he heard the smooth voice finishing: "So . . . like that . . . and if he had been one half minute longer . . . I was sweating all over when it was done." Ernst rose suddenly from his seat to stand for a time at the window, peering moodily into the full darkness outside. And then at last, the conversation came to the one subject to which it never failed to return sooner or later. In low voices, bitter voices, they ridiculed his latest follies, scoffed at his poses, rehashed again the rumors of his being a dope-addict, a paranoiac, a sadist. But even their common loathing could not keep them serious too long; soon they were laughing over him for the clown that he was. ("A second Bismarck, a Lohengrin-Siegfried!" scoffed Pogner, "Our deliverer and savior from that venomous vampire, the blood-sucking Jew . . . he's more like some overswollen Mickey Mouse, I say.") And so when it came time for Ernst to say good night and make his way down four dark flights to the street, he was glowing with a good humor such as he had not felt all day.

About an hour after Herr Dr. Tienus had left the house, after advising that the old lady should rest abed a day or so to recoup her strength, Frau Professor Roebels left her sister's room and went downstairs to put the house in order for the night. The door next to the kitchen stood open, and the room behind it was dark and empty; she wondered at this for a moment, as she went from room to room fastening the blinds, but concluded the girl must have decided to stay late with her friends in the village. Before putting out the lights, she set out her son's supper on the hall table: a piece of pastry left over from dinner, bread and cheese, a glass of milk; beside it she left a note for him, scrawled in her big childish hand: "Don't forget to take off your shoes, before you come upstairs."

The minute hand of the great illumined clockface, set like a cyclops' eye in the station's forehead, had not yet climbed to the hour, when Ernst turned breathless into the station square from a side street. So he slowed down, seeing he had minutes to spare, and turned to go through to the local platforms by way of the main station. In the confusion his eyes seemed out of focus; the glare and bustle dizzied him, as he drifted slowly through the moving crowd, reading the signs over the train-gates: 24 Schnellzug nach

Rosenheim, Salzburg, Linz, Prague, Wien, Budapest, Belgrade, Sofia; 23.35; 21 Personenzug nach Dachau, 23.05; 20 Schnellzug nach Zurich, Basel, Fribourg, Lausanne, Simplon, Mailand, Genua. . . . He knew them all as well as he knew the times of trains from the city out to Planegg; night and night again he had passed thus from one end of the station to the other, pausing at each gate, then going to the next, watching the travelers, wondering and reflecting, feeling within him a longing he could not check. Suddenly he was pushed aside by a shouldering porter, laden with smart new luggage, in whose wake followed two laughing young people, a young man in tweeds, a young girl chic in gray fur, carrying flowers. Bride and groom on their honeymoon, thought Ernst. He stared after them as they passed through the gate, pressing to the rail to follow them with his eyes as they went up the platform till they were lost in the crowd. A honeymoon . . . Annamaria and he. . . . He raised his eyes above the gate to read again the magic formula he already knew so well: Garmisch-Partenkirchen, Innsbruck, Venedig, Rom. . . . Innsbruck, Venedig, Rom. . . . Innsbruck, Venedig, Rom. The names echoed in his head, while he walked through the tunnel to the local station. Through the cold snow mountains it would go, through the gorges and passes in the night to Innsbruck; to Venice it would come then, to Venice glistening in sea and sun; and at last to martial Rome, where all roads lead, at last through plains of wheat to ruined Rome.

Elsa could hardly have known when she reached the garden gate, for only the instinct of feet long trained in a single daily path carried her home along the village road. A fat-bellied farmer, hurrying countryward on his bicycle through the night, laughed at the comical figure ahead of him in the road that walked like a puppet with wires on its legs, meandering an uneven course from side to side of the road. Too much beer, he thought to himself as he cycled past her; but he did not see her eyes. Inside the gate, she paused for an instant, as if not knowing where she was; she pressed a hand against the side of her head, running the fingers up over her scalp, while her eyes searched vacantly about in the darkness. Then she went on again with the same slow jerky movement, up the path, up the steps, across the porch to the door. There her wise hands went unerringly to the key where it lay hidden in a crack in the wall, and she unlocked the door, stumbled in, closed it, still without seeming to know what she did.

The dark was cool to Ernst walking rapidly into it from the area of light about the station. He turned up his coat collar close about his neck and swung his arms in time with his stride. Ahead of him the forest ranged dull black, the night sky a shade lighter above it; clouds hid the stars. When he had passed over the beams of light cutting his path from the high windows of a switch-tower and was out of sight of the station, he stopped by the roadside; then on again, walking as hard as he could, lengthening his pace and springing up from the toes with each step. He felt the road hard and rough beneath his feet, while the night was cold and moist in his face. Passing the pile of bark left by the pit-post shavers beside the track, he snatched up a strip without stopping, and shredded it in his fingers as he went; chewing a little piece of it between front teeth and tongue tip, he was glad for its bitter taste in his mouth. As he swung into the uphill stretch, he threw forward his shoulders, putting his whole body into the stride, revelling in swift flight through darkness, exhilarated in the thrust of his muscles against the night that pressed close about him, closed down above him, swept up to meet him from the ground.

Sometime soon after midnight the old lady in the corner room turned a little in her sleep, gasped a little, and died quite quietly. It was dark all about her in her room as she died, and the breathing of her little dog rose slow and calm through the darkness from the basket beside her bed. Ernst, opening his window before sleep, paused at the sill to stare out into the cool thick night. A train rumbled away to the left, drawing his eyes off into the darkness. For a moment moving lights flashed across to him through the trees; were gone; he stood still listening to the dying echo of its passing on the night. Then far from the heart of the forest a night bird cried once and no more. There was no sound but the great strong noise of the night's silence.

Soon the watchmen came trudging slowly down the road from the village. They paused at the corner of the roads to listen on the night wind that blew from the forest; but there was no sound. Then they turned down the other road back toward the village, walking slowly without speaking. They flashed their lamps on garden gates and house doors; once a watchdog growled low in his throat but did not bark. One figure stopped for a moment to pick up something from the road and then went on again. When they reached the house of the Herr Dr. Tienus, the watchmen turned to stare back down the road whence they had come. There was no light in the whole length of road, there was no light in all that darkness.

THE RIVER

You can go on moving around, thinking it's the place and not you, for a good while, trying the mountains and this city and that, even trying English country, which is about as far as an American can go, and then finally after you've spent most of your money and worn out two or three typewriter ribbons without getting anything done, you begin to see and know that it's not the places it's just you. Then if you have any sense you go back to Springfield and teach school or try to get a job in the bank and pretty soon the outlying cousins are saying how that crazy Carson is settling down and maybe'll come to something after all.

Craig and I wouldn't have come to be saying we didn't have sense, but when we got to Paris along about August, knowing then it wasn't the fault of the places where we'd been, we knew we ought to give up and go home, but we knew even more we'd rather do anything else. And so, as Craig said, rather than go home and start brawling with our families again, we would just sit still in Paris watching the sun shine and the Seine flow, hoping it wouldn't rain more than two days a week. We did and it didn't. In fact it was about the best weather we'd had anywhere, good and hot so you knew it was summer all right but none of those stinkers that you get in Wisconsin and hardly any rain.

The Seine was dirty, so dirty we didn't dare try swimming in it for fear of catching something, but it did flow in a quiet steady way that made me feel at home. (I've never liked New York because the river isn't in the middle of it where it ought to be. For me it has always been that a city that is a city is a city built on two sides of a river with each side about equal in importance. And Paris is like that. There are more of what the tourist maps call monuments on the right bank, but on the left bank you see twice as many people who look good for something, which keeps the two sides balanced. Then there is Notre Dame in the middle being a fulcrum, that is, at least, as far as I'm concerned it's a fulcrum.)

In Salzburg, where we had been in July, we had gotten used to a rushing roaring river, a river fairly blowing its head off to get wherever it's going. Wherever we went in Salzburg, even when we were stymied by one of those little bergs that crop up like pimples all around the town, we could feel the Salzach plunging along, almost jumping out of its bed. It was an excited river, and we were excited too, excited by being face to face with our futures, really alone with our future lives for the first time. The Salzach was an excited river. One day as we were crossing it Craig described the Salzach perfectly: he looked down from the bridge at it and said, "Yessir, she'll be comin' round the mountain when she comes!"

So the Seine seemed quiet to us when we first got to Paris, quiet and a little contemptible. (You'll wonder why we even noticed the river in a big busy city like Paris, but I'll tell you that water is such a thing to me that wherever I am it is the thing I see first last and longest.) But soon we were liking it better, soon liking it very well as we walked slowly along the quais in the late evening as the lights came on, and soon we were knowing that its slow steady flowing pleased us perfectly. Our time came to be the Seine's time, and again and again I stopped when crossing a bridge to lean over the wall and watch for a long time the brown water moving and yet staying, speaking but silent, hurrying yet delaying.

In Salzburg our living had been like the river there, intense and driven. We thought then we were going somewhere and wanted to hurry. We were pushed and pulled, pushed by the memory of what life had been like at home and pulled by the desire for success which would give us permanent escape. There was really nothing exceptional about our life at home (we lived in Springfield, Wisconsin); we were more or less typical— sensitive boys wanting to live a life of books and feeling smothered by the indifference of the people around us to the things we idolized. Springfield had a library, one of those Carnegie libraries that you find in small cities, but it had no books in it by Proust or James Joyce or Ezra Pound. Springfield had occasional concerts, but the pianists never played anything but Chopin and the singers sang "On the Road to Mandalay." There was an art shop in Springfield—it sold reproductions of "The Last Indian." There were pretty girls in Springfield but most of them thought Craig and I were flits and made us miserable; not one of them could have stood still or kept quiet for three minutes. How did we know about things like that? A teacher in the high school, a young English teacher. He was different. He came from the East. He understood. And Craig and I had become his intimates, draining from him his store of good things from the other world for which we came to long. We were with him constantly. He was a poet. And we were poets. We dreamed together—he was only seven years older than Craig and I—of life in Paris, of life in the hill towns, of a better, richer life far, far away from Springfield. Yet there was nothing exceptional in this; there are boys dreaming such dreams in every city in America. The exceptional thing was that we were able to try to live them, able to get away from the home we so despised while we were still young enough really to despise it.

It came about through Craig's grandmother. She persuaded our families to let us go. She understood us too. She could not understand the books we read or the things we talked about but she could understand what was happening inside us and put some sort of true value on it. Our parents could understand it in a way—we were not the first boys in Springfield to get ideas. But to them our leanings were just a phase, something annoying, like the measles, through which we safely would pass in time, to be in the end like them. Oh they understood us well enough! They were decent as could be. They let us have money for books and did not mind our being continually with Charles Herrick, but they were never for us. They never really thought it would be a wonderful thing if one of us should turn out to be a famous writer, or that it would be a better thing than our turning out to be moneymaking businessmen. But Craig's grandmother did understand us. She had never known a poet in her life but she could think of our being such a thing without feeling self-conscious about it. She was a larger mind than the rest, not a more developed mind, but one larger to begin with, capable of a wider natural knowledge. She was not dissatisfied with life in Springfield but she could realize that there were other places in the world where life could be as good and even better perhaps. That our parents could not do. Their imagination did not go beyond having the best house in Springfield. They might have filled it with expensive paintings from Italy if they had made that much money—they were not hicks, they made trips to New York and to California—they simply never thought of life anywhere else being possibly life for them. I imagine that they would really have rejected France because it had few bathtubs.

But Craig's grandmother got around them. She liked us. Without herself being in any way a rebel she could appreciate rebellion. She could sense that a distaste for life in Springfield might not be a weakness in our characters. She liked us. We often brought Herrick to her house and overwhelmed her with our immensities of superior wisdom. It was all Greek to her—she was not bookish—but she liked it. And she persuaded our families to let us go when we'd been graduated from high school. She persuaded them by saying it would be the quickest way to get us over it, to let us go and rub our noses in it. "They'll come back after a year and go to college and that will be the end of it," she told our parents. But those were not her real feelings, that was just her craft, a craft in which she was being perfectly honorable because she felt it was for our good. She didn't think we would get over it. She hoped we wouldn't. She wanted more for us than success in Springfield.

I think though that what probably finally decided Craig's father and mine (they were close friends) to let us go was the idea of showing Springfield that they were well enough off to give us trips abroad before we began college. I think the phrase "grand tour" and something of its connotation had permeated into Springfield.

And so we went. We were in the odd class that finished high school in February and we crossed over in March. And July found us in Salzburg, full of excitement, and confident of the wonders ahead of us. We weren't ridiculous. We had a sense of humor, if it was a little undeveloped. We didn't think that one glimpse of an oxcart would turn us into geniuses, but we were sure that things would be different in Europe, that the barriers inside us that had kept us from writing anything more startling at home than fairly adept imitations would somehow be moved away by the new life. In America we had known that what held us back was the atmosphere and not something in ourselves.

And we still thought so in Salzburg, in spite of the barren weeks in Munich (nice old atmosphere and lots of culture but not too much diversion), the Dolomites (what we need are the primitive realities—rocks and peasants), Ragusa (get out of this damn rain, get the sun, life force), Vienna (blend of Teutonic and Celtic spirits, just the thing), and Budapest (need more color). We still didn't realize that the only thing that stimulated us was finding good excuses to disturb the travail of composition. Craig had gotten around to justifying his obscurity (somehow his lines didn't seem to have much "style" when they had also to make sense) by saying that psychoanalysis had driven poetry to associational logic, and I had actually reached Chapter XI in my autobiographical novel, although somehow my scene had managed to get itself shifted from Springfield to the more exotic quarters of Vienna. As I say, in Salzburg, with the Salzach running itself ragged beside us and inside us, we were still energetically stubbing our toes on our own heels.

And then we had seventeen hours in a smelly third-class carriage to Paris with plenty of time to think and no mask of atmosphere or ritual between ourselves and the mirror. We didn't talk about it at all, we didn't even discuss what we'd do in Paris, but when we got there we both knew, though we didn't admit it at first, that it wasn't the fault of the places we'd been but just ourselves. All day we sat watching the rain-soaked country go by, watching the rain fall steadily against the gloomy station walls where the train stopped, while more and more the forced confidence of our early-morning start faded into uncertainty and doubt melted into despair. And after night came, hiding the rain and locking us tightly into our stale-smelling wooden box, there wasn't the least struggle left in us, in either of us; we were done for and we knew it and we didn't care enough anymore to mind.

So, soon the Seine seemed fine to us, as we were going no faster than it was, hardly moving at all, just letting ourselves be washed pleasantly along. At first we stayed at a fairly good hotel on the Quai Voltaire (the one where they say that an American lady saw a gendarme under her bed and moved right on to Berlin without saying a word) but that was too expensive and we moved to the Pretty Hotel in the Rue Amalie back near the Champ de Mars. It was an awful quarter to live in, not tough or dirty but just messy and sloppy, but the room was big and cheap and after all, as Craig said, if you couldn't afford the St. James et d'Albany the next most distinguished certainly was the Pretty. We were there almost a week before we caught on to the nature of the Pretty's principal business, though two or three nights the banging around on the stairs had woken us up, and not having our own bathroom we thought we would be better off the quicker we ditched the Pretty, which we did.

Walking down the Rue Saint-Dominique one day we'd seen a Chambres-à-Louer sign hanging out a window and we went there. It was an insurance agent who had his office on the second floor of an old apartment house; he had the whole floor and there were some little rooms in the back that he didn't use. We got two for less than we had been paying for one at the Pretty, which suited me fine because, much as I like Craig, I'd gotten tired of looking at his dirty shirts lying around in corners, and besides I have always hated to be looked at by anyone while I'm busy waking up in the morning. We almost moved again after a few days when we found out that one of the rooms down the hall belonged to a great big black man, but we finally decided that, as Craig said, miscegenation was better than moving again. So we stayed, and then in a few weeks we were calling the black man Josh and buying him drinks at the corner bistro while he told us about the war and all the French women he'd had in a mixture of broken-down French and even worse English that he'd picked up from an English spinster in Arles who had paid him well, he said, for just coming to sit with her of an evening. After getting out of the army, Josh had managed to marry a solid widow who politely had died at once leaving him enough to enjoy Paris for a few years before going home to his brother Senegalese.

So we stayed and the quiet waiting ways of Paris grew into us. We found a little restaurant in the quarter where they would cook eggs for us at ten in the morning, we got used to coffee with chicory in it, we learned the bus routes and got caught riding first class in the Métro, we didn't bother anymore to get our pants pressed, we began picking up some argot, and we even got used to keeping the covers on our typewriters all day.

As I say, the weather in Paris that August was all you could have asked for, sun every day but never so hot that you sweated when you walked the way you do in August back at home. We walked a lot, usually in the evenings when the coming darkness seemed to stir a breeze, not going anywhere in particular, just strolling along the quiet streets and busy boulevards, talking a little now and then about the things we saw, the people we passed and the houses, the people walking quickly to get somewhere, the people walking slowly as were we, the people sitting on little chairs before their doors, talking and watching, the houses we passed, the houses some hard, some soft, sometimes like pictures but more often not, walking and sometimes talking, walking slowly, talking lightly, not hurrying and not delaying, hardly thinking what we were saying; so walking and so lightly quietly talking, we often saw and surely came to know the way the light dies and the night comes softly on. And we sat.

We learned to like to sit and watch, to sit and sip, to sit and sit. For Paris is a sitting city.

There is no city anywhere that sits as Paris sits, that sits so much, so often, or so everywhere. And soon we were sitting and waiting, or sitting and worrying, as is the American way, but watching and gently talking. At first we sat when we were tired of walking and then we came to sit for sitting's sake. We sat a lot, in many places both by day and night.

We sat at big cafés on boulevards and at little ones on side streets. We sat on park benches sometimes and never on park chairs because we couldn't bear to pay the chairkeepers. In the mornings before lunch we would sit at one of the cafés near the Opéra, reading the paper and our mail if we had any, our mail from home that we rushed each day to the American Express office to collect and then never liked when we read it. We never liked them, the half angry half loving letters from our families back in Springfield, but we would always read them, each reading his own first and then reading it to the other. They didn't bore us or make us homesick, they only made us vaguely uneasy, because we knew that the life they told about would always be more real to us than that we were living, much as we hated it and wanted to escape from it. And they made us think of our families as we didn't want to, made us neither hate them nor love them, but only realize how wholly we were bound to them, how surely we would never cease to be what they had made us. We read our letters and then as we sat watching people come and go, sipping a vermouth or perhaps a Pernod, making up in our minds elaborate answers to them which we finally never wrote.

And as we sat and watched we read the *Paris Herald* through, first skipping from page to page, then reading every word. It was a daily ritual, completely meaningless and very satisfying, to read it all, to read the whole dull paper which was exactly the same every day. We read all the *Paris Herald* every day and never anything else, easily forgetting all about the solid classics in pocket editions that we'd carted around Europe to feed our souls on. We read everything in that paper and liked it. Just watching the news of the world floating by on the front page seemed to give us a sense of action, to establish us against time, and never did the editor fill space by printing the whole passenger list of an incoming liner but we read every name, never recognizing that of anyone we knew, but somehow enjoying the certain knowledge that these were their names. We read all the personal items in the society column and tried to figure out which ones had been sent in by the people themselves. Naturally, we had no way of telling, but sometimes from the name we could be sure it was that of a person who liked to see himself in print. We read the stupid Republican editorials that someone told us were written by Englishmen. We read the financial articles which we didn't understand. We read the letters from pacifists, puzzlemakers, amateur politicians, and ladies exchanging recipes, and thought up sarcastic answers to them which we never sent in to the paper. We read, as I say, the whole paper and liked it, but most of all two things: Sparrow Robertson and the baseball games. Back at home we would never have read the sports page at all as a matter of principle, but there in Paris at the big cafés, sitting and sipping, watching and reading, we came to be liking that part best of all.

There is one good reason why the *Paris Chicago Tribune* could never really rival the *Paris New York Herald* and that is Sparrow Robertson. You have got to read him to believe him possible. I suppose Sparrow Robertson would call himself a philosopher of sport, but to me he will just always be the great living master of American prose. If I were to quote things he has written, you wouldn't see what I was talking about. No, you have got to come on Sparrow Robertson's literary pearls by yourself, to stumble on them yourself in the middle of his dignified account of the last boxing match at the Palais des Sports or a hailstorm of statistics about horseracing results in 1910. Now I wouldn't want to give a wrong impression and have you think that Sparrow Robertson ever gave way to unnecessary rhetoric or even sporting jargon, because he is, I assure you, a very serious artist indeed. No, it is only that sometimes his enthusiasm for expression, his great affection for his subject leads Sparrow by the way of certain lapses of grammar, certain variants from the accepted order, which are so individual, or let us say, so quite apart, in fact so gorgeously and beautifully things unto themselves that there is I assure you nothing in the heavens nor on earth to measure the joy, the orgasmic abdominal joy, with which the reader thereof is instantaneously seized. For you see old pal Sparrow has a way of saying things that is really kinda funny.

But it was really the baseball that mattered most. As I remember that time it is this that I remember, the passionate way we felt about the Cardinals slowly catching up on the Giants. Now I couldn't even tell you who finally did win the pennant that year, in fact I think in the end it wasn't either the Cardinals or the Giants, but still there is something left in me of the way I was feeling about it then, the passionate death-and-destiny way I was feeling about the Cardinals slowly catching up with the Giants. There was no obvious reason for liking one team better than the other, but somehow the verbiage of the sportswriters who were playing up the race between them did its work on us, and we began to feel excited and concerned. Neither of us had ever been in St. Louis, but really the teams didn't mean places to us anyway. They didn't mean places or even ideas to us, it was their slow steady struggle, the tortured rising and falling of their percentages as they won and lost games, the gradual catching up, the sudden spurts ahead and falling back, the agony or joy of two games won or lost on the same day, the nervousness of games divided, the exciting certainty that the Cardinals would finally catch up mixed with the worrying doubt that their luck might change and they wouldn't, these were the things that were meaning so much to us then, this constant excitement of fighting against chance, assurance against doubt, ourselves and the Cardinals against the Giants and luck. It seems foolish that we should have cared at all, and yet even now, when suddenly something makes that time come back inside me, I can feel a little of the feeling that we had, the tense exciting feeling that we had.

So our morning sitting wasn't quiet, when we read the papers and the letters from home. But in the afternoons we had a very different kind of quiet pleasant sitting.

Then we went into little hidden streets, where at deserted bistros bad-tempered old women would serve us dirty glasses of stale beer that we could hardly swallow. In gray and dusty side streets we sat away our afternoons; watching the people come and go who don't walk for pleasure, watching the flow of life that does not see itself because its living is too close and real. Mornings and evenings we saw Gay Paree, but afternoons we saw Chelsea and the East Side, every shabby street from South Boston to Bucharest, empty of life and full of living, the quickslow fatlean oldyoung shabby ones who have no names. We sat and saw them endlessly ever and never the same, an endless broken-rhythmed movement from somewhere to somewhere and nowhere to nowhere. Each time we saw the kind of face or step or look we thought we knew, we knew the more we knew nothing. We thought we knew where we were, and then we weren't so sure; we only knew this moving, this coming and going, slow steady flowing from nothing to nothing, from zero to infinity. Dusty sunlight in a faded street.

"What does it mean, Craig, where are they going, where are we going?"

"You tell me, why don't you!"

Dusty sunlight and the noises far and near, city sounds that rise and fall and never die, a voice of many tones, speaking the words we hear but cannot understand.

"What can we do, Craig, to make it stop for a minute, to make the whole damn thing stop and look at us for a minute?"

"You're asking me?"

Dusty sunlight and the feeling of old stone and the feeling of blood, not the quick blood of a wound, but the slow, stale blood of life's endless seepage. "Look, Craig, look at that dog over there in the gutter; it's free! It doesn't see what we see! It doesn't have to try to understand!"

At night we sat at the big cafés in Montparnasse and tried not to look like Americans. "We can never do it," Craig used to say, "until we get suits with pointed lapels and stop wearing crêpe-soled shoes." We would have liked to do the boîtes on Montmartre, but we didn't have the money to waste; we had to go places where we could sit for a long time without spending much. So we sat at the Dôme and the Rotonde and wondered what they had been like in the good old days before all the Americans went home to Connecticut. There were still young Americans to be seen around in various states of intoxication, but they none of them looked as though they might be Hemingways or Harry Crosbys or McAlmons. Most of them looked as though they might be medical students or bank clerks, and certainly none appeared to be wearing the black hat very hard. We sat at the bright noisy corner and tried not to look like

Americans, while we talked about nothing else except America, and why we were Americans and what it meant and what we were going to do about it. I don't remember what we said anymore; there was a lot of talk about time concepts and the sensuality of motion, about the abstractions of materialism and deracination, about lack of resistance by tradition and even the melting pot. There was endless talk about the American Scene and Pure Art, and of it all I remember almost nothing. It was serious and completely unimportant, and we forgot what we had said one night in time to say it again the next.

We sat and watched and knew that we were waiting for something to happen, as every American must wait for something to happen, and gradually grew more and more content to have what was to happen be nothing happening at all. Almost we ceased to care to think we knew what we were waiting for. We sat and watched.

Naturally, as you might expect, the great diversion of our evening sitting was that of watching the girls. Back home in Springfield we had always heard the usual stories about the women of Paris, and now that we were there seeing them, we could see that there was a reason for all the talk. As Craig said, having looked over the Françaises he could understand why the frogs didn't want the Germans to get Paris. Sitting there at the Dôme and the Rotonde we saw some mighty interesting specimens, and seeing them we were wishing all the time that we were a lot richer and more experienced and less generally terrified of something that had been a continual source of speculation for years without ever ceasing to be a hopelessly insoluble problem. And so we watched and joked, savoring in imagination the thing we wanted but didn't dare to touch. It wasn't that both of us hadn't had the usual adolescent experiences, or that we didn't know, or think we knew, about all there was to the subject, but somehow there was an impassable barrier between the Springfield high school girls whom you pawed in rumble seats and the Paris *poules* who stared at you with unconcealed contempt. And so we sat and watched and wondered, yearning with mind and body, trying vainly to believe that we were being sensible and mature and only succeeding in feeling more intensely the frustration of our immaturity.

It's true that we did have one mild adventure, but that only served to increase our discontent, increasing desire without increasing confidence or removing doubt. It was nothing extraordinary—two obviously nonprofessional young females who gave us the eye one night as we were walking across the Champ de Mars and picked us up when they found we didn't have the *savoir-faire* to do it ourselves. At this point Craig took control of the situation, attaching to himself the better looking of the two and leading the way down one of the more obscure and less public paths of the gardens that lie beneath the Eiffel Tower. I can't say that I had a particularly good time. The girl was too eager and I was clumsy with her, but at least I found that the difference in language was a great help. Trying to say something in situations where absolutely nothing was to be said had always given me an unnatural horror of them. But that night, having only to talk with lips and hands, above all knowing that I would never have to see the girl again, I had less separation of mind and body, less the feeling of being a ridiculous fool. But after my heat had risen and then cooled, when repeated caresses were no longer a crescendo that swept along the mind in the body's ascent, when kiss after kiss was like the banging of a bad chord, mere product of inertia, when nothing remained of the first excitement but a boredom half disgust; when I had suddenly left the girl without a word, pushed her away, risen, turned, and gone away in a single motion, walking as fast as I could without once looking back until I had come to the edge of the river; then, as I slowly went along the bank, watching the water moving in the spots of mirrored light, feeling the stillness of the silent river in the sleeping night, I felt again, as I had felt before, that these things I had done, the things that had been done to me, could never really have importance, could never be all to me that I wanted them to be, all that I had read and sensed that they could be, until the person for whom they were done and who did them was one speaking to more of me than the body alone. For all of its being in Paris this was no more to me than had been similar experiences in the country roads outside of Springfield. It increased my desires without giving me any greater reason for them.

But with Craig it was otherwise, for he told me next day, though I had done everything I could to keep him from bringing up the subject, that his girl had been a "pretty hot little number" and that she had "given him a real good workout considering it was free." And I could see that the thing had started up in him a new kind of inside movement that had not been there before, for from then on, though he didn't say it, I could see that the half unhappy pleasure of our quiet watching waiting life in summer Paris was no longer so much for him as it had been. He began to get restless and he didn't talk in the same way as he had been talking; I could see that there was a separation taking place inside him and that he was no longer content to be drifting without a good American goal to hold on to. I could see growing in him the need to be working toward something definite. I could feel the American in him coming back to rule him, could see him beginning to feel that time was wasted in which something wasn't done and that walking and talking, sitting and sipping, watching and waiting, were not enough to make a completed life. He didn't start to work again at his poetry, but he read again and seemed hardly to notice the quiet life around him but only to notice the busy moving life, to realize that time was going on without him. He was changing, as I say, and I could see it but I didn't say anything, because I knew that it would only make it go faster. I knew what the change would be, and I was sorry for it.

Somehow I knew the day on which he would go, the boat on which he would sail, before he even tried to break the news to me. And somehow he sensed from the way I answered him, that there was no need for him to explain anything, that I quite understood and that I would not try to change his mind. I didn't and he bought his ticket. We agreed that he would tell my parents that I had joined up with two English boys whom we had gotten to know in Paris who were "very steady and quite all right," so that they wouldn't think I was alone and try to make me come home, and that he would spread the word around in Springfield that I was putting the finishing touches on a novel that a big London publisher was just waiting to publish. Craig left me his American razor blades, and the night before he sailed we celebrated the end of our partnership with champagne, but as we could only afford a half-bottle, we neither of us managed to work up much gaiety. I was sorry to see him go, but not as much as I should have expected if I'd known it was going to happen two months before. We have always been each other's best friend, and we still are, but somehow it seemed to me perfectly natural that we should come apart just as we had gone together, casually almost without any sentiment or excitement. Craig said he would write, and I knew he wouldn't and knew as well that the moment I saw him again we would be right away as good friends as ever we had been. So Craig went home the third week in September, and I stayed on in Paris with the slow-flowing Seine and the shadow of black Josh down the hall.

As the boat train was pulling out of the Gare St. Lazare, Craig leaned out the window and started to spout some sort of slush about what our being together had meant to him, but I said, "Stuff it, Alexander, stuff it!" and Craig laughed and shouted, "O.K., Boss," as the train rolled away from me down the platform.

For about a week after Craig had gone I felt as though something inside me was going around without any clothes on, but soon it began to get itself dressed, and by October Craig had gotten to be for me just part of Springfield, though often at unexpected moments I suddenly remembered things about him—the way he had of summing up a discussion with a bad epigram and the way he had of running his fingers along a wall or a fence when we were walking.

I had a long letter from him from the boat full of unconvincing explanations which seemed entirely natural. He said that of course it had been a wonderful experience, and that he couldn't thank me enough for all the help I had been to him, but that he was convinced that, although he would always want to live a life of the spirit and the intellect, he wasn't really gifted for poetry and that probably he had just mistaken sensitivity for something more. He ended up by saying that he knew I had real talent and that I shouldn't let myself be discouraged by what he imagined was just a normal interval of lying fallow.

I didn't reread his letter, but I didn't throw it away, because I could see that he'd spent a lot of time on it, probably making two or three drafts to get it right.

Then there was the letter from Springfield saying that the town hadn't razzed him half as much as he'd expected and that most of the people were really a good deal better sort than he'd thought. Later he wrote from Chicago that his father had agreed to put him through the university so that he could get a teaching job, and then there was nothing for about five months, until I got one of those fancy engagement announcements in two envelopes. It was a girl I'd never liked much, but her father had a big drygoods business and she'd been East to school. On the corner of the card Craig had written in pencil "How'm I doin?" with three big dollar signs after it. I thought about the dollar signs and thought about some of the poems he had written, and then I didn't think anymore because I saw there was really nothing to think about.

For a while after Craig had gone I went on with my quiet life, watching the flow of the city living, slow as the flow of the river, waiting for nothing, as the Parisians seemed to be waiting for nothing, and as their river the Seine seemed not to be knowing that it was flowing or where it was going. For a while, I say, things were as they had been, except that I was doing them alone and a little sadly. And then I too began to change, though not as Craig had changed. I didn't rebel at the movement around me, or fight against it as he had done, I simply began to become a part of it, to move with it and in it, to go as it flowed, to be one with it. Still I was watching the waiting, but now the two were one thing; the watching became my waiting. I was no longer waiting for nothing because I was watching, but because my watching was in time with my waiting, I was not waiting as Americans wait, waiting for something to happen, I was waiting as Parisians wait, awaiting nothing and yet always having something, having my watching and then finally another thing—my telling.

Yes, again the top came off my typewriter and I bought hundreds of sheets of white paper, and again my writing began. But now it was different than it had been before, it was a part of the very flowing it described. It was no longer a means to something, but something itself, no longer something I was waiting to have happen, to have succeed, to win me fame and escape from Springfield; it was, as I say, no longer this to me, it was a constant part of life to me, something I did each day as I ate and sat and talked and watched and waited. It came to be not telling life for me, but part of life itself for me.

And so as fall came on and the heat of summer fell away, I came to be working every day, telling the things I saw and what I thought I knew about them, making a picture of this slow and steady movement, this gradual onward flowing, this simple waiting that I felt and lived. As the leaves fell and the nights grew cold, as each day the lights came on a little earlier, as each day the air told more of winter's coming, as each day there was less struggle inside me between what remained of the life at home and what was building of my own life, I came to have, to really have and really know, what we had tried so hard to find and never found, I came to be a writer and began to be a man.

*T*he animals came in two by two,
The Elephant and the Kangaroo.
   At last Noah became downhearted, because the roof of the
Ark leaked, and many of the animals were sea-sick, and those
that were not sea-sick, quarreled incessantly among
themselves . . .

CHERBOURG

He thought he would just play a little trick on the customs
officers and smuggle in a few packages of Luckies and some
American pipe tobacco. After the bags had been examined and
chalk-marked, the inspector at the gate to the railway platform
asked if M'sieu' would permit that he examine the overcoat that
M'sieu' was carrying on his arm. M'sieu' was obliged to pay his
fine in francs, and when the money-changer gave him a bad
rate, he shoved his hat back on his head and stood glaring for
some moments with his mouth hanging open, unable to speak.
When the fine had been paid and the cherished Luckies and
tobacco surrendered, he came and sat down beside me in the
second class carriage. His face was dripping with perspiration
and required repeated moppings with a handkerchief.
   I hoped the train would start soon. It was tiresome watching

the people come and go on the platform. I could hardly wait to see if the women would be washing clothes in the little stream over which the train would soon pass. It would only take the train a few minutes to get there. I should have to be careful not to miss the place, as I had done once. Thinking of it made me remember how disappointed I had been at the time. I had kept on looking out the window long after Cherbourg had been left far behind, hoping that the train might not yet have passed the stream. (Maybe there wouldn't be any women there that day, kneeling at the water's edge, scrubbing clothes on flat rocks. Maybe they only washed at the stream on certain days, and they wouldn't be there after all.)

He said that he certainly would never let himself be caught in a fix like that again and be forced to take a bad rate of exchange. I asked why he hadn't thought to buy some francs from the purser, but he didn't answer me. He took out his pipe and tobacco pouch, preparing for a smoke. I pointed to the sticker on the carriage window. He put the pipe and the pouch back into his pocket, after deciphering the sticker and muttering something about "foolish restrictions." Then he stared out of the window and didn't know what to do with his hands.

I watched his hands while he tried to decide what to do with them. They were almost pudgy, and the fingernails were edged with grime. I wondered why he never cleaned them. (If he washed clothes in a stream all day, his fingernails wouldn't be dirty. The flesh of his fingers would be raised in little ridges, as was mine when I had stayed in swimming too long.)

The train made a false start; I thought for a moment it was really about to leave.

PARIS

He wanted to go to the Dôme, because that was the one place where we could see together all the various Parisian types. He said that the only way to understand the life of a great city in all its complexities was to become familiar with the different types of people that lived in it. This we could do at the Dôme, and it would be easy to get there by the Métro; we wouldn't have any trouble at all, for he had travelled all over Paris underground. Then we could sit at one of the tables on the sidewalk outside the Dôme and watch all the different types go by.

I didn't like the smell in the cars of the Métro. They smelt like the school gymnasium after basketball practice. There were too many people in the cars. Most of them were workmen in blue smocks. I supposed they were going home from their work for the night.

He called my attention to the diagram of the Métro system on the side of the car, showing me how we should be obliged to change at Palais Royal and Sebastopol to reach the station nearest the Dôme. In the hot car he began to perspire and his face grew lividly red. (Whenever his face was red, his bad eye seemed more blank than ever. Maybe it was because the good eye looked so angry, that the contrast with the other was increased. Often I was afraid to look at the bad eye. For sometimes I could hardly stop staring at it. Once I was sure it was about to roll out of its socket, drool slowly down his face, and drop into his open mouth.)

It was nice walking through the long underground passageways at the change stations. They were walled with bathroom tile like the big tunnel in Rome from the Piazza di Spagna to the Via 4 Settembre, running under the gardens. *I had wanted to walk in the gardens, but Malespino had said they were closed to the public. They were shut in, high up as they were, with white walls. But I knew there were gardens inside, because the heads of palm trees showed over the wall. That was like the picture of the Hanging Gardens of Babylon in the book about the Seven Wonders. . . .*

He couldn't find a vacant table on the sidewalk in front of the Dôme; so we had to stand on the corner. He didn't say anything, because he was pretending to be so busy studying the types of people sitting at the tables. Then too, I suspect that he was waiting for me to say how glad I was that we had come to the Dôme, and how fine a place I thought it. After a while he could no longer keep up the pretense of being interested in the people about us; he began to talk. He spoke of the Rotonde across the street; of the radical literati living in Montparnasse; of his previous stay in Paris, when he had lived at a little pension and been taken to dine with Ezra Pound.

I couldn't see many "types" around the Dôme. Almost all the people at the tables were Americans anyway. Of these, some were noisy because they were getting tight, others because they wished to seem to be getting tight. I soon grew tired of watching them. Perhaps it would be more fun across the street at the Rotonde; but when I glanced in that direction, it seemed little better than the Dôme. The people passing were at least silent in their motion, but even they didn't strike me as being "types." Except, perhaps, for the sleek girls in tight-fitting silk dresses with big floppy hats who walked by so very slowly. Sometimes they passed in pairs, going along arm in arm, seeming not to look about them or pay any attention to the crowded tables. I stared at them as they went by, watching the ripple of their smooth stride under the shiny silk. I was frightened when one of them noticed my stare and glanced back at me, as she passed along. I was frightened for fear he had seen her look at me in that way. But he hadn't. I wondered what he would do, if one of those girls looked at him in that way. I wondered what his bad eye would do, if one of them should look at him. I could guess what his face would do, and what his mouth would do. Perhaps his eye might roll out of its socket and slither into his mouth. Perhaps it might turn as red as the rest of his face. Maybe it might split in two and hang open like his mouth.

> (One eye blue
> And one eye red
> And one eye split
> Through the head head head)

He said that if we waited, we would be able to get a table, and then it would be more interesting.

But I replied, "Let's go back to the hotel; this isn't any fun."

(Boulevard Montparnasse as far as the Gare Montparnasse: Rue Vaugirard as far as Boulevard Raspail: Boulevard Raspail to Saint Germain-des-Prés: Rue Bonaparte to the quai: up the quai to the Pont du Louvre: Past the Tuilleries Gardens along the Rue de Rivoli: Rue St. Honoré, 259bis: Hotel de France et Choiseul: Chauffage centrale: Ascenseur automatique: English spoken.)

> *One eye blue*
> *And one eye red*
> *And one eye split*
> *Through the head head head*
>
> *One eye blue*
> *And one eye red*
> *And one eye hops*
> *Into bed bed bed*

(Also, though less clearly. *The butcher, the baker, the candlestick-maker. Shadrach, Meshach & Intobedwehop.*)

A SECOND-CLASS CARRIAGE

IN A TRAIN BETWEEN SPIEZ AND ZERMATT

I kept looking at the pipe he held in his teeth. No matter how much the train swayed it never moved. It grew out of his mouth like a strong tree, a tree that cannot be shaken. It was deeply rooted in his teeth and did not waver. It was as much a part of his head as his nose or his chin. The spaces between the front teeth were yellow, but the teeth themselves were bright and white. No matter how much he scrubbed them, the spaces between would remain yellow.

I listened to the regular sucking of his breath as he puffed. I watched the smoke curl up from the bowl of his pipe and saw little wisps of it eddy through the yellow spaces between his teeth. I could not keep from smelling the smoke; the carriage was full of it. It was a flat smell like long-dead cigarette ashes in an ashtray. The leather upholstery of the carriage seats had a flat smell, too, as if the heat of many bodies had ingrained the smell of ashes in the cushions. I sat very still, trying to keep that smell from eating into me. I knew that if I moved at all, it would filter through my clothes, coating over the surface of my body; that if I drew breath, it would come creeping and seeping down into my lungs, to lie heavily in them. I sat so still that I could feel the blood pressing against my skin in every part of my body, and feel the emptiness of my lungs, waiting for the breath which I withheld. Out of my stillness I watched his face and the slow-mounting puffs of smoke; watched his teeth with the smoke-wisps eddying between them; watched his good eye staring into space. And as I watched I knew that his good eye was trying to die too, trying to get out of life as the other eye had done before it. It neither moved nor wavered, but the light was ebbing from it and dullness was stealing into it. In a moment, if I did not stop it, it would cease to see at all; in another moment if I did not move, it would join the bad eye in death. Then he would be blind and never stop smoking. Those puffs would rise forever, and those firm teeth never release their grip on the pipestem. My lungs were rising up within me, surging up for breath, unable to hold out longer. An instant more I checked the gasp for air, feeling my whole body's tenseness, seeing still his eye's slow dying; moment of delirious agony, of wonderful waiting. Then a great frantic gasp of air, and his head jerked sharply toward me, recalling the near-dead eye to life.

When I looked out the window a moment later, I could see the peak of the Matterhorn up at the end of the valley. I held my head firm and still against the back of the seat, and its sharp white beak slipped slowly across the window with the train's turning. It moved ever so slowly like a house being dragged along on rollers.

VIENNA: THE DINING ROOM
OF THE HOTEL METROPOLE

He didn't say a word all during dinner in spite of my repeated jibes. (When I had wanted to rough-house up in the bedroom, he had stood staring at me with his mouth open in disgust.)

I said:

"Haven't you got anything to say for yourself at all?"

"For God's sake, why don't you say something once in a while, instead of just sitting there?"

I said a great deal more, as well.

He didn't say anything.

Between us, we emptied two bottles of Barsac.

BERLIN

He had another one of those guidebooks now, and with its aid he was explaining the significance of the monuments and public buildings which we passed along Unter den Linden. He supplemented the information in the guidebook with what he had doubtless learned in his college history course, giving biographical details of the early Hohenzollern rulers.

I said I would meet him around the block. Then I ran as fast as I could so that he couldn't see me, when he should round the other corner. I went past a synagogue and a great cathedral with towers like a Turkish or Russian mosque. I strolled into the courtyard of the palace of William-der-last-now-Hollander. At the gate to the grand hall I paid two marks; then, with big felt slippers over my shoes, I went skating over the glassy floors of the palace. I paid no attention to the guide, who was bellowing in German. Instead, I looked closely at the pictures of naked ladies and gents on the wall. I tried to guess what the German titles meant and laughed to myself at the immense buttocks of the many naked ladies.

When I got back to the hotel, I discovered him soaking his feet in a hellish pink broth, because he said he had athlete's foot.

BRUSSELS

He suggested that we should take a sightseeing bus out to Waterloo. It wouldn't take very long, and besides, Waterloo was one of the places we really couldn't afford to miss. Then he outlined at some length the historical importance of Waterloo.

While he was taking a bath, I sneaked down the hotel stairs and out into the street. Walking past the Bourse, I came to the Guildhall. Inside, was a museum dark and dusty, filled with musty old figures dressed in period costumes. I liked those costumes; they were so perfectly useless and impractical. They made me think of Fort Ticonderoga with its wax figures in bright British uniforms. But there was no costume on the Mannequin Pis, when I came to look at him in a little street below the Guildhall. But in the window of a nearby store I saw rows of postcards, showing him decked out in every imaginable kind of rig. And there were little tin replicas of him with suction balls attached. I wanted to buy one, but I was afraid to go in and ask for it. There were lots of "humorous" cards, too; one showed an old gentleman putting up his umbrella, because he thought it was raining. (However, this card was unjustified, since it was based on a fallacy; I found on inspection that the jet of water in question fell neatly into a basin fixed below it for that special purpose.) A little further on I sat down in front of a café and asked for a *bière*. The waiter brought me Walsheim beer, smooth and soft to the tongue, not too bitter, and just a bit oily. I drank it slowly, letting each sip swish around in my mouth before swallowing it. Then for a long time I sat quite still beside my marble-top table, watching the sun strike in odd shapes on the house-walls across the street. There was no one else in front of the café, and the waiter didn't seem to mind how long I sat there.

AMSTERDAM: THE PIER OF THE
HOLLAND-AMERIKA LINE

While waiting for the tender, he remarked that it "wouldn't be long now" before he could buy some good American tobacco instead of that damn European hay.

I sat slumped on my suitcase, watching the preparations for embarkation. In a few moments we would be allowed on the tender. Already the gangway was in place, and people were crowding toward it. But I did not get up to follow them, though I knew he was anxious to be off. I was watching little waves slap up against a piling. The water was muggy brown, laden with refuse. It sloshed despondently against the piling; rubbed itself catlike along the tender's side. But in a day or two, out to sea, it would be brittle and clear. It would raise itself in whitecaps in the wind. It would reflect the changing mood of cloud and sun. There would be sea-change and new birth by water.

After she had cleared away the dinner plates, Evelyn brought in the dessert. It was served in the kitchen, and she carried it in two plates at a time. Of the first two dishes she gave one to the Professor and the other to George. (For even the servants seemed to sense that George was the Professor's "Prize Cash Customer" and gave him preference accordingly.) Then all the other men, except John Gruer, kept making signs to Evelyn, as she came through the kitchen door, each hoping to be given his dessert before the others. But John Gruer never gave a thought to his food; sitting slumped in his chair, he ate and drank mechanically what was set before him, staring at the wall when he had finished. Even the Professor took a sly interest in the distribution. He didn't speak, but sat regally at the end of the table, half smiling, with his thumbs tucked under the edges of his waistcoat and his left eye squinted. The right lens of his spectacles was opaque, for the eye behind it was sightless, and I wondered often, as I watched him squinting, if the left eye were not slowly attracted into blindness.

As I didn't like the look of my dessert, a mealy baked apple, I began squeezing my napkin into its ring. This the others noticed at once; all except John Gruer, who was already eating his apple, digging into it methodically with his spoon. Danny Murphy fixed his beady little eyes on my plate, and Tim

Moynehan leered meaningfully at me. Being only hirelings, neither dared ask openly for my apple in the presence of their master; but when the Professor was not at the table, the two Irishmen would devour all the food they could lay hand on, and laugh greedily at John Lyon's off-color jokes. And it was to him that I ceded my dessert; I liked Danny and Tim well enough, but after all, they were only "damned Irish bloodsuckers," as George used to say, and there was little to be gained in showing them favors.

I left the dining room and went out on to the porch, where I sat down to wait for George. I hoped he would be finished soon so that we might get away for a walk into the woods before dark should come on. I sat on the edge of the porch, kicking my heels against its side and watching Fraulein Knaus. She was down the slope a little way between the house and the lake pitching horseshoes, while keeping an eye on Miss Benjamin, her charge. Miss Benjamin was standing beyond Fraulein by the lakeshore. She had a handful of stones and was throwing them out into the water. She couldn't throw them far; it was easy to see from her clumsy movements that she had never played with a ball. But that was not surprising, for she had been at the Professor's almost all her life. George told me that she was around twenty, but I should have guessed forty at the least. Her face was that of an old woman, and her matted black hair accentuated the darkness that ringed her eyes.

I expected George to join me any minute; when he didn't come, I judged that he had decided against walking that evening. Knowing the futility of any attempt at persuasion, I resigned myself to what other amusement might be at hand. That meant a book or Fraulein Knaus. I would have had to go upstairs to get a book; so I went down off the porch to where Fraulein was pitching horseshoes. Coming on her unawares, I picked one of her shoes deftly out of the air before it reached its mark. She pretended to be angry, and told me to go away and stop being a nuisance. I caught the next shoe, too, and told her that I could beat her pitching left-handed. That was a sufficient taunt, where one was hardly needed; we started the game. At first, I could not come near the peg, but when I gained some measure of control, it was easy to slip inside her wild, rolling pitches. Dull sport it was, but I liked to watch Fraulein and hear her talk. She was dressed in silk, fitted tightly over her plumpness; almost fat, but she carried her flesh well and it became her. I liked to watch her smile, especially when she was trying to catch some unfamiliar English word. How she ever came to work for the Professor I couldn't understand. She wasn't the least bit callous, and had certain little feminine mannerisms that were irrestistible. Possibly these same traits appealed as well to the Professor, senile as he was; for even in his moments of regal dignity I detected certain qualities foreign to that role.

Soon I was winning every round, while Fraulein was complaining about her bad luck. But she seemed to make singularly little effort to throw the shoes correctly, in the way I had often shown her. I spoke of it again; she tried for a little while to throw them the right way, placing the index finger on the end and gripping between the thumb and second finger, but then she fell back on her own method, saying that mine was far too complicated. I started showing her again, determined this time to make it wholly clear. I placed the shoe properly in her hand and then stood directly behind her, holding her wrist to guide the pitch. Thus my body was pressed against hers, while my arm half circled her. The shoe was pitched with perfect form, but Fraulein was squeezed with neither grace nor dignity, albeit effectively. She struggled very feebly indeed to loose herself and laughingly expostulated, "Let me go, you bad boy!"

Then I heard Miss Benjamin's shrill voice, "Ooo, you naughty boy. I'm going to tell on you. I'm going to tell the Professor what you were doing."

I was truly annoyed. I knew well enough that she would run to the Professor; tale-bearing was half of life to her. Then I remembered something.

"If you go telling the Professor things about me," I said, trying to look menacing, "I'll tell Ed Bridges what you said about Mildred Day."

My thrust was effective. "I never said anything bad about Mildred Day," she screeched. "You know I didn't."

"If you go squealing," I went on, shouting to interrupt her, "I'll tell Ed Bridges that you're crazy about him and so jealous of Mildred Day you called her a dirty, filthy little . . ."

I jumped aside just in time to avoid a handful of stones. Then I laughed at her, and she began to cry. Fraulein tried to look cross but didn't succeed. "You terrible boy!" she said.

Soon the tearful one was comforted (her fits of anguish and rage were frequent and short-lived), and when the Professor came out on the porch for his evening cigar, I was unobtrusively picking up the scattered horseshoes from the grass.

When I saw that the Professor had settled himself in his big chair on the porch where he would remain for some time, I decided to walk after all, even if I must go alone. I set off through the woods toward Day's, where the evening mail was always left by the rural carrier. On the road to Day's it was fairly dark. Here and there a little sunlight broke through the trees, but the sun was so low that it shone in my face, not on the road. I picked up a stick and began knocking the tops off tall woodland plants along the trail. The stalks of meadow rue broke easily and fell to the ground at the first blow. But the elderberry bushes were not so easily broken. I swiped viciously at them with my stick, but sometimes it took two or three blows to bring them down. I liked jewel weeds the best; they grew closely together, and I could wipe out a whole clump with a single sweep, cutting the stalks evenly as a mowing machine cuts hay.

Coming around a bend in the road, I saw two figures ahead of me, walking in the same direction as myself, only more slowly. They were Mrs. MacQuillan and Steubenroch, the German. Even before I caught up with them, I could hear the old lady mumbling to herself. She walked very slowly, talking steadily in a low voice. Nor did she ever give her companion an opportunity to reply. But now and again she would stop and turn toward him, as if to drive home some particular point. Then on again, still muttering. When I came up beside Steubenroch, he began to talk with me as if we were alone. And the old lady paid little heed to our conversation, till we began to talk about schools. Then she turned to me, though her eyes seemed to see nothing, tumbling word on word, "I know all about schools. Yes, indeed I do. I had just as good an education as any man. I was four years in the university learning to be a doctor. Everyone in this world has got to do something. That's the only way you'll ever be happy in this world. I'm a doctor, saving other people's lives. I could be a queen, if I wanted to. You don't believe that, do you? I could be a queen this minute, but I'd rather be a doctor. Do you know who my mother was? My mother was Good Queen Victoria. I could be a queen too, but I'm a doctor. I'm Dr. Dowling. That's who I am. I'm Dr. Dowling. I spend all my time curing people. That's what I do. You won't ever be happy in this world, if you don't cure people. I could be a queen if I wanted, but I'd rather be a doctor. I'd rather be a doctor, because a doctor's higher than a queen. That's why. I could be queen of England now, but I'm higher than a queen. I'm higher than a queen. A queen is higher than everyone else except a doctor. A doctor is the only one can save a queen from dying. I'm higher than a queen. I can save a queen from dying. I've saved lots of people from dying. I saved three people from dying last night. They all had typhus fever. But I saved them from dying. I knew how to save them, because I'm a doctor. I can bring in babies too. That's what a good doctor likes to do best. Bringing in babies. I've brought in lots of babies. I brought in two babies last night. Two new babies. I didn't let them die. A good doctor doesn't ever let any babies die . . ."

I couldn't listen any longer. I wanted terribly to put my arm around her and calm her into silence. But I knew that no one could ever give her silence. Steubenroch motioned for me to go on. I walked ahead as fast as I could, but I still heard her for a long time. I wondered how Steubenroch could bear to listen to her. Yet when I passed them on my way back with the mail, he was still walking slowly at her side, seeming to listen intently to that current of gibberish.

It was dark by the time I reached the house, and the men were all sitting in the living room, where the lamps were lit. There was the Professor squinting with his good eye at a newspaper, while the Irishmen played bridge with John Lyons and Ed Bridges. John Gruer was working on a crossword puzzle. He did the puzzle in the "Tribune" every night, and on the days when the papers were delayed in the mail, he was more gloomy than ever, sitting motionless by the empty fireplace till it was time to go to bed. He seemed to live entirely for his puzzles, since, only when working at one, did he show the least sign of animation or pleasure. I felt I couldn't stomach the living room. Besides, I was tired and ready for sleep.

Upstairs, when I had prepared for bed, I went into George's room for a smoke. He was sitting on his bed in a litter of papers and letters. All day these documents were locked in his shoe trunk, and every evening were brought out to be read over and again. Seeing me, George broke out, "Oh, there you are. Thought you'd be along soon. Want you to read this letter from Parsons. (How many times already I had had to read it.) Wrote me this just before that thing happened. Deliberately lied to me, whom I had trusted more than anyone. Just read it, and tell me if I've not been misused."

I didn't take the letter; I just said, "I'm pretty tired tonight, old man. I'll have a look at it in the morning."

He was already reading another paper and didn't answer; so I rested my hand on his shoulder for a moment, and then crossed the hall to my own room, where I got into bed.

The new butler had been in the house in Cam-
bridge, Massachusetts, only three days. The family was that of
a deceased Harvard professor, Alexander Lowell Whitten, not a
poor and earnest professor but a man whose name was in the
Social Register and who had had plenty of money from his
parents who had had it from their parents.

"You can see they have money," the new butler's wife had
said the first night they were in the house, "They have the
loveliest things . . . you can tell they cost plenty . . ."

They had been worried at first because the house was not
large. They took the place without even seeing anyone in the
family, just to get away from where they were, in a house in a
bad neighborhood. They wanted to be in a big house in Milton
or on the North Shore with the wife not cooking but only
helping upstairs or looking after the linen and the lady. They
were not quite up to this class yet, but they hoped to get there.
And Cambridge seemed a step nearer it.

The reason there was no interview was that the family had
been away for the summer in Europe and had written to the
agency from abroad to tell them to have a couple in the house
when they arrived. There were other servants of course, a little
Irish maid named Bridget, and an American laundress, a
woman from the country. The butler made it clear at once to

these two that there were to be distinctions in the back of the house. Everything would be friendly but there would be a line. This was not difficult to do because the maid and the laundress were very simple people, much impressed by the way the new couple came in a cab with fine looking luggage and an air of superior importance. It had always been an easy-going house because the professor's wife was very deaf. And there had never been a serving man in the house before. There had been chauffeurs and gardeners outside the house, but never a man inside.

What the butler and his wife were to the world was a dependable couple. They did not want to be this, and they weren't, but they appeared so. The man was not dependable. He read letters that were left lying about and he listened on the telephone. He profiteered on the small transactions that were entrusted to him. He didn't do this because he hoarded money, but because it was obviously the thing to do. His wife didn't do such things, but she knew her husband did them and never tried to stop him.

In fact they were not servants at all. Of course really they *were* servants; they had been servants, he for ten years and she for twelve, and they had been good ones, but they were not servants by nature. Sometimes someone who employed them would find herself thinking of them as visitors in her kitchen. There was nothing they did that was wrong, but they were interlopers.

Naturally Paul Usclavics did not use his Polish name. He had been born in Saugus, an industrial suburb of Boston, and there was nothing foreign about him on the surface. So he was able to take the name of Paul Martin and have no one except his wife, who wasn't the kind of person to care, know that it was not his real name. In looks he could easily have been English, except for the fact that he could not make himself be a servant type. He had a thinnish face that might have been called "sensitive" but was really more quick than intelligent. He had hair that was noticeable because its shade of brown looked like molasses. He had almost no beard and his eyebrows were so light as to leave his eyes unimportant. He was short and not heavy, thin in the shoulders, but very strong nevertheless and never ill. Altogether he was good enough looking to have married Rachel Wilson.

Rachel was not a servant either, though not in the way that her husband was not. She was intelligent as well as quick. Her cooking showed this. In most houses she could cook with more intelligence than the mistress could appreciate.

As soon as she finished high school she had to go to work to help support her family. The father was dead and the mother had ulcers and could work only off and on and there were younger children who had to be fed and clothed while they were in school. If Rachel's mother had had enough money to send her to a secretarial school she would have made a very good office worker, perhaps one who might have become a business woman by her own efforts. But because there was no money she went into the kitchen of a big house as cook's helper and in two years she could cook as well as the cook she helped. Rachel Wilson was able to get above the routine of kitchen labor and see cooking as something that could be done with the mind just as much as an office job is done with the mind (though of course she never thought it out like that for herself). And so when she was still in her early twenties she was cook in a good house on Marlborough Street in Boston.

Paul Usclavics came to the same house as butler after she had been there about a year. And in about a year from that time they were married. It was a courtship, not a seduction. It was not kisses in the pantry and a stealing into a dark room or a lying on the damp ground in spring but a neat matter of question and answer. "Will you come out to the pictures tonight?" . . . "Will you come to my folks for dinner the next night we're off?" . . . and finally "Rachel, will you marry me?" just like that.

Rachel Wilson was not pretty in any way, but she kept herself so well and had such an air of being somebody of importance that her husband steadily loved her. She had an instinctive knowledge of how to hold him. They had for a long time an intimate life together that was passionate in its inarticulate way. Usclavics was not peasant Pole but city Pole, so that in his lovemaking he was never simple and always a bit self-conscious. With anyone else his wife could have been truly passionate, but not with him. And this restraint was part of their bond—because it was in itself an attractive and to him enjoyable thing. It kept her for him always a little in the class of something rare to be won.

The Whitten family arrived home from Europe the day after the Martins came to the house and they were pleased with Paul at once because he seemed to have learned immediately all the habits of the household. The first meal, which the professor's widow had been dreading all the way home on the steamer, was managed perfectly. Paul used the right plates for the right things and got through the pantry door without its squeaking. As a matter of fact he had oiled its hinges the night before in the same efficient, mechanical way that he had gone through unlocked desk drawers in the upstairs sitting room looking at check-book stubs and old bills, and stolen a pretty piece of underwear with good lace on it from the room of one of the daughters to put on his wife. The thing about Paul Martin was that now he wouldn't steal anything more for a long while and perhaps never again in that house. The family would not notice things disappearing— they would just get lost every once in a while and not turn up again. He did not steal to sell, nor for pleasure. It was just a form of self-assertion, one of the many little ways he had of impressing his figure on the air about him, so that inside himself he could feel of consequence. To be a good butler, even a perfect butler, would not have made him feel important.

* * *

Yes, the Whittens were pleased with their new servants. All but one of the daughters who noticed that the butler's hands were "queer." She said it to her sister: "Don't you think he has 'queer' hands?" But her sister had not noticed them. There was nothing really wrong with them—they were clean and not misshapen—yet she felt about them at once that they were not the kind of hands she was used to see passing serving dishes around a table and that in a way she did not like to have her food from them. This was only a small impression on the part of the second daughter, whose name was Harriet.

There had been five daughters but one died. The mother had always given the impression of having more daughters than she knew what to do with. Perhaps the fact that she grew deaf when still fairly young had something to do with it. She seemed apart from her daughters in spite of loving them and worrying over them in the normal way.

The few days that the butler had been in the house had been extremely agitated. This pleased him because it gave him an opportunity to get a hold on the family at once by showing how efficient he was. There was not only the ones who came home from abroad, the mother and three of her daughters, but the fourth daughter, who was married and about to have her first child, arrived all unexpectedly in the house with her husband. They lived in the country, in New Hampshire. The husband was a writer, though not a successful one. Suddenly his digestion had gone bad on him, and they came to town to see a good doctor. No sooner had they arrived than he became really seriously ill and had to be in bed, with nurses and a doctor coming to the house several times a day. Add to this that of course all the friends of the family who had not seen them all summer had to come to call, asking "How was your trip?" and "Did you go to such and such a place?" and then not listening—

especially the young boy friends of the youngest daughter, Marian, who was very pretty in an easy way.

The new butler informed himself very soon of everything about the house and had its occupants all placed and accounted for—except for one—the daughter named Harriet. He found her rather baffling. He noticed first of all that she did more than the others about their mother, about seeing that she had what she wanted or had something to do. If she were left to herself Mrs. Whitten would spend most of her time reading a book or playing solitaire. And, except for Harriet the daughters more or less neglected her. But Harriet seemed really fond of her, or, if not fond of her, at least more conscious of a duty to her.

The butler had seen this at once. But there were other things besides that puzzled him in Harriet. Above all there was her voice—not an ordinary speaking voice at all, or like one he had ever heard before. It was extremely cultivated and yet not affected. Any one hearing Harriet speak realized that she had trained her voice and that it meant a great deal to her. She spoke beautifully, because she wanted to. Why? the butler asked himself. A voice like that showed him that life to this girl meant something very different from what it meant to her sisters, but he couldn't yet tell what it was.

She *looked* like any number of girls he had seen in the houses where he had worked—a little on the big side, good-looking without really being pretty, attractive because of the good finish on them, the well-keptness of them, rather than anything physical in them. Harriet was like this to start with, but there was much more—her voice, and a kind of radiance about her, and a way she had of not quarreling at the table with her sisters, even in the friendly way that sisters argue among themselves in public.

There were busy days in the Whitten household. The husband of the married daughter was really ill. The doctor had to come in the night, and Paul, though Mrs. Whitten told him it wasn't expected, stayed up to let him in and out. And there was the continual come and go of friends of the family. All this excited him. This was what he liked. Yet all the while he never long had the daughter Harriet out of his mind or ceased to be on the watch for a glimpse of her. He managed often to go into rooms where she was, or past the door of the room upstairs where she had her piano. And because of Mrs. Whitten's deafness he could go to her for household directions. But he was so deft in his management of these little expeditions that she never noticed that he was pursuing her. It never occurred to her that Paul had any interest in her; nothing he did was obtrusive enough to make her think much about him. She disliked him a little because of his strange hands, but not any more, say, than she disliked the postman who had a purple patch on the side of his face, and certainly not enough to have him on her mind or wish to get him out of the house. She paid no more attention to his appearances than does a person naturally accustomed to having a house full of servants, and she answered his questions with the pleasant detachment—an impersonality that would have seemed forced except for the way her unusual voice went well with it—that was characteristic of her. This detachment, and her voice, and her carriage as she moved or sat still aroused Usclavics more each time he encountered them. This girl was different and he must find out why! There was nothing about her physical appearance that drew him more strongly than the ordinary appeal of a woman's body, yet an attraction existed, of a kind that only a woman could have on a man still young, an attraction, a message, if you like—tacit, inarticulate, and instan- taneous. In Usclavics' mind Harriet Whitten was not yet a woman consciously to be desired, yet she was very definitely in his mind, and as a woman, not just as a person from whom to take orders.

Naturally he wanted to discover whether she were in love with someone. There were no pictures of young men in her room and none came to see her. A good assortment of them, most of them from the college, from Harvard, came to call on the other daughters, or came to take them out, but none of them seemed to be interested in Harriet. He watched her mail and there seemed to be no letters for her in a young man's handwriting. So he felt sure, perhaps because he wanted to feel sure, that there was no one. He watched her when she was with the boys who came to see her sisters. She handled them well. In the way she treated their beaus she was a good sister to her sisters. She made them like her without making them like her as a girl, as she might have.

So Paul had concluded that there was no one paying attentions to Harriet, and he was taken by surprise, and not pleased, when one afternoon, when he had been perhaps two weeks in the house, a voice on the telephone, a young man's voice, asked for her.

"Is this the Whittens'—is Miss Harriet in?"

As soon as he had announced the call to her, Paul hurried to the servants' telephone in the back hall and took off the receiver, very slowly, so she could not hear. The young man's voice was saying, in what seemed to Paul an affected tone, an affectation perhaps caused by agitation, "Why didn't you do what I told you?"

"Where are you?"

"Why didn't you?"

"Where are you now?"

"I'm out at school, out in Milton."

"Are you coming in?"

"Well, I didn't really know whether I would or not."

It was still the affected tone; it was contradiction. Paul could tell that the young man wanted very much to come in, and would most certainly come in, and was just fishing to be urged. The girl seemed to know this too, and not to mind being hooked.

"Well, we're probably having eggs or something for supper, but you better come in anyway."

"No, I don't think I better; I really ought to stay out here for supper."

"All right then, stay out there."

There was a pause. Paul listened with both ears, one for the conversation on the telephone, the other for the sound of some one approaching in the hall who might catch him listening. Then: "Why didn't you do what I told you?"

"I can't talk about that now. You'd better come in after supper and we can talk about it then."

"Oh, I guess I'll come in for supper."

"All right."

"Do you want to see me?"

"Of course."

"Well, I wouldn't have thought so from the way . . . ."

"We'll talk about that when you come in. Don't be late."

"O.K. Hold everything."

"Good-bye."

Paul put back the receiver on the hook at the same instant that Harriet put back hers and then hurried into the pantry in time to be there with his coat off laying out plates when she came in to say there would be one more for supper.

When she went out, Paul stood watching the spot where she had been. There was even more to her for him now that he knew this about her. He had been excited by what he heard and as she stood there in the pantry doorway it had been, for an instant, hard for him to be the respectful butler. Something else in him had almost spoken, something had almost moved as she stood there—but had not.

"One more for dinner," he called through the kitchen door to his wife, and went on with his work, his mind full of what he had heard. The whole picture was changed now from what it had been ten minutes before.

When the doorbell rang a little before seven Harriet was already dressed and downstairs and at the door before Paul reached it. But he caught sight of the visitor—a blondish boy, nice looking, rather short, dressed like all the college boys who came to the house in a tweed coat, striped shirt and grey flannel trousers. He heard Harriet greet him as "Tommy" as he retreated to the pantry . . . "Tommy" . . . he looked like a Tommy.

While Paul served supper he watched him and watched the way Harriet reacted to him. She was different with him; he changed her. Usually she was trying throughout the meal to pull up her sisters' chatter to a proper level of conversation. Tonight she almost seemed to want them to be silly. She was putting herself out more for this Tommy than she ever did for her sisters or girl friends. She was fond of him, that was clear, and wanting to please him, and perhaps a little afraid that she would not please him by being her ordinary self. So she made herself a foil for him in the conversation, leading it to the subjects he liked and holding it there, where he could talk to his pleasure. She even seemed to be putting herself forward to be walked on. She encouraged him to make jokes at her expense. And he did, repeatedly. But they were not so much jokes as sorties. On his part it was still the affected aggressiveness of the telephone conversation. This Tommy seemed to need to say things to her that were downright rude and unkind in order to fulfill himself. There was some sort of barrier in him, some obstruction of self-consciousness, which would not let him be natural. Paul could see that he was not mean; he had a gentle voice. But he couldn't be like it. It was as though there were something in his relation to Harriet which choked him, or on which he choked, making him not himself. It showed in the attacks that he made on her, for such his sallies were. Ostensibly they were entertainment—"cracks"—actually they were attacks, yet attacks not intended to end in capture, more feints, to bring out the opponent into the open. And they succeeded. They made her show herself, show that she liked him well enough to take blows from him. And it even seemed to Paul that she was not hurt by the boy's approach, but expected it and took a kind of pleasure in it, seeing it as a tribute, as a sign of her power that he should be put off balance. Certainly she exposed herself to his thrusts and did nothing to check him.

It made Paul uncomfortable, even though in his rounds with the serving dishes he caught the conversation only in snatches. They were talking about the trip abroad, and Tommy was riding hard on the idea that Harriet and her sisters had done only the most "touristy" things and been "regular little culture-grubbers from Peoria." Some of this was past Paul, but its tone was not, and its tone he disliked. It was as though the boy were wet and uncomfortable and trying to wring himself out. And it made Paul ill at ease to watch him doing it, made him shudder a little. But the others didn't notice it.

Paul served coffee in the living room. Then later while he was clearing the supper table, after his own meal in the pantry with his wife, he saw Harriet go out with Tommy and overheard that they were going to the movies. Paul watched them go from the dining room window. Tommy didn't open the car door for her but went around to the driver's side and got in before she did. Then two doors slammed.

Since there were no guests left in the house Paul could have gone to his own quarters. Mrs. Whitten had returned, just after Harriet left. And Harriet had her own house key. But he waited—for a glimpse of her when she came back. Sitting in the kitchen, he read the *Transcript*, but his mind was not much on it. It was on this unattractive youth who seemed in spite of his unattractiveness to be so interesting to Harriet. Interest . . . it was more than that. It had seemed to Paul that she really wanted this Tommy, wanted to have him want her, wanted his attention, his admiration, his affection. He read that in her performance at the table. It was nothing so patent as a girl's ordinary way of playing up to a man. What had been between them? How long had it been going on? What was the thing she had not done on which he had tried to force her over the telephone? Perhaps something involving another person. Or perhaps it was nothing at all—some trifle that his illness at ease had magnified. Yet no, he thought, there was something of substance hidden there. He had sensed an undercurrent as he waited on table. He had felt that something "wanted out," that something would "out," to which their nervousness, the strain between them, had been a natural preface.

He wondered if they had really gone to the movies. Probably not. More likely they had driven somewhere and then stopped to talk. Out Concord way probably. Maybe at that moment they were having it out. Would they be fighting, or talking in circles to each other, or even making love? The last thought inflamed him and dwelt with him. He pictured the scene: the car parked by the road somewhere, their talk growing slower and more self-conscious, possibly a little silly, looking at each other, looking hard at each other without feeling it strange, the long stare of love's investigation, eye to eye and hand to hand, and then the first light kiss, and then the hard kiss that follows it, and the protest and the denial of it, and the melting together in over-abundance of self and self . . . Paul shook himself free and leafed over his paper. But he looked at it only for a minute. It was he himself in the car with her, with Harriet, alone with her, by the Concord road. It was he, of course it was! . . . and of course it wasn't. But he knew now that he wanted it to be him. He knew now what she was to him, that she was a girl he wanted, that he much wanted, and not just a girl in the house where he worked. The coming of the rival, the successful rival, had driven him on faster than he would otherwise have gone, driven him across a space that perhaps he might never have crossed. And now here he was waiting in eagerness for her return, all trembling as he waited—waited, to see what? To see them come back eased of their strangeness toward each other, or stranger to each other than before? Yes, that would be it. They would have failed to find what they were searching for, failed to discover the bridge; Tommy would still be kicking around on his stilts, and she not herself, but he would go—perhaps curtly, perhaps clumsily lingering—and she would remain in the house—for Paul.

When he heard the car in the drive he went to the pantry window—the room was dark—to watch. They sat in the car for a moment before the engine was shut off and he imagined that Tommy would not come in, or even see her to the door . . . but no; they got out, came in and almost at once he heard them coming toward his place of lookout. They were coming to the pantry to raid the ice box. What to do? Should he show himself and help them and, by so doing put them on their guard and lose all chance of discovering what had taken place? No. Harriet would not suspect any one was still downstairs. He glided into the kitchen and snapped off the light there just as they entered the pantry. Their light went on, shining under the crack of the door. In the darkness he bumped a chair and the terror of discovery thrilled through him . . . but they didn't hear. He heard the door of the refrigerator come open with a soft click and the clink of a milk bottle taken from its shelf. He eased himself onto the chair nearest the door and listened. A cupboard door opened. Glasses were taken down.

"Hey, that's enough. You take the rest."

"Do you want something else?"

"What else is there?"

Sounds of rummaging in the refrigerator. If only he could see. Was he close beside her as she bent to the ice box, perhaps leaning against her, perhaps touching her? Chink of crockery.

"What's that?"

"Prunes."

"All yours."

"There ought to be some cold chicken left over . . . I guess they've eaten it all up out here . . . you'll have to nourish your vast frame on milk alone."

"How about cake?"

The cake box banged open and shut.

"No cake. Nice little place you have here—no cake, no chicken, no nothing . . . nothing but prunes and love—love pure and unabashed, especially pure."

It was still the affected tone, the acted tone, only now it hadn't so much aggression in it. This had been replaced by a kind of whine, a sound of self-pity, of injured innocence almost. It infuriated Paul. The girl's voice was wonderful—still beautiful, but now nearer, its aloofness gone, so human now . . .

"Drink your milk, it'll make your perty hair curl."

"Yeah, like crusts and carrots."

"You were a lovely baby."

"Ravishing. I ravished all my nurses."

"I still have that picture you gave me of yourself in the sandpile."

"Well at least I had some fun then . . . Oh, to be an infahunt back in mother's arrums!"

"Don't you have any fun now?"

"What do you think?"

"I don't know. Don't you? I do."

"So I notice."

Paul edged toward the crack in the door, but he couldn't see them. They must be sitting up on the drying table part of the sink. But he could tell from what they said that they weren't close together. The poor nut; he could be. She hadn't talked like this to anyone else. It was a long pause. A match was struck and flicked to the floor.

"Harriet."

"Yes."

"You know, I guess I have been happy tonight in a funny backwards sort of way."

"What does that mean?"

"Well, you know being with you I felt things again tonight. I really felt things the way I used to be able to. It wasn't what I wanted to feel exactly but at least I did feel as though I had some feelings in me still."

"Why shouldn't you have feelings in you?"

"Well I haven't, I haven't really *felt* anything for ages. It's been just as though I didn't have any feelings, for months, not since the time when you really used to like me."

"Tiens, c'est joli ça."

"No, really, that's not a line."

"I know it isn't, Tommy."

"Oh the hell with you!"

"That's nice, too. You always tell me the nicest things. You tell me much nicer things than my other fellers tell me."

"Oh, screw!"

"That's nice, too."

"I'm sorry . . . But goddamit, why can't it be now like it was. Don't you remember the way we felt then?"

"Maybe I don't want to remember."

"Well I do. It was wonderful. I never felt like that till then and maybe I never will again."

"Yes that was something, wasn't it?"

"Oh I thought you couldn't remember?"

"Oh I can't, I just imagine—what I read in books you know."

"Oh all right, don't!"

Paul gritted inside. The damn little nut . . . Why doesn't he stop talking about it and *do* something? . . . Can't he tell she's just working around for him, just laying it out for him? . . .

She's just waiting for it and all he does is blabber! . . . Sticking it right out on a platter for him . . . What's eating him?

"Don't you want some more milk?"

"No."

"And what does your highness desire?"

"You know."

"No I don't."

"Yes you do."

"I don't."

"The hell you don't!"

"No, really . . . or if I do maybe I know better than you what's good for you. You know you can't have everything you want even if you are Tommy Walters, Jr."

"Oh, so that's it now. All for my best? It hurts mother more than it hurts baby!"

"Well, maybe it does hurt me."

"Creeps! That's a pretty rash statement—sure you don't want to take that back?"

"Tommy, you're still quite a fool, aren't you?"

"Yeah . . . I guess I am."

You certainly are, thought Paul, you certainly are the prize fool! . . . Go for her! . . . Don't you know how? Didn't you ever kiss a girl? . . . Don't you know when they want it? Didn't you ever figure out they put you off just to make it better for them afterwards? . . . Jesus Christ, what a man you are! . . . What if she didn't let you neck her in the car? That's just because she was waiting to be necked twice as hard when you got her home. And there you . . . Paul was hardly in control of himself. Her voice, so full of wanting under the light words, had worked upon him, roused him, made him another person . . .

"Well, Harriet, you know I'm really awfully glad I've known you because later, in about twenty years, when you're an old maid I'll know how an old maid got to *be* an old maid."

There was no answer for a moment, and Paul heard her get down from her seat and turn on the sink faucet.

"Give me your glass."

"That information"—the voice was more false now than ever—"will really be of the greatest sociological interest to me; it's something I've always specially wanted to know, just how an old maid gets to be an . . ."

Paul heard her go out of the pantry, and then, in a moment heard Tommy follow. Paul rose in the darkness. He went into the pantry and opened the door a crack. Tommy was still talking in the hall, and she was standing watching him with an expression on her face such as Paul had never seen. It was not disgust, and it was not anger, and not hurt, and not love—but a little of all, and more. She simply stood and looked at him and said nothing to him, not a word. Nothing. Tommy faltered, stopped, stared too, went toward her, but she backed away, started to speak, stopped, raised his hand, let it fall, hesitated, turned, looked back, dropped his eyes, and went out the door.

Harriet stood where she was, motionless, staring at nothing with the look still on her face—deception, pity, anger, love— Paul couldn't have told what it was. He only knew it cried out to him, called to him, shouted to him. Before he realized it he was walking through the dining room toward her. He had to. He had to come to her. He couldn't help it.

He startled her.

"Why Paul, I thought you were . . ."

Her voice checked him.

"No, miss, I just came in . . . I saw the lights on . . . I thought . . ."

Her voice had checked him in his rush to her. For it had again in it—suddenly, unexpectedly—her old detachment that had been missing all evening. It took him by surprise. She was herself again. And he . . .

The car started and pulled away in the drive.

"Shall I lock up, miss?"

"Yes, please."

Yet she was not herself—she was not. The sound of the car's going had caught her back. She didn't move. She didn't start upstairs, but stood in the same place in the hall.

And as he locked the front door it swept over him again, again irresistible—her need for him, her need of the man in him, of the thing in which she had just been betrayed. He turned and looked at her. And she looked at him, for the first time seemed to look at him as though he were not just the butler—as though he were a man.

A moment no thicker than an eyelash, and he thought of a dozen things—among them that she would never dare tell anyone. Never. And he moved toward her, very slowly, looking into her eyes, slowly coming to her, moving toward her, the long look, the hand . . .

But she spoke: "Did Mother get in all right, do you know?"

He nearly fell. He nearly dropped with this shock. His mouth came open, his hand collapsed. It seemed so long before he could answer, as though he were travelling years and years, miles and miles, across a whole lifetime, back from himself to the butler. At last:

"Yes, miss, I think she did. I'm sure . . ."

"Oh, all right then. Good night, Paul."

Detached. Distant. She hadn't even noticed. The woman in her gone. Hopelessly gone from him, where he could never follow again. Gone.

She went up the stairs without turning.

Paul put out the lights and started for the back of the house. At the pantry door he turned to look back but there was nothing to see so he went on, through the pantry, through the kitchen, up the back stairs, to his room, to his bed, to his wife.

NIGHT WINDS RISING

It was hot that night, and no wind came in off the bay. Only the thick smell like rotting fish came in off the dark water. The waiters at the waterfront cafés had sweat on their foreheads, and no one was lively yet. It was so hot that people were not walking up and down along the sea-wall as they usually did. The sound of water sluffing against the bottom of the wall was very quiet.

I was sitting at a table in front of the Marsale with Laurence's wife, looking out into the black of the sea where two cruisers, bright with lights, lay anchored beyond the headland. They were flashing their searchlights along the shore, and the sharp white shafts of light cut open the night in bright gashes. My fingers were sticky from sipping a liqueur; I can never do that without getting my fingers sticky. Laurence's wife was smoking; she smoked one cigarette after another, going through them steadily, lighting the next one from the stub before putting it out. She said, "He's gone to watch the Muss go by. They said he was due to come by about seven, but it's all right, he hasn't got any money."

I looked at her eyes that were red all round the edges and stayed open so long between blinkings. She had a thin blue ribbon through her hair, and there was too much powder on her face. After a while I asked if he was writing again now.

"Yes," she said, "he started in on something yesterday and worked almost all night and today he slept all day. If he does some more tonight, he'll stop tomorrow when he wakes up and he'll want to go out fishing again. He says he's met some man down at the albergo who knows a publisher in New York, but if he does any tonight, he'll stop tomorrow anyway."

Suddenly one of the searchlights flashed full in our eyes, startling and blinding us; after it was gone her eyes still stared fixed and vacant into nothing, while her hand mechanically lifted and lowered its cigarette. I remembered noticing her one morning when she was sunning on the shingle; I guessed she would soon have another one, I couldn't decide just how soon.

"When he comes back," she said, "don't let him borrow any money from you. You'd better pay for your drink now. Last time he rode down to the albergo in a carriage and then borrowed from the cabby; he wasn't back till the next evening."

In a little while, after I had paid the waiter for my drink, we heard shouting and horns blowing up in the town; soon Laurence came along and sat down quite excited. At first he talked about the Muss and how he had nearly run down the town boys who ran before his car in the street; then he began the stories. First it was the one about the Princeton man whose wife divorced him for throwing butter-balls at the ceiling; he was still quite excited and quite charmed with his own geniality. His wife was lively now and laughed as though she did not know I had heard the stories before. Then it was the one about the crazy doctor who did abortions and played Chopin; he was still lively and pleased and not very restless. But when he was half along with the one about the old peasant lady who thought she had been raped by her son-in-law, he said all of a sudden, "Jesus, I need a drink." And he was very bitter at once, with the corners of his mouth twitching. "I suppose Clara's seen to it," he said, "that you don't have one bloody lira between you." Before I could say anything, he was up and gone, walking fast down the waterfront toward the albergo.

I didn't say anything, and she went on smoking; I took one of her cigarettes, though I really have no taste for them. A few people were walking up and down the sea-wall now; a little bit of breeze was drifting in across the bay. We sat smoking and didn't say anything. Two blond girls in scarlet pajamas walked by arm-in-arm. They weren't twins; their pajamas fitted sleek and close. Laurence's wife shivered a little in the new breeze, and I pulled her shawl up over her bare shoulders from the back of her chair. When my cigarette was short, I crushed it out slowly and deliberately, said good night in Italian, and walked down along the sea-wall toward the headland.

Up the old road before me paraded a half-dozen white-uniformed cadets; they stumbled along, arms linked across the width of road, singing very loudly in the quiet night. One fine clear voice sang verses and the others howled in chorus. They went along slowly, but I did not try to pass them, fearing they might notice me and do something, I didn't know just what. At last they turned off toward their tender-landing; following the shore road below terraced villas, I passed dark-molded figures seated on the sea-wall. Once a girl's voice came out of the darkness in startling American: "Gosh, what a tall guy!" The searchlights, chasing each other over the back-hills, caught brilliantly for an instant on a white villa, then dulled on again over the rough green. Close to shore a skiff with a light in the bow skimmed slowly over the shallow water; whatever it was the fisherman was bugging for, he didn't find it, for the skiff never paused in its wandering.

In the little cemetery under the big yellow church of the Infant Jesus, there were round lights along paths and bright shadows beyond. The black letters on the light-globes said to respect the memory of our beloved dead. Some days I would read all the names and ages of all the beloved dead on the little metal placards on each cross, but it was too dark to see them in the night. I went by another light with a globe that said to respect them, as I climbed up the higher path. At the top I came on two lovers lying together in the shelter of an old olive tree; I heard their startled breathing, as I passed, and felt their eyes glaring at me out of the darkness. I was frightened that he might come after me.

Sitting at the cliffshead at the end of the cemetery, I looked out over the sea. Nights when there were stars I could always tell the line where the sky began and the sea ended; that night it was all one black. I wondered if they had gone on and if they talked while they did it. Now the cruiser's search-lights were out, and, as I watched, the deck lights went out one after another. The riding light and red light of a tender glided twined across my line of vision. I listened hard to see if I could hear them. The night breeze freshened and I shivered inside. I turned up my coat collar; it was getting colder. I couldn't even remember in any part of me how hot it had been a few hours before. Going back through the cemetery by the lower path, for I was afraid to pass close by them again, I strained my eyes into the dark toward where I knew they must be. But I saw only sharp shadows cast from a light behind me that said to respect our beloved dead.

On my way home along the waterfront I stopped in at the Simplon Bar for a brandy to warm me up; but I paused on the threshold, seeing Laurence at the bar. He was high, and his coat and necktie were gone. He sat singing on a high stool with one arm clutched around a wriggling bar-girl. I went out before he should see me.

Passing the Marsale I looked up to see a light in the corner window third floor; her shadow moved across the blind. I started toward the door to go up to see her, and stopped. I started up again, and stopped on the first step. Turning, I went out again and crossed to the sea-wall, where I stood quite straight in the wind with my back to the Marsale. Waves were slapping briskly on the wall now, and the night wind was cold and sharp in my face.

A NATURAL HISTORY

Well they were real tracks this time, not like the ones Hank and Gussy had made the week before to fool Helena, and we followed them up the beach and found the turtle high in the dry sand, where the warmth of the sun hatches the eggs, already popping them. It was a big old bitch and she was half backed down into the hole she'd dug, dropping about two eggs a minute as near as I could time it. Helena started giggling, she hadn't ever seen one laying, and we'd come out a week before, too early, because she was so het up about it and wanted to see one before she had to go up back north again, and there hadn't been any, they hardly ever start coming up out of the sea before the end of May, so Gussy and Hank faked up a flipper track with their elbows while I kept Helena busy up the beach, and then they came running up the beach shouting that they'd just seen a big one going back into the water, the idea was to try to get Helena to dig for the eggs where there weren't any, but it didn't work because she caught on where Gussy had put his foot down a couple of times when they were making the track and the pattern of the sole showed on the sand, but Helena hadn't had to go north so soon after all because her old man, who is drunk almost all the time, had the d-t's just the night before they were going to start driving back to Illinois, and they'd had to take him down to Miama to the hospital to get over them, so she could stay on longer and we'd come out again when the moon got full because the old nigger who cuts the lawn for Senator Blossom says that's what gives the turtles the signal to come up out of the sea. Helena started giggling, and Hank slapped her fanny and said something I didn't catch that made her awful sore. "That ain't one bit funny, Hank," said Georgia. I could see, with the big moon, that Georgia wasn't liking it much, but Elsy was eating it right up. She got down in the sand to look into the hole. You could hear the eggs landing as they fell, plip . . . plep . . . plip, like that, like the slow drip of a faucet into a drain tub. "Wouldya lookit the way they bounce!" said Elsy. Georgia was looking like she was going to be sick any minute and Gussy said, "Isn't that cute the way nature makes them sorta soft so they can bounce like that and not get broke?" Georgia sat down in the sand and looked the other way; "Come on be a sport," said Helena, "You knowya wanted to come 'n you said how you came last year 'n what a laugh it was." Georgia didn't say anything. Plip . . . plep . . . plip . . . I was wondering how that poor goddam turtle must feel. She knew we were there all right, she'd pulled in her head under the shell, but once they get started laying they can't get themselves stopped, and there she had to go on with it knowing all the time that we'd cop the eggs just as soon as she got them dropped. Gussy was starting to fish some of them out of the hole already while she was still working. He gave one to Elsy and she turned it over in her fingers, fascinated with the way the air dent rolled around the shell as she moved it. "Look Gussy," I said, "Why don't you just put the basket down inside the hole? Save a lot of work." He tried it, scooping away some sand to get it down, but trying to work it under the turtle he must have scraped her behind because she struck out at him, quick as lightning, with her back foot and ripped a long bloody scratch down his wrist and hand. He swore at the turtle and gave it a kick which only hurt his toe. His hand was bleeding some and the girls clustered round. He was starting to suck at the cut but Helena said not to.

Elsy asked him if it hurt bad, Georgia couldn't take her eyes off it. "Wash it in the salt water," said Helena, "Salt's just as good as iodine." They went down to the water and I stood watching the turtle. Hank fetched back the basket that Gussy had slung away in his anger. Plip . . . plep . . . plip, the hole was nearly full now and the eggs seemed to be coming a little quicker. The turtle edged her head out cautiously from under the shell and jerked it back in again when she saw me. "How would you be feeling if you was this turtle?" I asked Hank. "I don' getcha," said Hank. "Well, having all your eggs swiped from you after you'd worked so damn hard to lay 'em." "Oh," said Hank, "Oh yeah, well I guess I'd be perty sore, I guess . . . hell, I didn't never think nothin, about it, I ain't no damn turtle." Gussy and the girls came back up the beach from the water, they'd tied a couple of handkerchiefs around his wrist. "Hey look," said Elsy, "She's going to fill up the hole." The turtle had finished laying and was turned around pushing sand into the hole with her flippers. Whether or not we were there waiting to steal her eggs she was going to finish up her job the way her instinct made her. She filled up her hole to the level of the beach and then hit right out for the water. And turtles aren't so slow either, she went right along with a quick jerking movement, the flippers pulling in front and the feet pushing from behind. Hank picked up Elsy to put her on the turtles' back, we'd filled the girls up with stories about how you could ride on the turtles' backs, how on real hot nights they ran a regular taxi service up and down the beach, how you could have races on them, but Elsy'd seen what that turtle had done to Gussy and she wasn't going to get herself within reach of it. Hank was carrying her along behind the turtle, trying to sit her down on its back, but she grabbed hold of his hair, he has long hair, when he combs it down the wrong way he can chew the ends of it, and pulled until he had to dump her or lose two handfuls of it. I followed the turtle as she scrambled down the beach, and the way she was going it looked as though once she got back in the water she'd never more come out again. A big wave hit her as she went into the surf, it rolled her on her side, but she flopped down again and pushed on out into deep water. For a little while I could see her swimming along the surface but then she dove under and disappeared. I watched for a while to see if she would come up again further out but she didn't. The moon on the water was something marvellous, like some sort of silver fire if there ever was such a thing. I stood there just watching it, it was so wonderful, and Helena came up behind me and leaned against me, rubbing her chin against my shoulder. "What'you think of that?" I said, "Ever see anything like that up in Illinois?" She rubbed her chin on the side of my neck and put a hand on my arm, I could feel her breath on my cheek and the softness of her pressing against my back. "Y'know I wish I weren't never going back home at all, I wish I was just always going to stay here with . . ." "Sure," I said quickly, "That'd be great, Hel, but y'know it get's awful hot down here in summer, it get's terrible hot, I think you'd pretty soon get fed with it down here in summer." She moved away from me and kicked at something in the sand. "Come on," I said "We've got to tote those eggs up to the car." She followed me up the beach without speaking.

Well, we got this stuff from a guy with a truck who'd killed a big turtle and couldn't get it up from the beach to the road it was so heavy. It's against the law to kill them but bootlegging them is worthwhile because the niggers love the meat, they eat everything but the shell, and one of those big ones, two or three hundred pounds of turtle, will feed a lot of niggers. This guy had come down from Stuart with his truck, and he'd located a whopping big turtle and been able to kill it by getting it turned over on its back with a crowbar and then taking an axe to it, but even at that it wasn't clean dead, a turtle is such a tough old bastard that you can't really call it dead till you've cut it in pieces, because as long as two pieces are still together they can manage to wiggle, I know because Hank tried to kill one one day, just a small one, and it took him over an hour with a meat knife and a hammer and screwdriver, its legs kept twitching after he had all the insides cut out of the shell, and the heart went on beating for about two hours after he'd cut it out and there wasn't any blood left in it, it just seemed to be beating on air, and when you'd poke it with a finger it would take on a spurt and beat faster for a while and then gradually quiet down again. Well we found this guy sitting on the fender of Gussy's car when we got back to the road with the eggs in a basket, and he asked would we give him a hand with his turtle. We had quite a job dragging it up to the road even though there were four of us because it was so big around there was no way you could get ahold of it, you couldn't get a grip on the smooth edge of the shell and nobody wanted to grab it by the feet because they were still jerking in spite of how its head was all mashed to hell and blood dripping over the sand. Finally Gussy got an idea, he remembered he had an old pair of chains under the seat of his car left over from the time when it was new and he used to drive people from the Beach out into the Glades to shoot. We got a hitch around the shell with the chains and that gave us something to haul on. Just the same it was some job to get it up that bank to the road, and while we were resting in the middle this guy brought down a big jug of this stuff from his truck and passed it around. And then when we'd gotten the turtle into the truck he'd brought along planks for that so it wasn't so hard, we had another round from the jug and he filled a quart bottle from it and give it to us to take along home. I don't know whatever this stuff could have been, it tasted something godawful, but it went down like a hurricane and hit like a landslide. It did the job all right, and by the time we got back to the beginning of West Palm we were feeling just fine and dandy and plenty left over to spare. Gussy had the old wreck wide open, you could have heard it a mile away, and we went down the boulevard like an itchy snake trying to scratch its back on both sides of the street at once. We were all feeling happy, hollering and singing and almost falling out of the car, and Elsy started throwing eggs at the cars parked along the sidewalk. Georgia tried to stop her, she hadn't kept up with the rest of us, but we all pretty soon forgot that we'd gotten the eggs to eat when we saw the way they splattered all over the cars as they broke. That was some ride I can tell you, and I guess there weren't two cars in twenty blocks that didn't get messed up the way we were slinging those turtle eggs. Then somebody thought of niggertown and it caught like a light, we were all yelling "Get those goddam niggers!" as we bumped over the tracks into Blackland. It was Saturday night and they were all still outside standing under the streetlights and sitting in front of their shacks. Gussy slowed down the car and we stood up and let 'em have it, all of us firing at once except Georgia who was sore and getting scared. We went down that old street like a mowing machine potting those damn niggers on both sides and you shoulda heard them swear and holler. A couple of them ran out and tried to hop our running board but Hank and I had a wrench and jack-handle ready and we let 'em have it right in the snoot. The rest of them all beat it back into their shacks but we went up and down a couple more times just decorating their windows. Then we heard a siren across the tracks, some nigger must have telephoned to the cops, so we scrambled out the back end of the street and beat it for home. When we pulled into Gussy's garage we were just too drunk tired to get out and go home so we lay there in the car, all but Georgia who went off by herself and left us. I was lying in the back seat, looking at the dark while the inside of my head rolled round and round in my skull, and Helena rolled over the top of me and started sucking my ear with her teeth the way she does. She was all set for it I could tell but I didn't try to get anywhere at all, I was so sleepy with the likker slowly wearing off, and we just lay there tight together feeling real hot and sleepy and good.

SALLE D'ÉTUDE

He sat for a little while staring at the head of the boy in front of him. There was a birthmark on the boy's neck just above the collar, and his hair came groping long and rank down toward it. He saw the boy's head, but he wasn't thinking about it. He wasn't thinking about anything. Somewhere in the back of his mind he knew that *étude* had begun and he must soon start work. But he wouldn't really think of that for a moment yet; he would sit quite still for a little while, slumped almost comfortably on his bench, his body warm and content in the fullness of the supper he had just eaten. It would be almost pleasant in the *salle d'étude,* if he could just forget where he was. The old brown walls were warm, and somehow friendly; there were soft shadows in the far corners of the room, for the overhead lights were not strong. *They're so stingy they'd let you go blind Butler said.* It was dark outside now, but the windows reflected the light so that he couldn't look out into darkness; but he heard the courtyard fountain splashing above the rustle and shuffle of the room. It was almost rhythmic in its quiet melody, fusing subtly with the emptiness of his mind. Later on, when *étude* would be over, lying in bed waiting for sleep, he would hear it beneath his open window, the only sound in a night noisy with silence. And in the morning . . .

"Bartol!"

He started into consciousness, as the sound of his name shattered his reverie. He had wholly forgotten Monsieur Valdonier, who was glaring at him now from the platform at the front of the *salle d'étude*.

"N'as-tu rien à faire, Bartol? Est-ce que tu t'endors déjà?"

"Oh, oui Monsieur, j'ai encore mon exercice à faire," hastily plunging into his desk to find his *grammaire* and *cahier*.

"Vas-y alors. Si non, je te don'rai des verbes irregulières à conjuger."

He bent his head over his book afraid to face the eyes that had turned toward him from all about the *salle d'étude*. It was lucky that Monsieur Valdonier had not given him "consigne." Then he would have had to sit copying verbs all Sunday afternoon, while the other went *en ville* to the cinema. He turned over the pages of his *grammaire* till he found the exercise for the following day. *That slimy skunk Valdonier Butler said he'll get you into consigne if it takes him all year to do it.* It was an "Exercice d'invention et de réflexion." That kind wasn't much fun, but at least it wasn't as bad as the "morceaux littéraires," where "les élèves réproduiront à leur manière le passage suivant" or the "Exercice de composition," where the élèves had to remember that "Ecrire avec noblesse, c'est éviter avec le plus grand soin toute expression triviale." He read the instructions to himself: "Copiez les questions suivantes et répondez-y"; it was called "Les vêtements et les chaussures." He opened his *cahier* to a clean page, put down the heading, and began the exercise, copying down the first question: "1. Quels sont les principaux vêtements?" Then he wrote down on the next line: "1. Les principaux vêtements sont les chapeaux, les habits, les pantalons, les souliers, les bas, et . . ." He tried to remember the French word for shirt, but he couldn't think what it was. Then he went over in his mind all the other kinds of *vêtements* that he could think of, but he didn't know the words for any of them either. Maybe he could look through his *Larousse* till he came to a picture of one of them, but that would take a long time, and there mightn't be any pictures of them anyway. So finally, he scratched out the "et" and wrote it in between "les souliers" and "les bas", smudging ink on the final comma to make it look like a period.

Then he glanced up from his work, furtively, in case Monsieur Valdonier might be looking in his direction. If he were caught once again, he would surely get the "consigne". But Monsieur Valdonier was staring away into the rear corner of the room, seeming not to see anything at all. He was balancing his chair on its two back legs and leaning his shoulders against the wall. If only the legs of his chair would slip and let him fall; that would take the wind out of him all right. Once Drasche, the Austrian, said he was going to rub floor wax on the platform to make it slippery, but he never did; probably he was afraid of the "consigne", too. *Anyway Drasche was a yellowbellied whitelivered sealouse Butler said because he was always threatening to beat up people behind their backs and if they heard about it and came around to start a fight he would always run away or go tell Monsieur Plaquet on them.* Monsieur Valdonier never sat quite still. First he would edge his chair a little further from the wall; then he would move it back. Now he would shift the weight to the right leg, now to the left. He couldn't seem to tilt it at an angle that was comfortable. Some of the other masters read a newspaper when they were in charge of the *salle d'étude*, but Monsieur Valdonier never did. Everyone hated him for that reason. No one ever dared throw spitballs or shoot paper-wads because of the way he had of running his eyes up and down the rows. *Butler said he was stuck on Ma'm'selle Meury the* garde-malade *because once when he went into the* infirmerie *to get his throat sprayed he caught Monsieur Valdonier in there . . .*

"Monrandière!"

"Qu-est-ce 'tu fais là-bas?"

All the heads turned toward the far side of the room where the boy who had been caught was trying to look surprised.

That was another piece of luck that Monsieur Valdonier should have seen someone else. He started writing again: "2. Quels vêtements sont faits en coton? . . . 3. Quels vêtements sont en laine? . . . 4. Avec quoi les boutons sont-ils faits? . . ." After answering a few more questions, he stopped writing to calculate his progress. There were twenty-eight questions in all, and of these he had done seven, just a quarter of the whole. He decided that if he divided the remaining twenty-one into groups of seven with a rest only between each group, he might get them done more quickly. Then he could put away his *grammaire* and *cahier* and read in his *chrestomathie*. That would be pretty good, because he could just skip over the words he didn't know, and the stories would probably make sense anyway. Or he might take out his *géographie* and look at the pictures in it; but that wasn't much fun anymore, because he had looked at them so many times that he knew them almost by heart and could guess just which pictures were going to be on a certain page before he turned over to it. He didn't know whether he would dare read *Twenty Years After*, when Monsieur Valdonier was in charge. He had bought it for four francs from an English boy who had fitted it inside the cover of a *chresto-mathie*. It had a few pages out of the *chrestomathie* glued in the middle, so that when the master in charge was walking up and down the rows, the boy reading it could just turn to those pages and pretend to be studying them, when he heard the master coming behind him. It was safe enough with most of the masters, and some of them didn't seem to care at all what went on during *étude*. Once Monsieur Aegiter, the German, had caught him reading and hadn't done anything about it at all; he had just laughed softly and said in his funny, falsetto-sounding voice: "C't un bel livre que tu lis là; je le connais bien, moi." Almost everyone liked Monsieur Aegiter pretty well, except the Belgians; they all said he was a *cochon boche*. But they all hated the Germans anyway. Once some *juniors*, mostly Belgians, had tried to hang a very little German from a limb in the park, and they would probably have succeeded in doing it, had not his screams brought Monsieur Plaquet to the scene. And another time, when Pulitzer, one of the biggest Belgians in the *moyens*, had beaten a German in a fight, he held him down and scratched his face with a pen-point till it was all bloody.

Three fourths of the exercise still remained to be done. He wished that he were half finished, instead of only a fourth. It was always much easier after the half-way mark had been reached. Then it was like sliding down hill after the long trudge up the slope. He began to write again, pausing after each question to see what fraction of the whole he had completed. Eight twenty-eighths. Nine twenty-eighths. Ten. Eleven. Twelve twenty-eighths. But that could be brought down to three sevenths. He wondered just how he would feel, when he should have come to the next to the last question, twenty-seven twenty-eighths, when there would be just one more to do before the end. Somehow it made him think of the night before Christmas—lying in bed, too excited for sleep, wondering if the morning would ever come and what it would feel like to be opening the stockings. Sometimes he had thought so hard about opening the stockings and taking the things out of them, that he had almost believed the morning were really come and he was actually doing it.

Then he happened to remember that there wouldn't be any stockings that year, nor many presents either. But surely his grandmother would send him some money, and he would be able to gorge on *meringues glacées* at the *confiserie* for weeks. Indeed, he never seemed to have enough money in his pocket, when the day came for the *juniors* to go *en ville*. Being only a *junior*, he had but two francs a week for allowance, and the *amendes* that Monsieur Fauré was always giving him, reduced that small sun to almost nothing. He hated Monsieur Fauré, at whose table he sat in the *salle à manger*. For Monsieur Fauré found keen delight in "riding" him. Again and again he would say: "Dis donc, Bartol, sais-tu que tous les américains sont bêtes?" Then, if his sally drew forth a retort, he would go on:

"Mais oui, je vois bien qu'ils sont tous des singes. V'yons c'qu'ils font. Ils n'aiment rien que l'argent." While, if he got no answer, he would leer grinningly, as he whined: "Oh, oui, je vois bien que tu le sais." Or sometimes he would declare that *les américains* were wholly incapable of originality, all their machines being but copies, and bad ones at that, of Swiss inventions. This remarkable dictum was frequently repeated, but evidently its author thought it so obvious that it needed no proof, for certainly one was never offered. Beyond these attempts at "whimsy", Monsieur Fauré seldom spoke at the table. When not eating, a function which he performed with amazing rapidity if little grace, he read the *Lausanne Gazette* and paid little attention to what was going on about him. His shiny black hair came down in a point at the middle of his forehead, while his black eyebrows tilted up at the ends so that he looked like pictures of the devil, but Butler said he had been a monk in a monastery until he had been expelled from his order for breaking his vows. Certainly his methods of discipline were simple, if not precisely monastic; periodically he would emerge from behind the *Gazette* to announce: "Un franc d'amende pour tout le monde. J'ne veux plus voir de bêtises." He would take down all the names in his notebook and then go on with his reading.

When he had finished the fourteenth question, the halfway mark, he stopped work again. Cautiously, with a glance toward the platform at the front of the *salle d'étude*, he raised his eyes from his work and looked about him. Almost everyone seemed to be studying except Braneovan, the Roumanian, who was reading from a book artlessly concealed beneath his *grammaire*. If only Monsieur Valdonier would catch him at it; then he would surely be "consigné" for two or three afternoons at the very least. No one liked Braneovan much, for he was dirty and furtive. *The slimy Roumanian wood pussy Butler said.* He never took a shower, as far as was known, and his sallow skin was yellow and oily. Every night he was said to rub bear-grease into his hair; certainly, his pillow was always a dirty brown where his head had lain. Some thought he was "nutty", because his room-mate declared that at night he lighted candles above his bed and prayed to them in a crooning sing-song, while he bobbed up and down like an Arab at his devotions. And everyone had been glad enough when Monsieur Laporte, the *culture physique* master, had once struck him full in the face for some "bêtise," knocking him down and making him cry.

Soon he set to work again, and found the questions somewhat easier, definitions for the most part: "A quoi sert la chemise? . . . A quoi sert le manteau? . . . Quand est-ce qu'on porte les caoutchoucs?" Suddenly he realized that here were all the words that he had needed to answer the first question. He thought of doing the first question over, and then realized that he would have to copy over the whole exercise, if he did that. Then he thought of writing some of the words in between the lines, but he decided that even that wouldn't be worth the trouble. What was the use of bothering to work anyway? He didn't seem to mind anymore whether or not he got good marks. What good did they do? Nobody seemed to care whether or not he did well. Each Monday evening after dinner in the *salle à manger* Monsieur Plaquet read out the marks of the whole school from his big record book, intoning each grade, with especial emphasis for those in *effort* and *conduite.* Each mark below a "six" was dully rewarded with two hours in the "consigne", but there was never a word of praise for a "neuf" or a "dix". Back in the school in Cleveland it had been far different. Good marks had brought freedom from afternoon study-halls, and the year he won a silver medal in Latin his grandmother had given him a bicycle for a reward. Thinking of Cleveland and his grandmother and his old school made him feel homesick again. Why had he asked to be sent away to school? What ever had made him think that coming to school in Switzerland would be some sort of an "adventure"? Why had he not been content to stay at home in Cleveland with the boys who had been his friends for as long as he could remember?

Soon he was pitying himself thoroughly. Indeed, he very nearly cried. And then, staring blankly out into the blackness framed by a window, he saw the darkness streaked with a long yellow line. It was a lighted train running along the tracks beyond the *terrain de sport*. It was going westward, possibly to Marseilles or even to Paris. And from Paris another train would go to Havre. And from Havre . . . This time he did cry a little, and long after the train had passed, he gazed blankly into the blackness, seeing nothing, aware only of his own misery.

But finally he roused himself. Things could hardly be as bad as he made them seem with his self-pity. For *étude* would soon be over and he could go to bed. It would be dark and quiet in his room. It would be warm and comfortable in bed. And he would hear the fountain splashing below him in the courtyard. Soft and melodious, its song would color his thoughts till he would fall away into sleep. Rather vaguely, he wondered what he would think about that night. Perhaps he might do his model city again, but he had done that so often. It was beginning to get a bit dull—thinking so hard about the avenues laid out in the form of a star, the big, pillared buildings, and the stores with marble facades. He had thought about them so often that the images were beginning to grow blurred. He could no longer visualize them just as they ought to be, all straight and square, marble-white and stately. Perhaps something more exciting would be better for that night. He might try being a young colonial officer in the Revolution, or a Scottish chieftain fighting the English for Bonnie Prince Charlie. Either one of those would do rather well.

But before he had reached a decision, Monsieur Valdonier got up and said: "Alors, c'est fini."

All eyes were lifted from the desk-tops.

"Remetez vos livres."

A rustling, a shuffling, and a creaking of desk-lids.

"A vos chambres; mais sans bruit."

A scraping of chairs and the clatter of running feet on the stone floor of the corridor.

As usual, Monsieur Beloeil woke up with a little jerk, wide awake at once. It was a habit surviving from the war. This was part of the "price of victory," never afterward to enjoy the delicious feeling of coming slowly awake, but always to wake up suddenly as though a shell had landed on top of you, to wake up with a start and feel for your legs. Eighteen years. You would think you might have gotten over it in that time. No, not the war. That would stay in him till he died. And now another one? A worse one?

Monsieur Beloeil woke with something in the back of his mind that he couldn't quite remember. Something was going to happen that day, something important; he must have been thinking about it as he fell asleep, but now it wouldn't come back to him. It was like a piece of gristle caught in a back tooth that the tongue could reach but couldn't loosen. What was it anyway? He shook his head, slapped it . . . *merde!* was he going to lose his memory too, the way his father had? Well, it would come back to him later. He touched the bell (Trac would start the tea) and climbed down from his high bed. It was built into the wall with curtains to hide it in the daytime.

Crossing the half-dark room to the windows he pulled open his glorious Chinese hangings. Just to touch them was a pleasure—so heavy, so rich, the texture so fine. Ten thousand francs apiece (the whole advance on his *Restif de la Bretonne*) but worth it, well worth it! They made the room; so many ladies asked especially to see them. Ten years to finish. Fifty swift fingers stitching away to make his golden dragons on their crimson field. Sunlight rushed into the room as he parted them.

Below, in the courtyard, the concierge's daughter was sweeping the flags. She must be fifteen now. "Fifteen and sixty," Uncle Georges used to say, the perfect ages of women. Before and after affectation. That little redhead, when he was lecturing in Clermont. . . . Two workmen came into the court through the street gate and stopped to joke with the girl, lighting last cigarettes before work. They were plasterers in white uniforms and caps. (Réquier, the jeweler, was doing over the main part of the old *hôtel* for his daughter who was marrying young de Seunes.) What sunlight! What a day! He must find time for a walk this morning; it would be splendid along the *quais*. Wonderful weather for March. He pulled up the window (Monsieur Beloeil took no chances with the night air; he'd had a touch of gas beside his leg wound) and took some deep breaths before going to start his bath.

The bathroom was his worst and most rewarding extravagance. Small, like the whole apartment, but there weren't a dozen like it in Paris—a real American bathroom with tile floor and walls, big mirrors, and a built-in tub long enough to stretch out in. The very day of his return to Paris from his first American lecture tour, he had called in the representative of the Crane Company and told him to "shoot the works" (Monsieur Beloeil's collection of American slang was always in demand on the Etoile). His bathroom was his treasure, but because of it his mother had quarreled with him for months. She was incensed by such waste of good money. "Here is your brother's own child with a *dot* smaller than the butcher's daughter and you throw out the door God knows how much for THIS. . . ." It had been upsetting, very. She had left in angry tears and been (or made herself) ill for a fortnight, while for weeks his brother Robert had been able to look more hurt and deserving and incompetent, and his niece Angèle more hurt and virtuous and hopelessly unattractive than ever. They had spoiled all his first pleasure in the new possession, and even now he couldn't altogether enjoy this warm and liquid relaxation because of them.

Monsieur Beloeil disliked his family but he couldn't escape them. He had always disliked them, feeling superior to them even as a boy—to all except his oldest brother Jean-Jacques who had died in the second Marne. He had despised his father, the *notaire*, because the old man was fussy and inefficient and his mother because she spoiled him without giving any tangible affection. As for Robert, he was an annoying nonentity. It was Robert's own damn fault if their father's business had dwindled to nothing since he took it over. Quite true the old man had lost clients in his last years by his doddering absentmindedness, but Robert had certainly added none. He was fair enough at the job itself, accurate and prompt—it took no brains to be a *notaire*— but his business manner was impossible. It was *paysanne* and then some. Robert was too friendly and always said ridiculous things. He had a "square tongue"; it made his clients uncomfortable and they went elsewhere. *"Mon frère,"* said Monsieur Beloeil to his old and best friend le Vicomte de Malvèzin, *"Mon très cher frère est un* FLOP!"

His family infuriated him. They bored him. They depressed him. But he couldn't escape. He was ashamed of them (as a child he had been miserable whenever they appeared at the fairly fashionable lycée where his father could just afford to send him) and he felt that this "background" was holding up his advancement in a certain quarter. Yet he couldn't break away. It wasn't their claims which held him so much as his own conscience. Or perhaps it was more instinct, peasant instinct. For the Bidots were not like city people, each able to break off from the trunk at will and root for himself; they were only two generations away from the land. They had second cousins in the Poitevin village of Beloeil (long before he had needed a distinguished pen name, little Edmond Bidot had been known to himself secretly as the "Chevalier de Beloeil") who were still farming the ancestral fields.

Even the final dropping of the family name ("the confusion," he had told his mother) had failed to dissolve the earth-deep tie that held him. He simply was not detachable. And so two or three times a month he would angrily cross the busiest part of Paris to the dejected neighborhood near the Porte Maillot where Robert lived, to sit for an hour in the stale parlor rudely answering his mother's stream of questions (she was so proud of the success he would not let her share) and trying not to explode over his brother's absurd opinions on politics. In his sister-in-law he had never discovered the least trace of intelligence and her daughter was equally void of curiosity. But the girl at least had the sense to keep quiet and he liked her a little for that. And she *was* such a good girl; he knew he should, and even would have liked, to do something for her future, but his good intentions seemed always to be being pushed aside by things more pressing—the secretary, the trip to India, the little Peugeot, the new panelling for the study. . . . Monsieur Beloeil blew up his belly till it rose out of the bath water and then let it slowly sink back again like a disappearing island. His last bank statement had been over forty thousand, and the new book (*New York, Tu es fou!*) was selling steadily. He really could afford to set aside a bit for Angèle now . . . but . . . just the other day he'd heard indirectly that Kahnweiller was cutting prices on his Juan Gris, and the way things were going on the bourse a good painting was really the safest investment, not to consider how it would "juice up" the study—there on the long wall above the shelves.

His mother had been particularly scornful about the big mirror in the bathroom door, but Monsieur Beloeil enjoyed it thoroughly. It was such a real satisfaction to stare at himself. It was a pleasure, even though he was ugly. Monsieur Beloeil made no bones about that; he was ugly. He was short and thin-shouldered, his wounded leg was twisted, his eyes were too little, he had dandruff. As a young man it had made him miserable. That was before he had learned to talk. He thought he would never get a girl; he was twenty-three before he did. And then his first book and a year in the salons had changed everything. But it was the wound that had done the most, that and the war's decimation of the male population. The wound brought out the mother in them. Their eyes followed his brave, pathetic limp. Marina was almost sadistic about it; she liked to touch the scar, she liked to hurt him and then be tender. He was her "*'tit guerrier*"; she made a fool of her rich husband for him. In June, she had promised, she would take him to the fjords to see the midnight sun.

On his breakfast tray he discovered what he had forgotten overnight, the thing that had puzzled him when he awoke. There in the lead column of the cultural page of the *Matin* was his attack on Morandière: "*Une Belle carriere se termine*" in big headlines and a picture of the "distinguished academician" underneath. The old lizard must be chewing his whiskers now! By noon it would be all over Paris. Monsieur Beloeil gurgled softly with glee as he reread his article: ". . . thus with a final (almost weary?) glance at his old haunts he leaves us . . . bringing to a fitting close a peculiarly brilliant career . . . the style that has so charmed us in the past . . . still evokes the faded elegance of another day . . . it is with genuine regret that we bid farewell to Monsieur de la Morandière . . . he will be remembered, we are sure. . . ."

The telephone ringing. It was Malvèzin. He had just seen the *Matin* and was frantic.

"What in God's name do you think you're doing? Here we are all working to get you put up for one of the empty seats and you start taking potshots at the pillar. . . ."

Monsieur Beloeil laughed (he had a special low slow laugh for the telephone that was very effective). "But you are wrong, my dear fellow . . . you will see . . . they'll take me in just to spite the old fool. And besides, you know how I love to fight; I couldn't let go a chance like this . . . I caught him right off his balance; a week ago he oozed all over me about my last. . . .

Malvèzin had hung up in irritation. Monsieur Beloeil rang for Trac; his tea had gotten cold.

"Il faut se battre!" That was one of Monsieur Beloeil's favorite apothegms. He loved to repeat it in company and was not afraid to put it into practice. A good enemy, he said, is worth two lukewarm friends, especially in Paris. He considered it a great part of his strength that so many important people disliked him. Their malice gave him a publicity he could not otherwise have attained. But it exasperated his friends (and he had friends too) who were forever tripping over the loose ends of his quarrels. Malvèzin, who was naturally conservative, had lectured him about it a dozen times. But Monsieur Beloeil was confident of his policy. Look where it had brought him already!

Monsieur Beloeil was not a first-rate writer (for all his vanity he recognized that; he was a sort of deluxe journalist—clever and impermanent), but he had first-rate results. He was known everywhere, and his books got as much space as Farrère's or Giradoux'. His aggressiveness was part of the whole scheme of his life. He fought with intention, with zest, with skill. He won because he was detached. It was an integral part of the "modern tactic" that had raised him from an obscure lectureship down at Clermont to a gilded man of letters who was sent on the first run of the *Normandie*. Monsieur Beloeil adored *sententiae*; he was crawling with them. "Travel fast and always attack," he would say; or, "Better buy a new shirt than wait to have an old one washed." He had learned about all that America could teach a Frenchman. And he believed fervently in advertising. Dress better than you can afford to. Don't stint on postage. Consider your apartment a show window; the richer the goods the greater the sales. Keep your taste ripe. And always see that your name stays in print and on the tongues of salon and café. If an editor gives your book only five inches, attack him so bitingly in your own column that he'll take his whole page next day to get back at you. Discover some youngster every year, preferably a Pole, and back him passionately till the next year; when he succeeds reverse your stand with equal passion. Raise an enormous stink after the award of every prize even if you helped engineer it. Keep women talking about you in the right places. And finally, never be caught asleep. *"Je dors,"* said Monsieur Beloeil, *"avec trois yeux ouverts."*

By ten o'clock he was dressed and busy at his desk. Like any Frenchman he disliked work, for its own sake. But his mind was as well disciplined as his ambition was compelling, and, unlike most Frenchmen, he could work at high pressure when he had to. Thirty-five letters or several thousand words of prose in a morning were nothing unusual. It had been hard to find a secretary who could keep up with him, and put up with him. But now he had a whiz, a bilingual Irishman, Parisian by voluntary exile, a regular young genius, when there was someone to direct his energies for him. He could fill in whole pages in Beloeil's own style; it was only necessary to give him a sketch to work from. He had his own room upstairs beside the kitchen so that he could be on hand at any hour of the day or night. Tergnier (who, like Malvèzin, had been a schoolmate of Monsieur Beloeil's) called it the "House of Nations": O'Meara, the secretary; Trac, the Tonkinese valet-butler; and a Swiss cook. The rumor that Monsieur Beloeil was bi-sexual, occasioned by O'Meara's habits and good looks, was specious. The Irishman was invaluable to his master, who therefore detested him.

Trac came in with a *petit bleu* hot from the *pneumatique*. Madame la Duchesse (Madame *the* duchesse) de Murviel-Palamède was short one male for dinner—she wrote—and could she impose on her dear friend Beloeil to help her out? He answered it at once with another, one that would seat him high at her table that night, and sent it out by Trac.

Monsieur Beloeil was a master of the *petit bleu*. He usually sent a half-dozen a day (there was a post office in the block) and he was vastly proud of his touch. Marvelous thing the *pneu*. Across Paris in fifteen minutes. So superior to the telephone, that was efficient but destructive of privacy. In America the women had their 'phones in bed with them and spent all morning gossiping over them. The *pneu* preserved a little of the old formal delicacy. It was an institution in his life. It was like sending a footman around through the Faubourg. He always signed his notes with a clever monogram and their wit was famous. Monsieur Beloeil had worked at the forge of language till words came to his pen molten hot, ready to be molded as he pleased. He wished he had time to make carbons of his best ones. With the names veiled they would make a devastating book.

Madame de Murviel-Palamède's was followed by others. A little torpedo to his publisher's sales manager: keep him from stopping the advertising on *New York, Tu es fou!* because it was selling well. "Double your bet when you win" was another of Monsieur Beloeil's standbys. Accordingly he sent a feeler to Kahnweiller about the Gris. Next a coal to a useful lady who was cooling, and an icicle to a useless lady who was warming too openly. Then some preliminaries for getting the *Prix Monceau* for Sicard. Sicard's new novel was as bad as his others, but his daughter was going to marry the owner of an important review in which Monsieur Beloeil, who was one of the judges for the Monceau award, was especially anxious to get a foothold. A regular page in the *Luxembourgeoise* would be invaluable for flanking movements. He had had a satisfactory conversation with Sicard (whom he despised) the evening before. It shouldn't be difficult; he was an adept at deals of this sort. One of the other Monceau Judges owed him a favor and another was afraid of him. He would swing it by fixing old Leiber. Leiber had a reputation for purity, but he was a gourmand. Monsieur Beloeil had arranged for a very special luncheon at the Belle Aurore.

He had just addressed an envelope to Mrs. Baldwin at the *George V*, when Trac announced Madame Bidot. He was annoyed. What did his mother want now? She knew how he hated interruptions during the morning.

"Make her wait," he said.

Mrs. Baldwin's sapphire was more important, it was a really wonderful piece of luck. Her husband was the vice president of a motor company in Detroit. He sat on the boards of large universities where lucrative lectureships were to be had. Mrs. Baldwin was Detroit's "cultural" hostess; she had even pretended to read one of his books in French. And now this little ($30,000) brooch. Would he mind taking it through the customs for her when he crossed next month? Couldn't he just pin it inside his coat or someplace? and bring it with him to Detroit when he came to visit her? He answered carefully. Baldwin neglected his wife. It would be best if she should think that he wanted in return favors more intimate than lectures at her clubs. His mother burst in before he sent for her.

She was not so much angry as passionately grieved. She was, he could see, "all worked up." He pointed to a seat, but she marched right up to his desk and stood over him. She began before he could speak. She was almost crying and her words poured out. It was about his going back to America again. He had tried to keep it from her but she had found out. It wasn't his doing so little for Angèle she was concerned with now but his whole attitude. America was ruining him, she knew it, she, his mother, could see where no one else could. It was hardening him, it was cheapening him; he was changed, he wasn't her "true son" anymore. She wanted him to give up this whole trip and stay in France. She was asking him to do this one thing for her, just this one thing—that would save him. He had plenty of work in Paris; there was no need for him to sell himself. His last book had disgusted her. It was cheap, it wasn't the best he had in him, what he really could do. She was asking him to see himself as he was, as his mother could see him, his mother who loved him. She was begging him to change while he could, before "those beasts" ruined him completely.

Anger rose in him as she talked—criticism, or even advice, infuriated him—but he let her go on without interruption, until she had spent herself and stood trembling and silent, her eyes burning at his. He started to answer, to shout at her, but her eyes stopped him. They stared at each other for an instant in thick silence. For an instant, a sickening instant, he knew she was right—he saw the sores on his infected soul—and then his pride came in again, and covered them. He helped his mother to a chair and slowly lit a cigarette before answering her.

Another woman would have broken down after such an outburst, but Madame Bidot was still herself. She sat tense in her chair waiting for his answer. She was a stiff woman, gray and straight, angular and severe, almost gaunt. She sat upright in her plain dark dress, in her drab correct hat, her hands clenched on her bag, her breath coming quickly. She looked at her son with anger and with love, with a great love, so deep and strong a love—a love that he had never given back to her since he was a baby. It was her very stiffness, her physical insularity, which had driven him from her. He had never been allowed to kiss her after he began, at five, to be a "big boy." She was always with him, teaching and tending him, but never touching him with any kind of love he needed. Her affection was intense and never reached him. He wanted the love that shields and surrounds, not the distant love of pride and perfection. She would never soften to him because that might weaken him. She wanted him to be always standing at attention. She knew he had better stuff than his brothers and she meant him to be perfect. She spoiled him with attention—and she lost him. It was a loss for which she could never compensate. It grew as she aged and as her son went forward in the world.

Monsieur Beloeil knew now that his mother loved him, but as a child he had never believed it because he couldn't feel it. She nagged him; that wasn't love. He knew now that she loved him, but his memories of childhood were too bitter to let him learn now to care for her. He felt sometimes that his mother had crushed out of him the capacity for real love, disinterested, spiritual love. Had he ever really *loved* the women who had loved him? Or did he merely *make* love to them to sharpen his vanity? Did he really *love* Marina? One thing he knew well: it was his mother's coldness which had brought him where he was today. She *had* taught him, though not in the way she had hoped, to shift for himself and make his way upward. Because she gave him no outlet for his affections all of his energies had gone into his mind. He had gone after books like a tiger after meat. Ambition had driven him like a man lusting for revenge. And success would be a sort of revenge: he would be showing his mother he could get along without her! . . .

"Well, what have you to say?"

He sat down on the edge of his desk, smiled at her, as though to an admiring audience, assumed his lecturing tone of voice, and began.

It was a little lecture on progress, in Monsieur Beloeil's best women's club manner. The Virtues of Progress. The Rewards of Progress. The Inevitability of Progress. How progressive and wonderful was America. How backward and ungrateful was France. How much he, Beloeil, had profited from America. How much France through him would profit from progress. He was, he liked to think, a missionary of the future, a link between the old world and the new, at once a Lafayette and a Franklin . . . who knew, might he not some day, like Claudel, who had begun as a literary man, be chosen to represent the Quai d'Orsay in Washington? And already look where his contacts with America had brought him! Had France, in the person of his dear brother Robert, come this far? . . .

It was a splendid lecture, so eloquent, so convincing—but unfortunately, Madame Bidot was not an American women's club. She listened with increasing disgust and then rose to go, before he had closed his cadence. At the door she paused.

"I see you know that what I said is true," she said, and went out as sad and angry as she had come.

Monsieur Beloeil felt no remorse. He knew he had been talking rubbish, but he had managed to get rid of her without too much unpleasantness and that was the important thing. It was time for lunch; he rang for his things.

Damn his mother! He had wanted to walk to the restaurant, the day was so fine, but thanks to her visit there was no time. So he took a cab, telling the driver to hurry.

As they turned into the Quai he caught a glimpse of the Académie and his heart lunged. How soon would he sit in there? Would he ever? Had he been wrong to attack Morandière? Fear stole into him for an instant, he went cold inside. But he thought of the meal ahead and the fear was gone.

Leiber was waiting at the door for him, his lips fairly dripping with expectation. La Belle Aurore is famous for its hors d'oeuvres, a meal in themselves, and Monsieur Beloeil had added *truites basques* and a pheasant. It proved a good investment; things went exactly as planned.

Over the shellfish Leiber was caustic: Sicard? Ridiculous! But after the pâtés (there were four kinds, all *au point*) he conceded the novel had its points. And when the pheasant had gone down on a tide of *Châteauneuf du Pape*, the venerable poet of Montmartre, the protégé of Mallarmé and protector of Radiguet, was certain that a better novel had never (well, hardly ever) been written. Monsieur Beloeil bundled him groaning into a cab, and set off toward home on foot, wishing he had not been obliged to overeat.

He hadn't been at home ten minutes when the telephone rang. It was Marina: "Can you come at once? I must see you! Please. I'll send the car around for you."

What could that be? This *was* a day of disturbances, perhaps bad stars were in conjunction. More likely indigestion; she had been quite calm when he left her the evening before.

In half an hour he was riding down the Avenue Kléber. It humiliated him to be sent for like this in her car, but he couldn't drive the Peugeot in traffic, and it wouldn't do to have O'Meara take him there. She was waiting for him at the head of the stairs. She had been crying. He kissed her cheek and they went into her little sitting room.

Marina (Meragniaro Sondheim-d'Anguersa) was a Venetian, without much doubt the descendant of a German emperor who had passed his vacations in the liquid city, an origin which she did not share alone. The golden beams of the Meragniaro palace are mentioned somewhere in the "Inferno"; Marina had red hair, nice instincts, and a wild temper. Her first husband, twenty years her elder, drank himself to death; her second, a black Roman whom she loved, was shot down in his plane above Cortina; her third, Señor Sondheim, a Semite, came out of the Argentine bearing many millions. Before their marriage a papal title was arranged, the name Anguersa being chosen at random from the pages of the *Decameron*. Sondheim had married to satisfy a romantic craving for high society. He bought houses in Rome, Venice, Paris, and London, and left his wife free, bored, and excessively rich.

It was her wealth coupled with her boredom that first attracted Monsieur Beloeil (she was two years older than he and by no artifice any longer good looking); he had hopes for a review of his own. But in two months he had found himself in love—with a woman who was ugly and who bullied him. She was the first woman whose mind he had really admired. She never read books, but no idea was beyond her. She never forgot anything, but she never said anything twice. Her wit he worshipped the most—it was unmercifully malignant. Three times a day she could tear her friends, him, and herself to pieces in a different way. She was vinegar and she left a sweet taste in his mouth. She was as small and as great as he was. Her elasticity was like her energy—amazing. With her he could be Marcus Aurelius and Tiberius in the same hour. He had met her three years ago in the spring. In October they had gone to Morocco. It was the first of four vacations together. He had started her writing, but she would not give him the review. "Not while I love you," she would say.

"What's wrong?" he asked her.

"Oh, nothing."

"Why'd you send for me?"

"I wanted to see you."

"But you've been crying."

"Yes."

"What about?"

"Nothing, except that I'm such a damn weak woman I can't get on without seeing you."

He laughed and took her in his arms and kissed her. It was broad daylight, cars were whizzing by below in the street, she was a wrinkled old woman with a bad disposition, and he loved her. He loved her, he loved her, he did, he did.

"I've got work to do. I've got to write a thousand francs worth of sweet nothing on modern literature for the *Franco-American Journal.*

"But you've got work here first."

"Not work," said Monsieur Beloeil, "I *hate* work!"

He was back at his desk by four but the sweet nothing for the *Franco-American Journal* was not progressing. It would not pour; it would not even trickle. For once he could not turn the faucet at command. He was fed up with this sort of thing. There was a limit to hypocrisy, even for good pay. He tried again, but revolted. Let O'Meara do it; have him write it and then touch it up a bit himself. But the decision didn't take away his feeling of enervation. He needed a change, he was in a rut. Then a thought came: why not walk out to see old Ribischka? Ribischka was always refreshing, he was real. They had served together in the infantry, bunked together, been in hospital together. Ribischka was no use to him—a sculptor of abstracts whom most people thought potty—but the friendship had continued. Sometimes he only went out to see him twice a year, but nothing had changed between them since the war. That much was static in his hectic world. Yes, a shot of Ribischka was just what he needed for a pick-me-up. He explained to O'Meara about the article and descended to the street again.

Traffic was thick at this time of day, everyone going home. The Boulevard Raspail was jammed; he could hardly get across it. The buses were packed to the steps with people hanging on behind. Horns honked incessantly. Monsieur Beloeil took to the back streets to avoid the noise.

It was chilly now that the sun was nearly down and he hurried along as fast as his limp would let him. It wasn't a painful limp, just a sort of pivoting on the wounded leg. (Friends noticed that the motion conditioned the rhythm of his speech; he loved to take long conversational *promenades à deux*.) He hardly needed a cane but he always used one. It gave him moral support; even at forty-five he was subject to attacks of shyness, awful moments when he thought people were staring at him or laughing at him, when he was afraid to speak to anyone for fear of seeming ridiculous. At such times he had to shake himself mentally, remember his position, and struggle into his self-assurance like a pair of too-tight gloves.

He was cutting across a corner of the old Faubourg St. Germain, deserted now by the great families that had been its glory. They had moved away to the hill around the Etoile, to fashionable apartments near the Parc Monceau, to the flowering chestnuts of the Avenue Foch. The old *hôtels* had been turned into cheap flats, or insurance offices, even warehouses. A wagon loaded with crates was coming out of the old Palamède place as he passed it. The Palamède lions, their heads embossed on the great bronze gates, kept watch before a courtyard littered with packing cases and straw. The good old days, thought Monsieur Beloeil—the peasant's grandson—*ces beaux vieux temps . . . on ne les verra plus!*

He stopped at a workman's bar in the Rue de Sèvres for a *cinzano*, then crossed to the Rue Vaugirard and followed it to the Impasse des Deux Anges. The streetlights came on just as he reached it, one after another they blinked on as far up the long street as he could see.

Ribischka had his studio in one of a group of sheds that had once been a livery stable. He had put glass in part of the roof and strengthened the floor to hold up his huge blocks of stone. Lilacs grew outside his door, blooming early in May. A neighbor kept chickens. The place might have been a hundred miles away from the Concorde.

Monsieur Beloeil pulled the bell string and waited. Someone was hammering in the next shed. The door was opened suddenly (Ribischka went barefoot; you could never hear him coming) and he was taken in. The old man did not greet him but his eyes showed pleasure, his eyes and his beard, his thick gray beard, square and curly. That beard was the most remarkable thing about him. It talked, it had a voice: everyone noticed it who knew him. It grew close about his mouth, almost covering it, and hid his chin completely. His hair was just as thick, growing low on his forehead and heavy about his ears. People always compared him to a faun, and his eyes were the ember-hot eyes of a faun—small, quick, and passionate. He was a little man but his eyes made him big. He was radiant, at sixty. He wore a brown, short-sleeved smock and white canvas trousers. His arms were hairy. His hands were large and constantly moving.

Monsieur Beloeil sat down on the only piece of furniture, a low couch, and Ribischka pulled up a stump of wood. He had been in the kitchen, he said, starting his supper (he did all his own work), wouldn't his friend share it with him? He came so seldom; he must stay a long time now that he was here.

Monsieur Beloeil lit a cigarette, leaned back on the couch, and looked around him. Ribischka did not expect conversation.

The studio was a sight—it looked like a stone jungle. Rough blocks of stone everywhere, all shapes and sizes, jutting like menhirs, or piled one on another. Above them, finished compositions on wooden stands—strange, abstract, symbolic shapes, polished till they glistened with light. And higher still, reaching up into the beams, Ribischka's curious, twisting columns, like totem poles, that he called his "Trees of Heaven," his endless towers.

Stone dust was everywhere. How could the man walk in his bare feet over all those chips and splinters? The light was failing and the sculptor rose to start the lamps. He had spurned electricity as he had spurned everything else that was alien to his native valley in the Grisons. He was still a Rhaetian peasant in spite of his good self-education. His French was full of Romansch twists, and his skin was still as dark as though he had just left the fields. Thirty years in Paris had not changed him; he had still the temperament of the mountains, warm-hearted but aloof. He shunned the salons, sending his work by an agent. He never read the criticism about him. He seldom saw other sculptors and never mentioned their work. He was courteous to visitors but never tried to sell them. He was haphazard about prices, refusing to sell the pieces he liked best. And except for the controversy over his tower with the exhibition architects, he had never been known, since the war, to mix in the life of the outer world. He saw his friends and in summer sometimes went with them on day-excursions into the country or the forests.

The affair of the tower had set all Paris to laughing, but it was the tragedy of Ribischka's life. His heart had been in his tower more than anything else he had ever done. His "Tree of Heaven" was a symbol of his deepest faith in the value of human life. He had been dismissed from art school, where he had come as a raw peasant of twenty, having hiked across Switzerland and France, because he refused to copy the Laocoon. "Suffering is not life," he said, "I will not do it." He believed that natural man was happy—"they make the pain themselves with their civilizings"—but he detested the whole Romantic movement. "The cult of suffering," he called it; ". . . those bodies, swollen, with their tortured muscles . . . decadent . . . do they make you feel good? Do they make you believe in life, in happiness?" And in his "Tree of Heaven" he expressed his faith in happiness, his belief in the *joie de vivre*. It was to be an endless tower stretching up through the clouds, like a great cathedral, a center of the people's life, a visible inspiration. "They will see the tree and they will weep no more. . . . *Dans leurs coeurs ils monteront aux cieux*."

But how to build it? Oh, that he knew, that was his discovery. The secret lay in a perfect fusion of the cube and the sphere. When you had found the exact proportion the balance was perfect, you could build it as high as you wanted and it would stand, ten times as high as the *Tour Eiffel*, when you married the cube to the sphere.

He had made experiments with these wooden columns here in the atelier. He had had to make dozens before he got it right. But it worked. He had one fifteen meters high in a friend's garden. And the balance was so perfect that it needed only ten centimeters of foundation under ground. That was where the engineers and architects had laughed at him. He had seen their drawings for a new tower for the next Exhibition, a hideous thing tapering from a huge base, and had gone at once to the mayor. He had brought one of his wooden models with him in a taxicab and the newspapers had all taken photographs. It became a national joke. There was a mock reception and a decoration. Ribischka was in heaven for a week before he realized the deception. The engineers said it was impossible. The fools, they wouldn't even come out to the garden in Senlis to see the model that was set up, to see for themselves. The defeat was terrible. For months he had been unable to work. He didn't eat, he saw no one, he sat in darkness. And then a new vision had come to him and he set to work again. He had not been humble; what could he expect of the deluded masses? This would be simply a small sculpture, a personal symbol, but it would be perfect. It was to be a flame: not the visible outline of a flame, but its inner reality, its hidden ideal. The flame of joy. Slowly he had shaped it from the raw stone, first with hammer and chisel, then by polishing. Seven months on it already, but time was immaterial. He would not show it to Monsieur Beloeil until it was finished. It stood under a cloth in the middle of the room.

Listening to Ribischka was a tonic for Monsieur Beloeil. "Sincerity" was not deep enough to describe him. He had an idea that perhaps the old man was right and the engineers wrong about his tower. Certainly there was no doubt that his sculptures were superb; they made the average abstraction look anemic. His flowers and plants, though they bore no resemblance to their namesakes, were beautiful and full of meaning. He walked about the atelier examining them again, while the artist went on with his preparations for supper. Monsieur Beloeil had explained about his dinner engagement and said he must run along soon, but he couldn't easily break away.

He felt a peace in Ribischka's jungle that he found nowhere else. In the smaller room, in back, the vegetation was even denser, as it served as bedroom, closet, kitchen, workshop, and library. There was a small forge and a talking machine fitted with double diaphragms on which he played aboriginal music— Eskimo songs and Polynesian dances. There was a workbench with tools and a hand-lathe. There were buckets of paint and piles of sketches. There was a trapeze on which he took his exercise.

The room fascinated Monsieur Beloeil; the house in Beloeil must have looked like this. He sat on the bed while Ribischka cooked and ate his dinner. They talked a bit of things that had happened during the war years but for the most part they were silent. The old man's joy at playing host was so evident and so delightful. He never stopped smiling. Dinner at the duchess's would be excellent, but Monsieur Beloeil couldn't resist his friend's invitation to try the stew. It was good. Afterward they drank brandy; it was cheap brandy, but he enjoyed it. Ribischka played some of his wild music on the machine and demonstrated on the trapeze. Monsieur Beloeil shook with laughter and let the time run on. This was marvelous, he must come here oftener, what a man! It was nine o'clock before he left, promising to come again soon. He would be late for dinner, very late, but what of it?

Ribischka loved to work late, sometimes all night. The silence of night enchanted him as he worked. His mind grew quiet, his thoughts flowed peacefully in halftime, turning on themselves, leading back and back into memory, dreaming forward to fame; and all the while his hand steadily polishing—shaping with endless love the inner, deeper, transcendental form. Polishing, polishing, polishing: on and on, heedless of time as a Chinese lacquerist. Polishing, polishing: hour by hour, hour on hour.

It was deep night, but Paris never manages to fall asleep. The silence brought the city's muted voices close around him. *Minuit on dort*: the long slow bells of St. Clotilde, spelling it out. *Une heure*: rattle of a market train bouncing along the car tracks of the boulevard towards Les Halles. *Deux heures*: unsteady footsteps in the street; stray whiffs of vineal song. *Trois heures*: a lonely dog howling far away; a single taxi horn; a child crying in a house nearby; leaves brushing against the dark windowpane.

In summer Ribischka would wait for the dawn before going to bed, but in March it came too late. Near four he stopped his work, stood for a moment outside the door, and then put out the lamps.

And at about the same time of night Monsieur Beloeil, still wearing his dinner jacket, but his hair much ruffled by the pangs of genius, was finishing a remarkably clever piece of prose. It had come to him at dinner. He had been describing his comical friend Ribischka to the lovely metallic lady on his left. She had laughed and laughed; how funny, how priceless, how fantastic! Why not do a comic portrait of him for the next number of *Le Boeuf sur le toit*?—something etched in quicksilver, a little overdrawn here and there . . . he had it half written in his head before he got home. Ribischka would never see it unless someone brought it to him, and even then it wouldn't penetrate. The man was indifferent to everything except his work itself. It would be a knockout.

Near four it was finished, and O'Meara was sent back to his bed. Monsieur Beloeil took the piece into the bathroom with him and read it over as he lay soaking in the tub. It made him gurgle with glee. Nobody else but he could make so much out of a thing like that! It *was* a knockout! Especially the parts about Ribischka talking with his beard or swinging on the trapeze like a chimpanzee. He would have all Paris laughing. . . .

Ribischka got up from his bed after a few minutes in it and lit a candle. He had to have one more look at his work before he could sleep. He held the candle high and its light flickered on the gleaming stone. He trembled a little as he looked at it—his flame, the soul of flame, the life-flame. He *had* caught it! He was sure now he had gotten it. It was there, permanent and unchallengeable, his vision of life, held in the stone, forever, forever.

Quatre heures: Paris is quietest now, it nearly sleeps. But hush! you can hear the river beating through its heart.

For a minute I thought one of them was going to come right in the window. They had been rumbling around the sky all afternoon, I couldn't see any of them out the window even though the hospital is on the highest hill in town, but there must have been twenty of them at least, they made so much noise, and then all of a sudden I heard one coming right at me. I mean it, it was coming straight at the corner of the building where my room is—God, I thought, what a swell piece of irony: you crack hell out of yourself in a ski race, and then when they've almost got you screwed together again along comes a big load of bombs through the window to blow you right back to where you came from and then some. . . .

That night I was talking about it with the man across the hall. He has one leg off just above the knee and the other one coming, but they put him in a wheelchair and he navigates all over the floor. Sometimes in the evening he comes in to listen to the radio and tell me about his legs and the football games he played in when he was at Syracuse. He'd been reading about the air raid in the evening paper, about how "aeronautical experts" had decided which side had won, that the bombers had bombed everything in town before the pursuit planes could get rid of them.

"What I want to know," he said, "how does anybody know which side wins if they don't do any real shooting?"

So I had to start right in and explain it all to him and even then he couldn't get it.

"You mean to say that it's all fixed beforehand? that no matter what the planes do the army will say they need a lot more of them?"

"Sure, that's the way it works."

He thought about it for a while but he couldn't get it down. Beyond a certain age people never can get it down. Some of them, the "broad-minded" ones or the "open-minded" ones, will look at it, maybe even look at the inside of it, but they don't really try to get it down. Because they couldn't; it just isn't for them, any more than our children's ideas will be for us.

He wasn't an old man at all, only about forty, I guess, (and the nurses were saying that the other leg would have to come off within a month), but he couldn't get it down. He didn't like the taste of it at all and it was beginning to irritate him.

"That's no way to talk about things, you haven't any proof, you just think it's like that because somebody's been filling you full of. . . .

"All right," I said, "I don't have any proof, I don't know definitely who paid who how much to say what, but I've seen this thing working before and I know how it works."

And then I told him how they worked it two years ago in Paris, when business was bad for Tannery and the *Forges* because the Left had been squawking and people had started listening a little. It took just about two weeks, I remember, just two weeks, and you could watch it happening in people's faces, you could watch their minds change, see them stop thinking about *pourriture* and economy and start being worried about the Boches dropping bombs all over the Belle Patrie, especially the particular arrondissement where each happened to live. (There was one politician, Colonel Somebody, who got himself elected in the next city polling, entirely on a platform of installing enough anti-aircraft guns to protect the quartier des Invalides from Goering's collapsible airships.) They would send the planes over in the morning when people were all going to work and by noon the papers would be full of descriptions of the destruction—number of people dead from gas, the Louvre in flames, Notre Dame in ruins . . . and then in the evening they'd send them back again just to give people something to think about that night and talk about in the cafés after dinner.

Inside of two weeks there had been a face-about in the Chambre and a huge appropriation voted for armaments—the cash, of course, to be borrowed at eight percent from private banks, commissions first and taxes later. . . . One of the floor nurses who spends a good deal of time attending to me wants to go to Paris.

She wants to go to Paris, not to stay, just to see it, and she even washes her own uniforms to save up enough quicker. How much will it take, she wants to know. She has four hundred in the bank now and she thinks she can double that in a year; she and her roommate have a single line telephone, but next month they're going to go on a party line and that will save quite a bit right there. Once she had an insurance policy, she paid premiums on it for five years, and then she got tired of scraping and decided to have some fun. She and another girl cashed in on the policies and bought a car to drive to California. They were there about a month and then they got terribly homesick. California was fine but it wasn't home, and they were lonely and longing for the things and the people they had always lived with. So they sold the car one day and flew home the next; that was the end of the insurance money.

"But you wouldn't like Paris any better than Hollywood, you'd get just as homesick and you wouldn't be able to fly home from there."

Yes, probably that was so; but she didn't want to stay long anyway, just see it and look around. Finally it slipped out: she had always wanted to go to Paris and hire a gigolo for a week "just to see what it would feel like."

I couldn't help laughing and at once she was sorry she'd said it. She tried to cover it up by saying how awful it must be to have to go around with some fat old woman, it would be like going out with an old man.

"But you could do that here, you wouldn't have to go to Paris to find a gigolo."

Yes, but it would be *different* in Paris.

The man in the next room rang his bell and she went out to attend to him. His name is Mr. Murphy and he has a lot of money. Three different nurses have told me that: "he has a lot of money." Yesterday he gave the orderly who has been shaving him ten dollars. He had a heart attack but now he's getting better and is able to run his business by telephone. His voice carries through the wall. He must be about sixty but he's a big man and still pretty tough. Last week the Somerville office grossed fifty-six thousand. This morning a woman and her husband came in to see him, I saw them go by my door. She did almost all the talking and I soon had figured it out that she must have been his secretary before she married. She must have worked for him a good while because she talked to him like a daughter. She was telling him he should rest now and take it easy, he had as much money as anybody needed and what would he do with any more? Money, she said, was just good for what you could do with it.

Eight hundred dollars and a whole week in Paris with a big Argentine gigolo! Half an hour later the nurse came back in with my orange juice; oranges are supposed to be good for growing calcium.

When she was in training she used to go around with Harvard medical students. I found that out fairly soon. The first week or so we talked about my crack-up and the doctor and how long it would take. Later on we would talk about her cases and life in hospitals. When she was in training she lost her cap for two weeks for holding a pillow in her teeth while she changed the case. She doesn't much mind having her patients die if they are old, but once she had a young boy die on her. He was just a kid, she said, he drove a truck, and the day he was going he would hold onto her hand and say: "You won't leave me till I'm well, will you?" That was bad. She doesn't think much of the Harvard students; they talk funny and wear "sloppy gray pants and their socks fall down over their shoes."

Then finally I began hearing about her boyfriend; that was after about five weeks of talking to me while she was feeding me my meals. We were talking about all the drinking the Harvard students do, just talking casually, and then all of a sudden she told me all about him. It just came out naturally, in bits at first and then all together.

He's a lawyer and he's real clever and makes good money and they've been going together for almost five years. She likes him a lot, she guesses she loves him, and he's been after her to get married for two years, but she won't till he really stops drinking because that's just the one thing she can't stand. He's so wonderful when he doesn't, and sometimes he'll go for a month without, and then he'll take too much and make a fool of himself or get in trouble and ruin everything for her. Just the other night he came around in a taxi to her house and rang the bell. She met him staggering up the stairs and just turned him right around and marched him back into the taxi. She told him then she didn't ever want to see him again, and that she'd rather have someone come tell her he was dead than that he was drunk. And they've been going together five years and she's had to give up almost everyone else for him because he's so jealous, but she knows that if he won't give it up before they get married he won't after. Often he tells her she could reform him if she just went at it the right way, but she thinks when a person is on their feet ten hours a day they don't want to come home and start in reforming somebody. And she's called him all kinds of awful names when she's mad with him but he keeps coming back for more and he'd marry her right now, any minute she said the word. But he's the kind who always gets in some sort of a fight or trouble, and it used to make her so miserable she would come home and cry all night. One Thanksgiving they were at the Copley, sitting at the bar, and he started a fight with some man who was drunk and sat down beside her and tried to talk to her, he started hitting him and then he fell down and cut his head on a stool and she had to take him to the Mass General for emergency treatment. After that she wouldn't see him for two months, she would just leave the receiver off the hook at night because she knew he would try to call up, but finally he came to meet her one evening coming out of the hospital, and she was so glad to see him she just couldn't get mad at him, and he was sweet to her and didn't touch a drop for over a month. But then one evening he called up and she could tell from his voice he'd been drinking so she just locked the door and went to bed. "That's life for you," she said.

That's life, and the man across the hall is slowly losing his. He's going to die, he's going to be dead. One leg is off and the other is starting to swell. He rubs it all the time, hoping that will stop it, and soaks the foot in a bowl of solution. He sits for hours watching it soak. But that isn't going to save it and he knows it, much as they all try to keep it from him, and sometimes he sits there, the nurses say, just looking at his foot with the tears running down his face. He played football for Syracuse and all the nurses love him because he's such a good sport . . . and the foot is swelling a little more every day.

The night nurse is a Venetian, she was born in Soldano in the foothills back of Venice, and she speaks Italian with a cold in her head: "mio fradelo m'a scriddo una ledders, m'a dedo" . . . that they don't think much of the war there in that part of the country, that the boys that get called up from the mountains would rather try their luck getting across to Austria than get burned up with sun and thirst in Eritrea or have the natives chop them in little bits for stew-meat. But they all hate the English like hell just the same, it's the English have taken the food away; it's not bad for the mountain people who never eat anything but castagne anyway, but it's hard on city people— nothing but pasta anymore, pasta for dinner, pasta for supper, pasta, pasta, pasta. . . .

"Come sta sdazera, va meglio?" When I get ready to go to sleep she turns me over onto my face; the cast gets me in the ribs that way but it's the only way I can get to sleep. I couldn't fall asleep lying on my back no matter how tired I was, it just doesn't work that way, I can hardly get my eyes shut on my back. So I lie in the dark on my belly, just as I used to when I was little at home, flat down with my face turned to the right and my hands palms down each side of my head. It was a white wooden bed with spiral flutings in the head of it. I can still remember the feel of them, I used to run my fingers up and down the spirals while I was waiting to fall asleep. There was a bit of paint off the back of one of them and my finger would catch on the place. They left the light on in the closet and the door open a crack because I was so afraid of kidnappers. When I was asleep my mother would come in and turn it off. There were bars on the windows because I had bad nightmares and they were afraid I would get up and fall out sometime. But I thought the bars were there to keep the kidnappers out, and some nights I'd wake up screaming thinking one had gotten into the room. I had the idea then that the darkness outside the house was full of kidnappers, that they were always prowling around looking for ways to get in. In the daytime I almost never thought about them, and in summer it was all right because I would go to bed while it was still light and fall asleep hearing the click of croquet balls on the lawn outside and the murmur of the players' voices.

* * *

It began by my trying to remember the books that I'd read there. For weeks, since the crack-up, I hadn't even thought about it. I'd sold my skis to Kelley and that was all I thought about it. It was finished. I saw it snowing outside the window but I didn't think about skiing. I read the Olympic results in the paper, but it was all impersonal. It was finished. And then, that night as I lay in the dark room waiting for sleep to come, I started seeing it all again, first the trains, and then the faces of people who were there, and then everything—the snow, the sun and snow, the whole high world of snow, the big schusses and the woodpaths, the gipfel and the alpine garden, the corniches, the gullies, the buried chalets. . . . I saw them all, I saw them as though I were there, as though there were no space and time between, as though nothing had happened and I was standing again on the ridge of the Weisfluh, waiting to put on my skis and looking across at the Silvretta.

I always carried a book with me to read during the ride back to Davos on the train, a Tauchnitz or an Albatross that would fit into my sitzplatzsack along with my lunch and waxes. From Kublis or Serneus back up the curving valley to Davos is over an hour and making three or four runs down a day I got in quite a bit of reading; I had to get a new book every other day. People I was skiing with, especially Negroponte and Agranoupoulous, thought I was crazy to waste my time reading when there were so many girls in the train. They were on holiday from diplomatic school in Paris (all the Greeks and Egyptians and such go to the Ecole des Sciences Politiques), and they just couldn't see what I was after. But reading and skiing make a perfect life, if the snow is good and the books are good. Sometimes I couldn't tell which came first; I put a furious concentration into both. Once I had grabbed a seat in the train at Kublis I wouldn't wait a minute to be at my book; I would eat my lunch while I read without looking at my food. And the minute the train got into Davos I would be running to catch the next funicular up the mountain for the next run down . . . for the next ride and read back and the next run down; on good days, when it wasn't blowing up on top, I could get in about twenty thousand feet of running and two hundred pages of reading. And the two fused together so that I remember it now the way you remember a tune from one spring as the whole season.

Negroponte was the perfect Greek, beautiful and dirty. He loved his food and the sun and girls; Agranoupoulous told me Negroponte had been a father at thirteen and I really don't doubt it. His appetite was always on edge and between times he was busy chewing his cud. He was killed last summer near Brindisi in an airplane crash.

The two Greeks had plenty of money (Agranoupoulous' uncle deals chemin de fer at the casino in Saint-Raphaël), so they stayed with the snoots in the Derby Sport Hotel. In Davos a "Sport" Hotel means that no lungers are allowed there in the winter and that they fumigate it when the summer crowd is turned out. Now almost all of Davos-Dorf is "Sport" in the winter since the Parsenn Bahn up the mountain starts from that end of town. The Greeks stayed at the Derby along with a Peruvian married to an American copper heiress who had ten pairs of skis and two private guides. I stayed for a while at the Parsenn Sport, where most of the guides stay, but I had to move out of there because there was always a terrible racket going on below me when I wanted to get to sleep, a thumping and bumping and rhythmic thudding that shook the whole house. Before I left I found out what it was: the second floor of the hotel, the ballroom, was rented out to the Davos Gymnastic Society who practiced vigorously every evening. I poked around a little and found, besides leather horses and Indian clubs, four dressmaker's dummies, the wire and horsehair kind; I don't know just what the Gymnastic Society did with those.

I kept on having my meals at the Parsenn Sport because I knew most of the guides and they let me sit with them at their long, uproarious table, but I moved into a second-floor room

across the street above the confiserie. And there in the next
room was Bul-Bul.

Bul-Bul, as she made no effort to conceal, was waiting for
something to turn up. She had spent the fall very pleasantly
with a Swedish baron in the Greek Islands and now had decided
that Davos would be a pleasant place to spend the winter. As
yet, though it was February, nothing had turned up, but Bul-Bul
was not downhearted; she enjoyed the snow and the sunshine,
she looked wonderful in skiing clothes, and she had made
pleasant friends among lively young people of many countries.
Besides the rent above the confiserie was not heavy and her
room had a pleasant balcony overlooking the street, where she
spent a great deal of time, enjoying the sunshine, greeting her
friends as they came to the Parsenn station to take the funicular
and chatting with them while they waited for the car. Toward
noon she would ride up the mountain, though she owned no
skis, to have lunch on the terrace of the summit restaurant, and
there she would spend most of the afternoon if the weather was
fine, greeting her friends as they came up in the funicular with
their skis and chatting with them while they smoked a cigarette
before starting the run down. Later in the afternoon she would
take tea at the Derby Sport where there was tea dancing, but
after supper she would never leave the house alone, and I soon
found that she had a much larger selection than I of Tauchnitzes
and Albatrosses.

Bul-Bul was beautiful and her disposition was perfect. She
spoke five languages so well that I couldn't tell her nationality
until I asked the proprietor (her name was Courdeveaux), and
her smile was constant and delicious. She looked as good to eat
as the cakes in the confiserie window and she ate enough of
them to have the delectable plumpness that only goes well with
blondness when it is French. Why she was called Bul-Bul no one
seemed to know, and though everyone knew her no one knew

who had known her first. She was there when I came, she was there when I left—the most pleasant person in Davos: smiling, chatting, enjoying the snow and sunshine, and waiting for something to turn up.

I got to know her quite well, though I never learned anything about her life (the Greek Islands were part of general information), and when I was leaving Davos she walked to the station with me, "to get a paper," but didn't wait till the train left to say goodbye. I expect to meet her again as an old woman in Carlsbad when I am old enough myself to be taking the cure.

You climb up and you slide down, up and down, up and down, or you ride up and slide down, and the more you do the more you like it and want to do. Tired as you are you're sorry when darkness comes, and each morning you rush out with only half your breakfast to catch the first car up the mountain. Up and down, in sun and storm, day after day all winter, until one day in April you notice all of a sudden that in all that world of white and bright sky-blue there is no green, no living green thing at all; there may be gray rocks or brown houses or the dead green of pines, but there is no living green of spring—you feel this all of a sudden and at once your desire is gone, you wouldn't go up another mountain for anything; you pack your things, block up your skis, and run for the valleys and spring. But in midwinter the snow makes the sun seem brighter and warmer.

Get up early in the morning after a night's fall of new powder; make the first track down a long open slope with the snow spraying out in a cloud behind you and your ski points cutting the fresh surface as a ship's bow cuts the sea; there is no wind, there is no sound, the sky is clear, and in its emptiness the sun, the great sun, the white sun, the sun . . . nothing is like this, nothing you know or can imagine—not the color of water or the color of air at sunset—this is the furthest you can go.

And the wonderful thing is that you can always go there again. It's true there will be days of storm when you can't see two feet ahead of you, when the snowflakes burn your eyes and you feel as though you were going down blindfolded in an elevator. There will be days when wind has swept the snow into crusts and drifts that pitch you on your nose. There will be icy surfaces where a fall hurts like a hammer blow on the bone. There will be thaws when no wax will give you speed, when the snow sweats and you sweat and you pole in vain to carry the run-outs. There will be rain turning the snow to soggy mashed potatoes. All this will happen, but you don't really mind because each day you're thinking: tonight it will snow and clear tomorrow. And when it does clear and the new snow sinks under your weight. . . .

For eleven days running we had new snow every night, sometimes ten inches of it, light and dry, the kind you dream about. Each turn in that snow was like a kiss, a whole kiss with the lips and the hands and the eyes, and you could never have enough of them; "a hundred and a hundred more and then another hundred." It was like that. And then each night the new snow falling quietly in the darkness. At bedtime I would stand for a long time at the window watching it endlessly falling.

"Ancor svegliado?" It was the night nurse, the Venetian, come in to put on the extra blanket.

"It's late," she said, "Mezza nodde . . . what are you think-ing about?"

"I'm seeing things."

"Seeing things? . . . did you have a nightmare?"

"No, not like that, real things."

"What sort of things?"

"Montagne . . . neve . . . sole . . .

"Do you want a pill to make you sleep?"

"No, I don't need one."

"You can have one if you want. The doctor said to give you one anytime you couldn't get to sleep without."

"No, not tonight."

She tucked the blanket in around my feet and shoulders and then felt my forehead for fever. "You're crazy about your skiing, aren't you?"

"Yes, pazzo," I said, "Plumb pazzo about it."

"Did you ask the doctor today?"

"Yes."

"What did he say?"

"Nothing much . . . nothing definite."

"Well, it'll be all right then. Next year. . ."

"No," I said, "It won't be all right, I could tell from the way he looked . . . he just doesn't want to tell me until I'm better."

"Purdrobo. . . . . ." She stood by the bed for a moment, her hand on my shoulder, then went out, holding the doorknob so the latch wouldn't click.

No matter what position you get into the cast will stick into you, or itch you, somewhere. It's like one of those iron maidens that you see in torture chambers. (When I was about six a prison ship came up the Ohio to Pittsburgh and anchored under the Point Bridge, an old English prison ship, a real one, that some promoter was towing all around the country with a tug. All the children were taken to see it. They had an iron maiden in the foremast and of course my brother had to shut me in it when no one was looking. I got scared and banged my head on one of the points so that I had to have two stitches in it. He got put to bed without any lunch or supper and had to learn three Psalms by heart.) The only thing to do with the cast is to lie absolutely still in it; that way you soon get used to the place where it pinches and it stops hurting. In Davos I tried to locate the sanitarium where Hans Castorp must have been. There are hundreds of them there, but I had one thing to go on: I was sure that the

Magic Mountain was the Silvretta, and you can only see that from the hillside above the town. Finally I picked out one sitting high above Davos-Platz near the Schatzalp Bahn that seemed to fit the description as I remembered it.

On days when a hurricane was blowing on the Parsenn side of the Weisfluh we would ski on the back side of the mountain, the side just back of the town. Coming down there we would go past a number of the sanitaria, where people were lying out on the porches and balconies in spite of the weather, bundled up in blankets. It was bad enough to see them there, lying still as a brick all day while we skidded all over the mountainside, but the terrible thing was their cheerfulness. As we went by they would always call out to us. Some of them must have been in the last stages (Agranoupoulous claimed that one night late, about three in the morning, when he was coming home from some-where past the station, he saw them loading caskets into the death train, the one-car train that runs down from Davos every night carrying the dead back into the valley) but they all would shout and wave to the skiers. Some of the girls would stop for a while and talk to them because they felt so badly about them, but I could never do it: their eagerness frightened me. Once I took a good header in soft snow right behind the Soleda and they all hissed and clapped and shouted advice to me as I tried to get untangled. They say that as the disease progresses their spirits and animation increase, and that not long before they are to die they are fuller of life and gaiety and real happiness than ever before. Having them there, knowing they were there even when I didn't see them, never depressed me as it does some people. Somehow it gave the life there completion. Their shadow on the snow made the action more wonderful. Perhaps that is the way you feel in wartime, I don't know. I would sing out "Skiheil" as I went past the balconies, but I never stopped to talk because I couldn't ever forget that night in the train, that ride to Aix in the third class carriage. . . .

I had been sick myself for almost two weeks, one of those

bugs you pick up in foreign cities that don't trouble the native inhabitants but raise hell with the stranger, and I was only able to get on the train because Marianne practically picked me up and put me on it. She said that if I didn't get to Italy that week I would die the next day and that bad as I was alive I would be three times as much trouble dead. All afternoon I lay on the couch while she packed my things and wondered whether there really was a place where the sun shone; it had rained every day for a month in Paris. We took a taxi to the PLM, which she wouldn't let me pay for, and then she sat in the compartment with me till the train left. She had brought sandwiches for me to eat and a bottle of cognac to keep me warm when the train got to the mountains. She sat across from me while we waited and kept telling me how hot it would be in San Remo and how the change would fix me right up and I would be swimming and writing again in no time. We had been fighting for weeks but now she was so sweet to me that I began to want to stay. The idea of leaving her began to hurt me and add to my misery. I think if the whistle hadn't blown I would have gotten out of the train no matter what she said. Just as it was leaving—she was standing outside under the platform lights—she kissed one finger and pressed it against the window-glass. There was no one else in the compartment so I pulled down the blinds and stretched out on the seat with my coat over me.

But at one of the suburb stops, maybe it was Asnières, I don't remember, these three girls, girls about eighteen I guess, got into the compartment; two convent sisters put them on the train, looking rather suspiciously at me, and kissed them goodbye. Since there was plenty of room for them on the opposite seat I didn't bother to sit up. Pretty soon, since they thought I was asleep (they had turned out the light and only the faint blue of the corridor light shone on the celling) they began chattering to each other. It seemed that they hadn't known each other before, they came from different parts of Paris, but they all had consumption and now they were being sent down to Aix to work as maids in a big sanitarium down there. It was the only way they could get out of Paris, as they came from poor families; they had never been away from home before, and their excitement was feverish. They rattled away at each other like a field full of crickets, and all the time they were laughing and giggling with gaiety.

I lay on my side of the compartment with my eyes shut, feeling terrible, but hearing everything they said. Soon they were comparing case histories, exchanging notes on their common illness, telling about other patients in the hospitals where they had been—and all with a gay animation that made the stories of their suffering more grotesque than ghastly. The girl on the window side could hardly suppress her laughter as she told about her pneumothorax operation, how it hurt and how awful it felt when they were putting the air in. But now everything was fine, they would all get well in Aix; she had known a woman the doctors in Paris had condemned who got well in six months in Aix. There would be snow there and bright sunshine all day long. When the train stopped at a station and its lights shone in the window I got a glimpse of her: she looked to me as though she would last about a month. Her skin seemed too thin to hold in the bones behind it, and she couldn't keep still for a second; she was holding the middle girl's hand, almost tearing it to pieces with her restless fingers.

The train clattered on and the girls were never quiet. Obviously they had no intention of trying to sleep at all that night. They kept undoing their bundles to get at the foul-smelling bits of food they had brought with them. Finally—they were sure I was asleep—one opened her blouse to show the others a huge operation scar beneath her breast. The nervous girl had to feel it with her finger and the proud owner described her ordeals all over again while her audience gasped and giggled. Somewhere past Nevers I was able to drop asleep for a while but I was wakened at Dijon where two workmen with toolboxes crowded into the compartment, obliging me to sit up to make a place for them. They put their boxes on the floor between their feet, they were stonemasons, and sat straight up on the hard seat, staring at the girls. Though they didn't speak for a long time I could see at once that they were Savoyards: they had blond red hair, blue eyes (very small) and enormous Italian mustaches. They sat with their hands on their legs staring at the three girls as though they had never seen anything like them before. But instead of being silenced the three became more excited than ever, whispering to themselves with glances at the masons and finally laughing right into their faces as though they were walruses in the zoo. And I don't think anything in the zoo could have smelt worse than those two Savoyards. Probably they had been away from home on the job in Dijon for at least a month and, since they had no baggage besides their tools, it was obvious that they had not changed their clothes in that time, and having no clean clothes why should they have bothered to go to the public baths of Dijon, fine as they are?

The walruses stared, the girls grew more and more hilarious, and I huddled in my corner trying not to see or smell. It was like a stale cheese sandwich raised to the tenth power. It was too cold to open the window and my legs were too weak to hold me up in the corridor. The next few hours were pure hallucination and horror. But finally I must have fallen into a feverish sleep, because I woke up feeling terribly cold in an empty compartment with an Italian bersagliere asking to see my passport.

When I was not skiing I loved to walk through the streets of Davos-Platz because they were almost completely empty. Sometimes you could go for ten minutes in broad daylight without seeing anyone. Hervera used to say that it was like his native city in Nicaragua during the hour of siesta. But of course the snow was piled everywhere and the names on doors were all German. It was like the towns through which you walk in dreams, like the towns of Chirico's paintings, unreal, mysterious, and frightening. Even the occasional people whom you passed were dream people—invalids deep in furs, who walked as though they knew they were really not moving, and sometimes a thin, thin doctor in a long black coat, hurrying to get to the patient before death did. When you met a postman or a delivery boy you almost wanted to speak to him to be sure that he could answer you with a living voice.

Do you remember Hemingway's story of the trout stream? How the "tenente," lying sleepless in the dark, could fish every good hole in miles of stream, all in his head? It was like that the nights before races. I could never get to sleep. I would have spent hours on my skis, waxing them till they sounded high E when you pulled your finger down the surface; and then read a little before putting out the light . . . shall I take the big schuss straight? how many swings should I make on the toble? will the waldweg spill me the way it did this afternoon? will it be frozen or slushy at the bottom? I knew every foot of the course, every bump and angle and possible line. And down it I would go in my head, over and over again, trying different tactics, imagining what would happen, making it happen as I wanted, taking it faster and faster each time, until finally I would be running a six-mile course in a fifth of a second, actually seeing the whole run simultaneously, every schuss and carry and drop and bend of it before the mind's eye at the same instant, the way they say Toscanini can see a whole symphony at once.

The Parsenn starts with the steep bent schuss from the gipfel of the Weisfluh to the saddle. To carry the saddle you must schuss the top, but to schuss the top you must be good, or you can't hold the bend and bump at high speed. Better to take a few swings high on the schuss and not risk a fall just before the saddle where you'd lose a whole minute pushing across the flat.

Then the run falls in a series of roller coaster dips, everything open of course, you are far above the tree line, where the line you choose will make a difference. If you follow the markers (and how you love those markers when you're coming down in a snowstorm, when, without them, you'd be snow-blind and lost forever in five minutes!) you'll lose speed, but if you work the drops against the slant of the slopes you can gain seconds. And remember the Canadian crouch when you're caught in a headwind; it looks terrible and it cramps your thighs but the streamlining makes a real difference.

Wherever you are in the world of skiing you'll hear people talking about the Derby schuss; it comes about two miles down the Parsenn, just beyond the fork where a run branches down to Serneus and Klosters. In Sanct Anton, in Cortina, in Megève, in the huts of the Oetztal you'll hear about the Derby schuss: how Furrer ran it the year the Derby was raced in a blizzard; how somebody "took it straight right down from the rocks and held it. . . ."— "the hell he did, he took two checks in the rocks, Lantschner saw him. . . ."; how it compares with this schuss and that schuss—"is it as bad as the big one on Maroi Kar?"; "it's not like the top of the Festkogel above Gürgl"; in funiculars at Kitzbuhel and Sestrières, over the glühwein in gasthofs in Garmisch and Mürren and Zell am See, you'll hear about the Derby schuss, and when for the first time you see it you'll undoubtedly stop short, look once, and go around the easy way.

If it were like the gipfel schuss, with a long flat carry to absorb your speed, it would be all right. But it isn't: right at the bottom is the gully, right at the top of your speed you must go across the nastiest ditch this side of purgatory—it's deep, it's bumpy, the banks are steep, and it's rough with shell-holes (and often littered with splinters from broken skis). There is a way to take it, a standard line, but few are the legs that can hold it under any steam. Better to stem on the schuss than crack up in the gully, but better the feeling of making that gully with speed than anything else in the Grisons.

Not far below the Derby schuss the trees begin and you come into the Alpine Garden and the bumps. Here the track winds and falls, drops and twists, between trees and over hummocks; your legs begin to feel like taut strings ready to snap. And when you come to Schwendi, a little hamlet of chalets, if you aren't racing, or making a train at Kublis, you'll be ready to stop for a rest. If the sun is out you can have some beer and go to sleep awhile. But beer hits you in the legs. Better stick to skiwasser: it slakes thirst and doesn't sweat much.

Below Schwendi the bobruns begin; the trees thin out, you are in the upper fields, the terraced hay fields high on the sides of the valley. Above Schwendi you are in the world of sky and snow; below Schwendi you come back to man. You run through fields past hay-huts and chalets. There are winter-bare hardwoods and, if it's March, the bottom of the valley beneath you may be green.

The bobruns are layers of terraced ski tracks made by the hundreds who don't run straight but curve back and forth down the steep slopes holding hard to the hang of the hill. By January they are so well worn and formed that they last through all the remaining snows. In your first days on the Parsenn you follow the bobruns, getting your sport from sharp cutbacks from one level down to the next. But later you'll see a kanone cutting straight down across them, bumping from lip to lip, half the time in the air. After that the bobruns seem tame; you may have to keep stopping to rest the agony of your legs, but you go down straight, trying to make it appear as though nothing at all were there. It's easy here to break a point; best to carry a metal makeshift in your pack.

At Conters, a hillside village, the track runs right through the main alley. People will be watching you from the windows, and sometimes traffic is jammed by cows or a horse and hay sled. Just beyond the village you go through the front yard of a chalet where a man with a red beard and a long pipe is always chopping wood. Any time of day he will be there, splitting up the wood that the villagers drag down the mountainside from the belt of firs above. He stops chopping to watch each skier come through, but long ago he must have gotten tired of answering their greetings, for now he only rests his ax and looks.

Below Conters the course traverses the side of the lower valley to Kublis, following cart tracks and footpaths, with a final swoop down a field to the river at the bottom. It is a half mile walk from here to the station, and there are always a lot of little boys waiting to carry your skis for you, if you look prosperous. When you get to the station it's always a good idea to dip your skis in the horse trough to clean them off and then stand them up, points down, in the sun to dry.

If you mean to run the maximum you can't loiter. There is always just time to catch the next train back up the valley if you hurry and don't fall. But for me the best part is the waiting at the start, the poise before the plunge, the instant before you bite into the cake, the bloodhot hush before the first caress. Then your nerves are all alive within you, your whole body is keyed for the run, and you wait, prolonging delight and agony, wait as the others jump from the ridge and flash down the schuss to disappear beyond the saddle, wait as you feel the sun and wind on your head, wait as you look across the great valley below to the distant glistening mass of the Silvretta.

A VISIT

MacDonald found a spot for his car not far from the house. The town was growing. Since his last visit, two years before, they had installed parking meters. He put in his nickel and crossed to the little frame dwelling that stood on a raised bank, with concrete steps going up to the door from the sidewalk. It was April but the bushes around the house weren't in bud yet, and the strip of lawn on the bank was more brown than green. The house had been recently painted—a light gray with dark green shutters—and looked neat if not handsome. MacDonald knew that it had been built for the Evanses just before the first world war and that they had lived there ever since. Although Evans had tapered off his practice some ten years ago, his faded shingle was still mounted beside the door: HOMER C. EVANS, Attorney-at-Law.

MacDonald rang the doorbell and in a moment a small, old colored woman in a cook's apron let him in. He threw his coat on a chair as she called up the stairs: "Mister Evans . . . man here to see you," and went back to the kitchen. MacDonald went into the living room—it wasn't large but light came in through tall windows—and studied the paintings on the wall while he waited. They were all good ones—gifts to Evans from painters he had known. There was a lovely, delicate Demuth of red flowers and green leaves—very abstract in its design and the colors subtle. And a strange Graves bird—no kind of a bird you could name but very much bird—a dark form, only the feet and the beak drawn sharply, on a soft gray wash; it had an oriental feeling. And a Hartley, a forest scene, the logs and rocks like crude chunks, thickly painted with heavy black outlines. And over the fireplace a Marin, a view looking out over some beach that must be in Maine—those wonderful free slaps and slashes of the water-color brush, an inspired jumble of bits and patches of pure color with the white of the paper left showing between them. Evans had been friends with all these painters. He had written poems to most of them.

The furniture in the room was in no way "interesting," no particular style and heavily worn. Evans' daughters had grown up in this room and now brought their children there for Sunday visits. At one end of the room was a tier of shelves built across the corner that always attracted MacDonald. There, filling nearly four shelves, were all of Evans' books, from the first little green pamphlet that had been printed at his mother's expense by the local newspaper printer to the collected volumes of his poems and essays. And the three books about him, and runs of the magazines he had helped to edit, and the translations into foreign languages. MacDonald had read most of them and had copies of many of them at home. Five of them had been published by his firm.

As he moved about the room, taking it in, he heard a noise from upstairs that he couldn't at first identify. It was a series of regular, repeated sounds—first a kind of soft scrape and then a little thump . . . then another scrape and thump. Suddenly it struck him; Evans must be dragging himself downstairs, holding onto the bannister and dragging one leg that had lost its mobility. It had gotten to that, the poor man could hardly walk anymore!

MacDonald rushed into the hall to see if he could help him, but Evans was already down and moving carefully toward the living room. MacDonald had an impulse to embrace him, to

throw his arms around him, but he checked it. He did take
Evans' hand in both of his and held it as he greeted him.

"Gosh, Hank, it's great to see you, it's really great." And
without waiting for Evans to speak, "You're looking wonderful!" MacDonald said this because it seemed the cheerful thing
to say to a man who had been through the mill with his
health—two years of one thing after another. But as they moved
into the living room and he could study him in the light,
MacDonald saw that his remark was true. Evans looked older
and his hair, what there was of it, was white, but his figure was
erect and his face ruddy and little lined for a man in his late
seventies. He was wearing spectacles with much thicker
lenses—the last bout in the hospital had been an operation for
cataracts—but the magnifying effect of the glasses made his eyes
appear even more lively than usual.

Evans had wonderful eyes. People remembered his eyes. He
had always been rather handsome in a crisp, lean-faced, eager-
looking way, but his eyes—gray-green with a dancing light in
them, a merriment in them—were the dominant feature. He
could never have been much of a poker player with such
expressive eyes. Every movement from a mind that was constantly in motion came through them. And now the magnifica-
tion of the lenses brought this play of feeling even closer to the
person near him.

They sat down together on the old sofa and Evans told him,
speaking very deliberately (MacDonald had been warned by
Mrs. Evans when he telephoned to announce his visit that the
worst effect of the illness was in her husband's speech), that he
had missed seeing him and that he was glad he had driven out.

Evans was sprucely dressed—perhaps even for the
occasion—in a rather sporty tweed jacket, a dark blue shirt and
a pert little bow-tie of the same shade of blue. This must be the
garb of retirement, the final break with the profession of law, for
MacDonald couldn't remember ever having seen him before in
anything but a conservative business suit.

In his poetry and in the essays—those "Letters from No-where" with which he had peppered the magazines for years, having his say in free-wheeling style about anything that caught his eye or crossed his mind, from the new book by a young unknown to the probable effect of syphilis on Beethoven's music, Evans had always been as unrestrained in language, as unconcerned with taboos, as the newest would-be Rimbaud in the Village or North Beach. He had kept young with the youngest, and this had been a part of his appeal to successive generations. He didn't date. In his writing there was neither pontification nor withdrawal to a protected height. At seventy he could still be playful, at times a little ingenuous. But in his personal life he was very much the respectable, small-town lawyer, and he had always dressed the part.

To his neighbors in Hampton, Evans was still more the man to whom they had gone to write their wills, or whom they could still call for free advice if some woman driver dented their fender and her husband wouldn't pay up than the poet who had won a Pulitzer Prize. Of course there had been quite a stir in Hampton when Evans had been homogenized with a picture story in *Life* (an accolade of banality which had had the curious effect of prompting some of his townsfolk clients to pay their bills for his services which had gone forgotten, and undunned, for years), but he had never in the least resented this lack of local recognition of his literary stature, this public separation of the halves of his life.

In fact, the busy mixture of two full careers had been the taut spring that kept the mechanism turning. A vintage portable Corona had always sat at one side on the desk in his law office and phrases for a poem or ideas for a "Letter from Nowhere" would be pecked out on it between calls when they drifted into his head. And some of his best poems had had their birth in the county courthouse in pencil scrawlings on the margins of a brief.

With Evans creation was a matter of spontaneous (and sometimes almost continuous) combustion. Even on weekends he seldom had time to sit down to write with an open space of a whole morning before him. He had to catch the sparks as they flew. And how they flew! It was as if he were under a rain of cosmic rays, invisible pellets that showered him from God knew where, leaving marks on the sensitive plate in his mind which were immediately translated into images made of words. And the greater the pressure of law work, the more intense the bombardment. On vacations, when he did have free time, he wrote less than during the crowded rest of the year.

This way of writing had certainly influenced his style. With its ellipses and leaps from image to image it was almost a poetic shorthand. There was something skeletal about his poems, even the long ones. Evans had no time to hammer out ornamentation, or to fashion much flesh between the bones. Part of the power of his poetry was in its very rawness, the fresh bite of the perception coming through to the reader as directly as it had to the poet in the simple, uncluttered phrasing. Of course, there was an elegance too; a man with an ear doesn't work with words fifty years for nothing. And it was not automatic writing; Evans did revise and rework. In the evenings, or on weekends, he would tinker with the sheets of drafts, trying different sequences and combinations. But he had never won the good opinion of the professor-critics for whom a poet must be as intricate as a complicated machine. Evans' work was not a happy hunting ground for the exegetes. An Evans poem said what it had to say at first reading. It offered no temptation to the academic maggots.

The force of this life that had put together two such different impulses—the down-to-earth setting things in order of homely law work and the wild escape into free imagination, into a kind of intentional disordering, of poetry—came across to MacDonald as he sat close to Evans, more or less silently studying him as the old man searched for and found his words. A frail but electric little man who all his life had had command of words, could summon them instantly to his use, and now, like the nightmare of a runner who cannot move his legs in his bad dream, a very nasty joke of fate, had to fight to bring them from his brain to his tongue. MacDonald could see how this injustice hurt Evans' pride. The poet became silent and began to look at his hands, rubbing one with the other. The hands were the only part of him which really betrayed his age. They were mottled with dark spots of brown and some of the veins stood up like blue vines on the skin.

"I've been rubbing Helen's neck for her," he said. "She still gets those bad stiff necks and they can't seem to do anything about it. So I give her . . . I give her . . ." and the word that he wanted simply wouldn't come.

"Massages," said MacDonald. You had to help him, you had to. At first you didn't want to show in any way that you took notice of his problem. But then you had to answer the appeal that came in the eyes that turned to you as the tongue searched for the word.

"I give her a little massage sometimes," said Evans, going over it as if to show that he could do it.

Then he laughed. And that was another thing that people always remembered about Evans, the way he laughed. It was a soft, musical bark which carried his voice into a range where it had a special timbre. It made MacDonald think back to the sound of a gong he had once heard in a Burmese temple. He had given a coin in alms to an old man sitting cross-legged on the stair landing of a hill pagoda in Mandalay and the man had struck a small bronze gong with a little hammer as a prayer for him . . . and MacDonald had recognized Evans' laughter. A laugh and a prayer.

"It's tough, Marsh, it's tough. And it makes you mad. I don't try to go over to the city anymore. I still want to see people, I want to find out what's going on over there, what the painters are doing now, but I can't handle it. I try to talk to people and it wears me out. I have to let Helen do most of my talking for me now."

MacDonald couldn't find much to say. He just kept smiling at Evans, looking into his face and smiling. Somehow it seemed indecent to make useless conversation, even if he could have, when Evans had to fight so for every sentence. And if he only had half an hour with him it didn't seem right that he himself should take even a minute of it.

"She reads to me, too. The kids all send me their books and she reads them aloud to me. Some of them are good, too. That girl that you published what's her name . . ."

"Campbell . . . Daphne Campbell."

"That's the one. She's all right. I think she's got it. A lot of them have got it. They've figured it out. It's taken thirty years but they've caught on. It's American now. It really sounds the way we sound. It isn't just warmed-over England anymore. You know what I mean, we've talked about this before. There was Whitman, and then . . . the Chicago fellow, cats' feet . . ."

"Sandburg," said MacDonald.

"Yes, Sandburg, and then the rest of us. But Pound never looked for it . . . all that Greek and Italian . . . and his crazy Chinese, singing Chinese to himself down there in the bug-house. He's the end of the other thing. And Eliot just going backwards as fast as he could pedal—let them have him over there if they want him."

"You were the one, Hank, you really broke it loose. You know that."

"Well, I tried all right—God damn it, I tried. It took me ten years to find out what I wanted to do, to get out from under all that load of crap they piled on me in college . . ." Evans laughed again. "No, it's not crap, it's beautiful. I still read it. Helen reads it to me. We were reading Marlowe the other day, it was marvelous—it gave me the gooseflesh. But that wasn't for us you see, it couldn't do anything for us with what we were up against. We had to find out some way to do it for ourselves, some way so that it would sound like us. Ezra just dug in the backyard. The best ear, but he didn't want to listen to people talking over here. It was always music to him, hearing the music in all those old languages he boned up on. I don't think he knows yet what I was up to—the arrogant bastard! But you've got to hand it to him . . ." Evans shook his head. He was still rubbing one hand with the other.

"But these kids know what they've got to do and they're going on with it. I don't want them to copy me you understand. I give them hell when they're just doing what I did. They've got to go further with it. I don't know if I ever really made it a metric. But what is metric anyway? I read all the books about it once and I still don't know. But I know you've got to have it, it has to be there. It has to be speech and something else, too. It's nothing to do with scansion or tum-tee-tum but there has to be a base under the way the lines fall. I thought I had it the way I wanted it in 'Long Night,' I thought that was as far as I could go with it, but I'm not sure. I've still got more to do . . . and how am I going to do it now?"

"That was a great poem you had in *Poetry* last month," MacDonald said, "you never wrote anything better than that, Hank. That's a great poem."

"Well, I keep after it. I'm still pretty good with my left." Evans held up his hands in front of him and looked at them, as if they belonged to somebody else. "This one is pretty well shot—the fingers won't do what I want them to anymore. But I can still type with my left. I peck it out—without the capitals, it's too slow to hunt for that shift—and then Helen fixes it up for me. It still wants to come out. You'd think it would quit when everything else is going but it's still there. Some mornings it even wakes me up. I can't wait to get dressed or eat my breakfast. But it takes so long now to work it out. It's there and I know the words I want for it but I don't have them. I just have to sit till they come out of that fog in there. She can't help me on that. Sometimes it takes the whole morning to work it out, just ten or twenty lines in a whole morning—or I have to go back to it the next day."

It was almost more than MacDonald could bear. There wasn't a shred of self-pity in it—Evans wasn't asking for sympathy, he was just telling it like facts—but it made a pain come in the back of MacDonald's throat as if he were going to cry.

"Does it bother you if I smoke, Hank?" He had to break it up.

"No, go ahead. Say, would you like a drink of something? We've got some bourbon around. They still let me have that, thank God."

"No, thanks, Hank, I've got to drive back to town." MacDonald took out his pipe and filled and lit it. This business helped him over the hump and he got ahold of himself. But Evans had more that he wanted to say.

"It's a funny thing that I can't quit. I sit here and take it . . . and you know I've never been able to write about death. I never had anything to say about it. All those poems and almost nothing about death in any of them. I don't like it, Marsh. I'm afraid of it. I have to rest a lot now but I don't sleep much. I just have to lie there and face up to it—that pretty soon now I'm not going to be around. That's just a lot of shit about people being ready to die. And you know I've never been able to get anywhere with the idea of anything coming after. You go out like a light and you're out. I believe that. I don't expect anything else. But this thing won't stop. It's as strong now as it ever was, maybe stronger. And I don't think it's just habit. Maybe it is, but I don't think so. It's like there was somebody else in there. Look at me. I can't talk, this is more than I've talked in six months. I'm ready to fall apart, but this thing is at me just as hard as ever."

MacDonald couldn't take any more. It was outside him, it wasn't happening to him, but he couldn't deal with it. He got up and looked at his watch.

"I guess I'd better get moving, Hank. I have to be back in town for dinner."

"Wait a minute now. I know Helen wants to see you."

Evans got up, hobbled into the hall and called up the stairs to his wife. She must have been waiting for his signal as she came right down. She shook hands with MacDonald, rather formally but with warmth in her greeting, and they sat down again in the living room. She was wearing a red silk dress with little black figures in it—a young woman's dress, MacDonald thought, but it suited her.

Helen Evans was nearly the same age as her husband but she too had kept herself young looking. As a girl—MacDonald had seen pictures of her then—she had been trim and slender, and she still was. You would have called the young woman in the pictures pretty; now she was something more than that—not beautiful perhaps but very close to it. In the past MacDonald had thought her a little prim. Compared to her husband who talked easily, almost intimately, to anyone, she had always been reserved, seeming to hold herself back, whether from shyness or because her mother had trained her in oldfashioned ladylike dignity MacDonald didn't know. But now she appeared much more relaxed, smiling and talking to him as if to a close friend. He wondered whether she might always have been a little in awe of her husband, easygoing as he was, deferring to his genius, or rather to her conception of it, for certainly modest, self-critical Evans would never have wanted to be put on a pedestal. Now that his illness had made him so dependent on her in his writing she was growing more self-confident, more sure of her right to be the wife of a man in whom she had always seen so much more greatness than the world had at first recognized.

There was really no reason, MacDonald thought, for her ever having had any feeling of insufficiency except, probably, the very great love, the devotion, that had made Helen Evans the good wife that she had been. Evans had never made much money and she had worked hard for him, cooking meals, keeping house, raising their two girls. The servant who had answered the door was something new in the household. A small-town lawyer does not earn large fees, even if he collects them all, which Evans could never force himself to do. And he was always taking on legal problems for indigent writer and artist friends without any fee at all. Nor does a poet, even a Pulitzer Prize winning poet, take in from his writing in a year, or three years, what a writer of popular fiction will get for one story in the *Saturday Evening Post*. What there was of extra money after living expenses and the annuity premiums were paid went to the girls, putting them through Barnard and Bryn Mawr and helping them get settled in their own homes as they married solid young men, but with small starting salaries, one a professor and one a lawyer, and began having children. It hadn't been a hard life—they had had many friends and never been in debt after the house mortgage was paid off—but it had been a life of hard work and little leisure. And now, when literary recognition had finally come and at the same time retirement from the law, there had been Evans' sudden loss of his health, completely unexpected as he had never been seriously ill before. Yet she seemed to MacDonald to have blossomed under this pressure. A happy woman was talking to him and the thing that made her beautiful, as she now was, was the radiance of her fulfillment.

They talked about her children and grandchildren and about MacDonald's children while Evans listened in silence, resting. MacDonald had a daughter who was reaching the age to be interested in boys—a phase which he was anticipating with some alarm—and Mrs. Evans had some good (and humorous) advice to give him on the problem. Evans did not add to the conversation but a few of his wife's reminiscenes about their daughters brought out his laughter. Fearful of tiring him, MacDonald soon took his leave. Evans got up from the sofa to see him off. Then they both stood out on the stoop, saying their goodbyes, as MacDonald went down the steps and crossed to his car.

The indicator of the parking meter showed red—he had stayed longer than he planned to or should have—but there was no ticket. He felt cheerful again as he pulled into the traffic of Elm Street and headed back toward New York. The talk about death had made him grieve for Evans, but now the glow of the man's wonderful spirit had driven the pain away. Driving along, MacDonald found himself fitting together bits of what Evans had told him with lines that came back to him from the poetry. Particularly he remembered passages in the one attempt which Evans had made at a novel. This book came along fairly early in Evans' career, and had been billed as a novel but was really more a long series of lyrical reflections and descriptions, largely autobiographical, something in the nature of an interior travelogue. What plot it had concerned a young man's struggle to reconcile an overwhelming urge to write with the practical demands of conventional life. There was a girl whom the writer loved, though not with the same intensity that he gave to his writing. In the book the girl had left him—and the man in the book had not much cared. MacDonald thought about that (when he had first read the book this exit of the girl had seemed very unconvincing) and about the scene he had just witnessed—a love scene indeed, if you weren't afraid of being sentimental: a pair of lovers who had really come through together, who had really "made it."

MacDonald was well outside Hampton when it suddenly came to him that he had entirely forgotten the main purpose of his mission. It had completely slipped his mind—though he had thought about it long and seriously before coming. He had wanted to tell Evans that he was sorry.

There had been trouble in their relationship of author and publisher, rather bad trouble. MacDonald, as a young man starting in business for himself, had taken on Evans at a time when the poet's career, or at least his acceptance by the public, was in the doldrums. It was soon after the Depression and no one of Evans' early publishers wanted to continue with him. His name was well known in highbrow literary circles but poetry was not selling. For three or four years Evans had published no new books and most of his older ones had gone out of print. MacDonald had seen the opportunity to start his list with a writer who could give it literary prestige, who could set a standard for what he hoped would follow. He brought out Evans' backed-up books and re-issued some of the best that were out of print. He put Evans back into active circulation, for which the poet had been very grateful, the gratitude taking the form of a kindly and generous friendship. They grew very close, with Evans assuming for MacDonald the role of a literary father.

This was at first a wonderfully exciting experience for Mac-Donald, but as time went along, without being aware of it, he began to take Evans too much for granted. As his business grew he became interested in other writers and, perhaps only because they were demanding, while Evans never made any demands—it just wasn't his way—he had worked harder at promoting these other writers' books than he had ever done for Evans. He went on publishing Evans, but, without intending to, and always thinking of him as a dear friend whose work he venerated, he neglected him. It came to the point, during the war, when paper for books was rationed along with most other commodities, that he put Evans off when a new book was ready, pleading the paper shortage, although it was obvious that he had paper enough for books by S. and B. (whose work happened to be easier to sell).

At the time MacDonald had had no understanding of what he was doing to Evans, so it came to him as a brutal shock when Evans, as tactfully as he could, suggested that he might best accept an offer that came to him "out of the blue" (he had not gone to look for it) from another firm. MacDonald took it hard. He had come to feel that Evans was almost a personal possession, something to which his merit in publishing him when others were not eager had given him title. MacDonald was a great believer in his own virtue and fully expected his just rewards for it. He had illusions about gratitude and had always expected that Evans' gratitude would go on forever.

MacDonald imagined that Evans had betrayed him and wrote some bitter letters in which the word "knife" was prominent. Evans had replied with restraint but MacDonald's tone confirmed his decision and he went his way. MacDonald assumed a posture of injured benevolence, complaining very caustically to his intimates of the bad treatment he had received. His correspondence with Evans dropped off to a trickle of business letters. If they met at some gathering MacDonald was formally cordial; Evans was good-humored but at a loss for much to say to him. MacDonald could usually put up a good front of equanimity but inside he was a brooder. In certain moods his thoughts would focus, as if magnetized, on someone he supposed had wronged him and he would indulge himself in fantasies of revenge—nothing violent, but complicated stratagems for humiliating the offender. And he would snap at his wife if she happened, quite innocently, so much as to mention one of these occupants of his doghouse.

Things went along thus for several years—no drastic rupture, but their old friendship in abeyance. Then one morning there arrived on MacDonald's desk a large manila envelope addressed in the familiar Evans hand. Inside it was the typescript of a new manuscript, the sequel to an earlier poetic narrative which MacDonald had published, with a note inquiring if he would not like to undertake it since he had already on his list the earlier volumes in the sequence. MacDonald read it through without opening the rest of the day's mail. It was beautiful poetry which brought all his true love for Evans' work, and for Evans himself, flooding back. Within the hour he had Evans on the telephone and it was as if nothing had ever come between them—all the hurt, and the resentment, disappeared as if it had never existed.

Sometimes, in the following years, MacDonald would remember what had happened, but it did not cause him pain. It was like remembering his automobile accident—something unpleasant that had occurred, leaving no recollection in the flesh of the actual pain. And nothing was ever said, or written, between them about it. They saw each other now and then, wrote to each other frequently about all manner of things, but were careful to skirt the subject of the break. Yet MacDonald had begun to feel that something should be said about it. He felt no need that Evans should bring it up but it grew on him that he wanted Evans to know that he, who had been in the wrong, had finally realized where the fault had lain. He wanted to tell Evans that he was sorry he had been so blind, and so ugly.

That was his real purpose in going to Hampton that day. Somehow in his absorption as Evans had talked to him he had forgotten all about it. But the need to go through with it was all the stronger now because Evans had been so affectionate with him, had confided so much. As quickly as he could MacDonald swung his car off the highway and turned around. It was late, but he had to go back.

Mrs. Evans answered the bell at the door. "Oh, Marshall, it's you. Did you forget something?"

"No, not exactly. Excuse me for bothering you, Helen, it's just that there was something quite important I meant to say to Hank and I didn't. It won't take a minute. I know he's tired, but I won't stay a minute."

Mrs. Evans seemed a little more than surprised, almost annoyed, but she let him come in. "Well he's gone up to rest before supper. I hate to get him down again. The stairs are so hard for him now. Couldn't I give him the message?"

MacDonald was stumped for a moment, then came out with: "Please, Helen, let me go up to him. Just a second. It's something sort of just between us."

She must have read what was in his mind because her manner changed. She gave him a smile and told him to go upstairs. "You remember where his room is, don't you, Marshall? To the right of the stairs." MacDonald raced up the stairs without taking off his coat. The bedroom door was ajar. He gave a light tap and took a step inside. The room was half dark but he could make out Evans lying on the bed, on his back, with a blanket over him. Was he asleep? If he were, he couldn't wake him. But Evans heard him and asked, "Supper ready?"

"It's not Helen, Hank. It's me, Marshall. May I bother you?"

"What's that . . . Marshall? I thought . . ."

Evans raised himself on his pillows and snapped on the bedside table lamp. He was in his shirtsleeves with his tie off. He fumbled for his glasses on the table. MacDonald put them in his hand and sat down on the bed beside him. His words came tumbling out.

"I'm sorry to disturb you, Hank, but I forgot to tell you the most important thing, what I really came to see you for. You see I . . . I don't know just how to . . . well I have to make sure that you knew that I was sorry."

"Sorry? I don't see what . . ."

"About what happened between us. Only really it was what I did to you. I can understand that now and I wanted to tell you I was sorry I wrote those letters . . . and all the rest of it."

Evans had been startled at first—he had been lying in the gloom with his eyes closed thinking about something that happened a long, long time ago, something that happened in Venice when he was only . . . how old had he been, twenty-four? twenty-three? . . . it was the summer after law school that he took that trip . . . he had been sitting at evening at a café table in St. Mark's square, with the flocks of pigeons wheeling through the dusk—he was startled, but then he took it in and he began to laugh. It wasn't the big laugh this time, but a little, soft prolonged chuckle, and his head nodded from side to side as he pulled the good left hand out from beneath the blanket, felt for MacDonald's hand and covered it with his.

"Why, Marsh," he said, "you didn't have to come back here to tell me that. I knew that. I knew it when it happened. I knew you didn't mean all that stuff you wrote me."

"I guess I did mean it then. But I shouldn't have. And I don't now." He gave Evans' hand a squeeze and got up. "I'll get out of here now. I'm sorry I woke you up."

"You didn't," said Evans, "I was just lying here . . . thinking of . . . of . . . Venice, of all things." And as MacDonald left him, "But I'm glad you came back."

It was Saturday and most of the mill wasn't working. Bad times again. Recession they called it this time. But there was a rush order of light sheets to get out and the skin-pass stand was running to finish them up.

They have to have them out today, said Riordan, will you check them over after the skin press? They have to be perfect they say or they won't take them.

Who are they for?

They're for tombs, said Riordan, they're for the dead.

Mausoleum shelves?

That's it. They just paint over them to look like stone and it has to be smooth.

O.K.

The skin-pass stand is way down at the end between the loading platforms and the tin dip. A crane went over me as I walked down the mill. It had some of this job in its mitten. The mill was all quiet and you could hear it coming way down the line from the annealing ovens. This stuff had just come out of the ovens the night before. The crane stopped by the skin-pass and let the sheets down with a clatter on the rack. They were just small ones. Then it hauled up and went rolling back down the mill with sparks shooting out of the bottom of the cab.

*   *   *

. . . He would always take me down to the mill on Thanksgiving morning and on Christmas. Those were the good old days when they ran day and night without a stop and the sky was red as blood all night and there was plenty of money. Mother couldn't come because she's a girl and girls can't go in the mill. They might catch their dresses in something and get set on fire. It was smoky inside and terrifically noisy and the smoke made me cough. We had to put on dark glasses to go near the furnaces and when they opened the door the heat would make you run. Then there was the man throwing salt on the molten slabs. Bang! The mill would bang down on them and the fire would fly up like fireworks and then when they came out on the rollers the man would throw on the salt and a big cloud of smoke would burst up and the salt would hiss and fizz like bacon frying. I liked to watch that but I liked the cranes best. With everything running you couldn't hear them and they had to blow their sirens so people would watch out and not get hit by whatever they were carrying. I wanted to ride in them but it was against the rules, but one year he let me and we climbed up a ladder to the track and got in the cab and rode up and down the whole mill carrying things and turning the siren. . . .

No need for a siren today. The mill was so quiet you could talk in a natural voice and hear the traffic outside the wall. Big Frank was on the skin-pass. There are two Franks. Poles. Brothers. Big Frank and Little Frank. Little Frank has another name but nobody can say it so they call him after his brother. Big Frank was adjusting the measure screw on the rolls.
Got them fixed?
Yum.
Ready to shoot?
Yum.
How much is there?
Bout tree hunner sheet.

O.K. let's go.

There were two fellows to pull the stuff off the rack onto the moving rollers. And one to watch what came out of the skin-pass and stop anything bad from going on through the smoother and then two more to tote it over to the marking press where I would check on it again before it went to load.

Big Frank started the skin-pass, but they couldn't feed fast because the sheets were stuck a little from the annealing. The fellows on the feed had to give three or four yanks at each piece to get it torn free. The stuff isn't very stiff after the annealing, but steel's steel and that feeding is some job when they stick—a nice big sheet the size of a double bed to play with.

The skin-pass stiffens it up to the hardness that the fellow who's going to make something out of it wants. Then it goes through the smoother to take the kinks out and comes out looking shiny and beautiful. Up to that point it hasn't looked like much of anything but it comes out of the smoother as pretty as tinfoil. Then if they oil it it will shine even better. But there wasn't any oiling on this lot because it was to be painted later.

I checked over each piece for flaws and marked the good side with a chalk cross. Both sides are never the same. One will be a little rougher because of the way the rolls are set in the main stand. So you mark the good side for them to use on the outside. Then it went through the marking press to get trade-marked—a big red brand of an oak tree and

MACDONALD STEEL LASTS FOREVER

I had two fellows moving the stuff. If they kept going they could just keep up with the skin-pass. So they were glad when I would find a flaw and they could rest while I tried to clean it up with a piece of emery paper.

One of them was a fellow I knew, I'd had him in my gang before. Name of Mihacsek. A Croat or something, but born in Pittsburgh. Nice guy. Just about my age. He'd had one year in some college before he came to the mill. Got married and had to work I guess.

Not much on today, he said.

Nothing but this.

They say Carrick is all shut down.

Yeah I guess they are.

I read in the paper General Motors was laying off twenty thousand fellows.

Yeah I read that too.

Looks bad don't it?

You're damn right it looks bad.

What's your old man going to do? Work two days a week?

What can he do? There's no good making steel if you can't sell it.

I had to stop quite a bit and use the emery paper. There were quite a few flaws. Pretty soon I noticed they were all in about the same place. Must have been a rough spot on a roll somewhere.

I hear your dad's pretty sick, said Mihacsek, one of the cops was telling me.

Yeah he had to go to the hospital.

What's he got?

Some sort of a bug. He got an infection and it got into his blood.

That's bad, ain't it?

It's real bad; I was over to see him before I came to work and he's about the sickest looking man I ever saw.

Hell that's too bad. I hope he gets better all right.

Thanks. I guess he'll pull through. He's a pretty tough customer physically.

Never was sick before was he?

No, never had a sick day in his life except when somebody dropped a piece of tube on his foot.

Yeah I heard about that. Out at Braddock wasn't it?

Yeah.

Well, I sure hope he gets better. I suppose he has a lot of doctors and specialists.

Yeah but they can't do much for him. They haven't got any cure for this bug. They say he's just got to fight it out for himself.

Well if he fights it hard as he fought the union. . . .

They say if he can drive the infection out of his blood before the fever weakens his heart he'll get through all right.

Got a bad fever?

Just about burning up. He's sweating all the time like the guys on the open hearth.

I stopped rubbing with the emery paper and looked at the next sheet coming up. The flaws were getting worse—bigger—and all in the same place.

This is no damn good, we can't rub these out, they'll take five minutes apiece.

I hollered over to Big Frank and he stopped the skin-pass and came over.

That's a spot on a roll isn't it Frank?

Yum.

Well, we'll have to dump these, they won't take them with that scar on them.

Yum, that's a bad one.

Look Frank; you go up to the main stand and see what you can find, see which roll it is. They'd better change it before Monday, and I'll ask Riordan what he's got lying around that we could cut down to this size.

Everything was quiet now as we walked up the mill. It was almost dark. No lights turned on and a gray day outside that sent no light through the windows along the roof. Big Frank walked with a roll like a sailor, his big shoulders rounded over and his head down.

Cigarette, Frank?

Danks.

We stopped to light up and then went on. Past the annealing ovens. Past the pickling pits. Past the coiler. Past the cooling rollers. And through the main stand. All still. No smoke. No noise. No fire.

Riordan came out of his office just as we got up to it.

Say I was just coming down after you, the hospital's on the wire, guess you better talk to them.

Oh—sure—

It was Dr. Morris.

Is that Mr. MacDonald? Mr. MacDonald, we've been in consultation here and we think it might be advisable to try a transfusion now.

Is he worse?

No, there's nothing to worry about, no change in his condition, but Dr. Althaus and I feel that a transfusion might help him.

Yeah I see—well do you want—

And we thought if you would care to be the donor. It's generally customary to have someone in the family.

Oh sure, absolutely, anything at all I can—

Well if you could come right over Mr. MacDonald we could test you and see if you'll do.

All right, be right over.

I told Riordan about the flaw and drove right over to the hospital.

It was over on the other side of town, across the hills that rise between the two converging rivers, over by the Allegheny. I took short cuts to avoid the traffic, winding around through slummy back streets. A transfusion. Yes, he would need that. New blood. He hadn't lost any but his was full of germs–streptococci. They could tell from the counts they made. They counted the white cells. They were the fighting cells that got created automatically to fight the germs. When the germs killed them that made pus. They took so much blood and then counted it under the microscope. You were supposed to have only seven thousand white cells and he had twenty-some thousand. So the infection was bad. And the fever. Burning up. Hot to touch and having to change him every few hours because of the sweat. Sweating blood all right. New, clean blood. Mine would mix with his and maybe give it the strength it needed to fight off the infection. How do they do it? Hurt much? Give you anesthetic? Stick a tube in you and run it into him? Why wouldn't it run the wrong way? His run into mine? That wouldn't be so good. I can do without those bugs. Maybe they put you up higher and it has to run down. How do they get into the vein? Or do they have to use an artery in you and a vein in him? And what closes it up when they're finished? People that make a regular business of giving blood. Policemen do it a lot. And that fellow at college that did it when he missed getting his scholarship. Maybe they're better. Might be better to get one of them for him. No the doctor said the family and that means me. Why not? Scared? What if it does hurt? Think what he's suffering. That's the least you can do for him. And whose blood is it anyway? Isn't your blood his to begin with? Without him and mother there wouldn't be any you at all. No you. No me. Nothingness. Non-existence. Like the way you felt when you were little about dying. Thinking hard about it and suddenly getting that awful terrifying feeling of not being anymore. Like the feeling when you shut your eyes to pray and had to get right up to God. Nothing between you and God. No you anymore. Will he die? No. But he's awful sick. Most people do die of this, when it's this kind of bug. No. But if he does? What then? Mr. Jenkins would take over. He's trained him for that. Till I'm ready. Till I'm forty or so. No. I can't. I can't do it. I'm not like him. That's not what I'm made for. I'd try but it wouldn't work and then I'd ruin everything he'd done. I'm not like him. I'm not good with people. People don't follow me. I can't fool them. They know I'm not sure. Like at camp when I couldn't get my points for leadership and at school never getting elected anything and at college not making Ivy. That hurt him. Does he know I can't do it? Is that why Jenkins? No Jenkins is just for till I've learned the job. But he won't die, he won't. He's too tough physically. Never been sick a day in his life.

At the hospital—St. Thomas'—Dr. Klauss was waiting for me downstairs. I liked him the best of the lot—a youngish man with a nice easy way to him, not so doctorish as the rest of them. He was always a little bit sloppily dressed and stood on one foot with a hand in his coat pocket. It irritated Aunt Eleanor and Aunt Margaret but I liked him. He had the soft, relaxed movements of a good athlete. Must have played football in college.

We'll go right over to the lab and see what's what.

It was in a building by itself across the street.

You've been feeling all right yourself, haven't you? Not run down or anything?

Hell no I'm fine.

Well you'll never notice this then. It's wonderful how your body can make new blood for you. You'll have it all back in twenty-four hours.

As soon as that?

Yessir, you eat a good roast of beef tonight and tomorrow you'll be ready to lick Dempsey again.

We went upstairs to the laboratory.

How is he since I was here?

Not any change that we can see.

Does that mean he's worse?

No, I'd say he was holding his own.

Hmm.

That's more than most of them do at this stage, your dad's a strong man.

Yeah, I know. Are they up there with him?

Your aunts?

Yes.

Yes, they've been here all day. They've taken the next room to his.

That must be a big help.

We went into a big room with a long bench under the windows where some interns and a sister were bending over microscopes. One of the interns got up. Jewish looking. Glasses.

Dr. Silverman this is Mr. MacDonald.

Glad to know you doctor.

Now if you'll just set down here on this stool and lend me your little finger Mr. MacDonald. This won't hurt a bit.

He took a glass slide from a case and marked on it with red pencil—II and III—and drew a line dividing them. Then he dropped a drop of clear liquid out of two little flasks on each side of the line.

What's that stuff?

Those are serums made from two of the four main types of blood. We'll mix a little of yours with them and tell from the reaction what type you are.

What type is father?

He's a type II.

Are you usually the same as your father?

No, only about thirty percent are the same.

And if mine isn't you'll have to get somebody else?

Yes. Now let's have your finger.

He rubbed my fingertip with alcohol and before I knew it had jabbed me with his needle making a little ball of black-looking blood swell up from the skin.

There we are, said Dr. Silverman. Dr. Klauss was looking out the window, leaning over the workbench with both elbows on the ledge of the frame.

Two drops of my blood were dropped onto the two drops of serum and then the slide was rotated quickly, held in the doctor's fingers, so that they would mix.

I can't see anything happening. Don't you have to use the microscope? No we can tell without it, it takes a minute or two though.

. . . Maybe I won't be the same and then I won't have to go through with it. They'll have to get somebody else. Afraid. No I'm not afraid. I've been hurt before. Afraid. You're afraid. No. It's not that, it's just that I. . . .

There we come doctor, this will do the business. I looked at the slide.

I can't see any difference.

Sure you can, look. Look at the right one now. See?

Oh—yes—

As I watched something was happening. The reddish smear was coming apart, the red was breaking up into tiny little dots, leaving the rest as it had been before.

He laid down the slide.

That's a help, said Dr. Klauss, that'll save us a lot of time.

But that's type III that did that, you want type II.

No you're type II all right, that's the way type II affects type III. If you were a I or a III or a IV that wouldn't have happened like that to III.

Oh—pretty complicated business.

Not for us, said Dr. Silverman.

How soon will you do it?

Oh, we have to make some more tests first.

How come?

Well we'll do now what we call a cross-agglutination to make sure your blood isn't bad for your father even if it is the same type. And then we'll do a quick Wassermann.

Wassermann? . . . But that's the syphilis test . . . you don't have to do that for me do you?

Oh, you never know, said Dr. Silverman winking at Dr. Klauss, sometimes some of the very best people—

It's the routine, said Klauss, it's part of the state law, they require it.

Oh.

Would you like to look around here while he's doing it? We've got some pretty interesting things here in the lab.

Sure, you bet.

We moved over to the sister who was at work over a microscope and she got up. All in white robes and a little round baby-pink face popping out from the starched veils about her head.

This is Sister Mary Joseph. What do you have here sister, pneumonia?

Yes, pneumonia doctor, we get such a lot of that this time of year.

She's typing the germ. We have thirty-two types of pneumonia and serum for some of them.

Gosh. Thirty-two types that must be some job.

Oh, here's your father's star boarder. Dr. Klauss had picked up a little covered glass dish with red stuff in the bottom of it. Take a look at that, and held it out to me.

You mean that's the bug he has? Yes, we're growing them to study, we're still looking for a serum for those.

Spotted about the red stuff in the dish were little circles of a lighter color.

Are they as big as that?

No, those are colonies we call them, maybe a million or so in each of those little dots. That red is his blood mixed with something to feed the germs on.

And here they are in the bottle, said Sister Mary Joseph, bringing up a flask full of amber-colored liquid, stopped at the mouth with a wad of gauze.

They grow better in broth, the doctor explained, that seems to suit them better.

Nice beef broth, said Sister Mary Joseph, just the same as we eat.

But you just have these things lying around loose like this? Aren't you afraid of catching it?

Oh no, not from these. They seem to lose their virulence when they leave the human body. We can make them reproduce but they get harmless pretty soon.

A telephone rang, it stood on the workbench, and Dr. Klauss answered it.

Hello.

Speaking.

Well, what's the matter with him?

Is he bleeding?

Well, sew him up.

No, I can't come over, I'm busy here.

No, I can't, you do it. Just clean up the edges and sew it up the way you would anything.

Well, you've got to learn sometime!

He banged the receiver back on the hook.

Some butcher whacked himself with a meat ax.

Look, doctor, I don't want to keep you from—

Oh, that's all right. Intern's on the job, he's just scared of it.

But hadn't you better go—

No, he's got to learn sometime. Have a cigarette?

No thanks.

I caught Sister Mary Joseph's eye but it showed nothing. She smiled as we left. I do hope your father gets better, she said.

Thank you sister.

Show you the zoo, said Dr. Klauss. No, wait a minute, I think they've got some cancer in here. He went into another room and put a slide under the lens of a microscope. There, have a look at that.

I looked and saw something blue—a little piece of something covered with thousands of tiny blue lines and dots, all woven together.

Why is it blue?

That's the stain they used to make it show up. This is a very thin slice of diseased tissue embedded in paraffin.

Oh—but where's the cancer?

Those round things, do you see them? That's the cancer, those are cells.

That's what cancer is—cells growing where there oughtn't to be any. Those flowing lines are the healthy tissue. The way it ought to be.

I looked up from the instrument. So that's cancer.

That's it. He picked up the slide and put it back on a card, a hospital form. I glanced over his shoulder at the writing on it.

"Name: Marie Hemlinger.

Symptoms: Has been bleeding since abortion three months ago."

It stuck in my head. . . . Abortion. Bleeding in the womb. Must have gone to one of those unlicensed doctors that do it for fifty dollars. Bleeding. That girl in *Sanctuary*. . . .

As we walked upstairs I noticed that I was trembling a little. . . . Afraid. No, just the hospital feeling. Always hated them. Always terrified. Having tonsils out. Fighting the ether. The smell of them and glimpses of sick people through half-open doors. How can the nurses and doctors stand it all the time. How can they eat with that smell around them. Damn nice of this Klauss to try to amuse me while I have to wait. He knows what it feels like. Good egg. Like to see more of him after this is all over. He'd be damn good on a party. Ask him up to the house. Wonder where he went to college. Maybe better not to ask him. Maybe he went to some little dump.

On the top floor of the laboratory there was the stink of animals and rows of little wire-covered boxes on shelves. White rats. Guinea pigs. Rabbits.

We use the rats for pregnancy tests, said Dr. Klauss. Little soft white things with pink noses huddling against each other in sawdust.

Funny thing is you have to use them just exactly when they're nineteen days old and only the females.

Sounds like magic.

Yes—how they ever found that out beats me. But that's the way medicine is. They're looking for one thing and all of a sudden they stumble on something entirely different. That's probably the way it'll be with the germ your father has. Some fellow in a lab will be hunting for something entirely different and all of a sudden he'll make a cure for strep.

I turned and looked at him.

Look doctor, tell me straight, what sort of a chance does he have, is this thing going to kill him? Will this transfusion fix him up?

Klauss had taken a guinea pig out of its box and was holding it upside down in one hand running one finger of the other along its belly. He held it, looking at it, not at me, while he answered.

We don't know, Don, we can't tell. We know a good deal about it, but we haven't any cure. We know what course the thing will take and we know how to give your father all the help we possibly can and how to keep him from suffering. But it all depends on his strength. It can be licked. I've seen half a dozen fellows lick it. But not many. Most people can't beat it.

You think—you think he'll die then.

No—I don't think I do. Klauss looked up, looked me in the eye. The odds are against him all right but something tells me he's going to be the lucky man. That's just a hunch I have. I really think that. I think your dad's going to get over this.

God, I hope you're right.

He put back the guinea pig in its box, then picked it up again and put its nose near a piece of lettuce.

Eat it.

It doesn't look hungry.

Guess it isn't. We shot this one with some of your father's culture, about four days ago, he's beginning to feel it. About tomorrow he'll be a mighty sick little bunny.

What will that do?

Probably nothing. One of the boys here is working on it, he has some serum he cooked up he wants to try.

God, if he only had it ready now.

It may take him years, maybe all his life, and maybe he won't ever get anywhere.

Well, would it hurt to try it though?

We couldn't do that. That isn't the way the game works. That would be like throwing a pass on fourth down. You see medicine is a lot different from what people think it is. They come into the hospital and see somebody they love dying and all they can think of is the individual. But we don't see it that way. Oh, we try to be sympathetic and human, but we just can't think of the individual, if we did we'd all go crazy. We have to look at the bigger picture. We have to see the thing itself, the disease itself, that each case is just an example of. And we know that we won't win our fight against the thing by luck, by taking shots in the dark. We've got to go at it slowly and systematically and all in the right order. That's what science is. Science is order. We don't have an inspiration and then find a germ. We make about fifty thousand tests according to a logical system and then we study what we've found and narrow it down and go at it again. And that's the reason—

Dr. Klauss—a voice calling up the stair—we're ready now.

Come on we'll go down. No, wait a minute, I want to show you Rameses.

We went out onto a sort of roof terrace and there a big gray sheep came trotting up to us. It must have been white once but the smoke of Pittsburgh had turned it battleship gray. It rubbed its head against Klauss's knee.

We use his blood for serums. Strong old sonofagun, he's been here longer than I have. They bleed him about once a month and it never seems to faze him at all. The nurses make quite a pet of him but once in a while he gets rambunctious and butts them. Knocked one of them out flat last year, didn't you Rameses, laid her right out!

As we left the terrace the sheep followed us to the door and tried to come into the building. Its nose was sticking inside with the near-sighted animal eyes looking up at Klauss. He rubbed its nose with his knuckle and pushed back its head to close the door. But the sheep stayed at the panel window watching us as we went down the corridor.

Dr. Silverman met us on the floor below. It tests fine, he said, no reaction at all. Do you want to see?

We went to the microscope and Klauss looked in. Fine. Take

a peek. I looked and saw a sparkling golden-brown surface, made up of thousands of tiny round cells that looked, in their brilliance, like Chinese lacquer. As I watched I saw that the cells were moving, playing around among each other in ceaseless activity. It was beautiful.

God, that's pretty!

That's your father's blood mixed with yours.

I looked again. It was beautiful—a rich golden red, and the whole shimmering in its movement like sunlight on water.

Dr. Klauss was telephoning. Will you have them get ready for Mr. MacDonald's transfusion, say half an hour?

With Dr. Klauss I crossed the street to the main building. We'd better see what that intern's doing, he said. We went down long twisting corridors full of the smell and activity of sickness to the emergency room. I hesitated outside the door. Come on in, said Klauss, you don't mind blood do you?

I went in. A young fellow in butcher's white was on the operating table with one bloody thigh exposed and a fat intern working over it. The man's eyes were closed in pain and his fingers were gripping the edge of the steel table. Dr. Klauss examined the work and the intern straightened up, wiping the sweat from his face with his apron and beaming. He was pleased with his work.

I hunted all around in there for arteries but I didn't find any so I just went ahead.

No, there wouldn't be any there.

What should I do with him, keep him here?

Sit him out in the recovery room a while and see if he bleeds, if he doesn't you can send him home.

The man opened his eyes for a moment and looked to see who was speaking, then closed them again without saying anything.

O.K. Then there's another there that just came in, back there.

Klauss pulled aside a screen. An old man, rough-faced and gray, in overalls, was lying there. Over one eye was a deep square hole, black with blood. Klauss leaned over him and the ash from his cigarette fell on the man's cheek. He stooped and blew it away, then put his cigarette on the table edge, and studied the wound. Suddenly the old man began to talk, in a broken, mucous-clogged voice.

It doesn't hurt much, he said, and smiled. He was pleased with himself too.

I don't know what it was, he went on. I was just workin' at my wheel and all at once something flew up and hit me. But it missed my eye all right. I can see fine. That's the first thing I did. I opened my eye to see if I could see with it and first I couldn't it was full of blood but then when they wiped that out I could see just the same.

Dr. Klauss had finished his examination and left the man still talking to himself as we went out.

You can find your father's room from here, can't you? I'll meet you there.

In father's room I found my aunts, Aunt Margaret and Aunt Eleanor, his older sisters, clustered about the bed with the nurse.

How is he?

They didn't answer. They had been crying again. They looked at me and then reached for their handkerchiefs.

I stood by the bed and took hold of his hand that lay outside the quilt. So thin. You could feel the bones right through the skin. How much had he lost? Forty pounds? That was the fever. Burning his flesh off him.

The eyes were closed but he wasn't asleep, his breathing was uneven. So wasted. Like a skull. The eyes sunk deep back into their sockets, the lids drawn tight, the skin thin over the bones, the nose standing out like a beak, the mouth falling open as he breathed, the tongue swollen.

He's been like this all day, said Aunt Eleanor, just too tired to open his eyes. He can't even move his head by himself.

But as I pressed his hand the head did move, turning toward me on the pillow, and the eyes came open, blind-looking, the pupils enlarged, staring. I bent my face close into his vision. The eyes shifted, seemed to concentrate, seemed puzzled, then— recognition. The lips widened slowly into a smile, into a grin—a big grin with the teeth sticking out. He knew me.

I squeezed his hand. Hi Pop, how's everything?

Grin. Life in the eyes. Then struggle in the throat and a voice—not his voice, but a voice—mumbling but intelligible, just fine, son, first-rate today.

That's the stuff, I said, you're looking better today.

Yes, feeling better today. And that was all. Exhausted. The smile went away. The eyes dulled and then half-closed again. I stroked his hand and then stretched it back on the spread.

The two aunts were sobbing. I went to the window and stared out. All of a sudden the back of my throat went tight and the tears were in my eyes. I let them fill and the tears wet my face. Like a pain, a feeling like pain, and the tears blinding your eyes.

Two sisters came in and went to the bed.

Well, Mr. MacDonald we're going to take you for a little ride, do you want to come for a ride?

Are they ready?

Yes, we'll just wheel him up in his own bed.

Aunt Margaret took my hand and squeezed it in hers. Oh, dear boy, I think you're wonderful to do this, I just hope it—she broke into sobs again.

Now you two get some rest while we're gone, we won't be long.

He never stirred as the bed was rolled down the hall and into the elevator.

We gave him a little hypodermic so he wouldn't want to move around, said the nurse.

Out of the elevator and into the operating room—the same room that had terrified me out of my senses as a child—but now it was all right. They couldn't hurt me now, nothing would hurt now. These were all good things now—these big lights and mirrors, these cases of shiny knives, these people all dressed in white.

Dr. Althaus was there now and Dr. Klauss and another one—a little round pink one with gold spectacles and a cloth tied around his head like a handkerchief.

This is Dr. Marker, Don, he's our transfusion specialist. We shook hands.

You're not feeling nervous, Don, said Dr. Althaus, you'll hardly notice this.

Naw, he's not nervous, look at him! said Dr. Marker, squeezing my arm. Now you just come in here son and we'll fix you up. This may seem silly but we have to dress you up like a patient and lay you down here on this table just so it'll look like we're doing something wonderful. Matter of fact there isn't anything to it. Just take off your coat and shirt and get into this outfit.

I put it on and lay down on my back on the gurney. This was fine. Nothing to it. Nothing to this. The nurse wheeled me in beside father so that my head faced his and my left arm lay next to his. On a table between us was a simple little gadget that looked like an eggbeater, with a circular crank and two pieces of red tubing coming out of it. Already one of these led to father's arm where a glass needle pierced the vein on the inside of the elbow. The blood showed black in the glass and the blue vein pulsed against the pale white of his arm. So white. And the two bones of the arm, curving into each other, showing under his skin. He had not moved. Just his breathing and the slight opening of the eyelids to show he was not fast asleep. His head square on the pillow. The profile like an Indian's now, just like an Indian's.

The little round doctor fixed a tourniquet about my upper arm, and tightened it.

Now make a fist.

He dabbed the inside of my elbow with alcohol and suddenly

jabbed the needle into my arm before I expected it. It didn't hurt so much.

There we are now, that wasn't so bad was it?

Look, I said, trying to be funny, I'd just as soon you pumped the right way.

Oh, you needn't worry about that, put in Dr. Althaus, the pump is adjusted so it will only flow one way.

Then it struck me what I'd actually said—that wasn't funny, that was just something you didn't say. I felt like saying I'm sorry I said that, but there was no one to say it to. Father lay quiet as ever as Dr. Marker began to grind his little machine and my blood went over to him through the tubes.

I didn't feel anything happening, just discomfort where the needle was in me. I pushed up my head with the free arm to watch what was happening. Click—click—click—click went Dr. Marker's machine as he turned it. There was a counter on it that counted the rotations.

How much is each click? I asked.

Those are centigrams. He answered without taking his eyes off the tubes.

Dr. Klauss explained, he's watching to see that it flows right. Those are very thin rubber tubes and if there was a stoppage on either side it would show right away.

Click-click-click-click.

How is he taking it, Doctor?

Dr. Althaus was at father's side feeling his pulse and watching his face.

Don't notice a thing.

Sometimes there's a bad reaction in these things, said Marker, sometimes the new blood gives them a chill, but he seems to be taking this fine.

Click—click—click—click. My blood in his veins now and he so still.

How much are you going to put in?

Well, we usually take about a pint, that's about five hundred centigrams.

How do you feel? said Dr. Klauss.

Oh, fine.

Click—click—click—click. You know, said Dr. Marker, I've done my darndest to get rid of that clicking noise. Except for that this would be a perfect little machine. But I can't seem to get around it. When you put rubber cushions on there they come off when you boil it. Great little machine otherwise.

Click—click—click. Silence except for that and the bright lights and all the white figures standing so still, watching. Click—click—click. The fat little man's fat little wrist turning rhythmically and his funny serious expression underneath the thing like a handkerchief tied around his head. Watching the black blood in the needles, watching its flow through the tube, watching father's eyes for a sign, and my mind as empty as though all life had stopped and I were far, far away—not a thought, not a feeling, simply watching—far away somewhere, somewhere we have gone, like that time when I was little, somewhere like another world—click—click—click.

And then the clicking slowed and stopped. Well, I guess that'll do it, said Dr. Marker. Any chill? asked Dr. Klauss. No, doesn't seem so.

Well, that's just fine, said Dr. Marker, that's the way we like to have it go.

He pulled the needles out of father's arm and out of mine, dabbing the little black holes with collodium to stop the bleeding.

And that was all there was to it. It was all over. My arm hardly hurt at all and father was still just as still, breathing deeply now as though asleep. A nurse pulled down the sleeve over his arm and lifted it back under the bedcover; it lifted jerkily, like something inanimate and heavy. And then he was wheeled out of the room.

I started to get up, but Dr. Klauss pushed me down again.

Hey there, you've got to take it easy for a bit, you might just keel over if you got up now.

We want you to stay lying down for fifteen minutes, said Dr. Marker, and then you sit up for ten minutes, and then if you feel all right you can get up.

Oh, I feel all right.

Well, you'd be surprised, you just lie there.

I lay back on the table and let them wheel me into the next room.

I'll see you downstairs, said Dr. Klauss.

I lay on my back, looking at the ceiling. My mind was still empty. A peaceful feeling without knowing why.

One of the nurses came in, an operating room nurse, very thin-faced and efficient-looking.

Do you drink? she asked.

Sure.

Whiskey?

Sure, anything.

She went out and came back with a jigger of whiskey. Here, she said, and raised my head with another pillow. I took it down in sips, burning my throat. Bad whiskey.

She filled two tall glasses with water and put one on a table, giving me the other.

You want to drink all the water you can, she said, that will make new blood for you.

You mean that blood's nothing but water?

Oh, it's more than water, but the water will go right into your bloodstream and be the base for new blood.

I started in on the water. Not thirsty, just get it down.

You want to have some roast beef for dinner, she said, good rare roast beef with plenty of blood in it.

She stood surveying me for a moment, sizing me up.

I guess you'll survive, she said, and went out.

I worked away at the water. Two little nurses in blue training uniforms went through the room, looking at me as they went by, and started fussing with something in the next room. Banging around with cans of something. They were talking busily, something about some other nurse and what she said and then I says and she says and if she thinks she can get away with that stuff—they went out. It was quiet now except for distant sounds at the far end of the building. The lights in the operating room were off. It was a dark day outside, making almost twilight where I was. . . . Wonder if it's done him any good? How soon will it take effect? Certainly didn't have any when it went into him. No chill either, maybe he isn't as bad as they think. . . .

When the water was finished I sat up. It felt all right. Didn't even feel weak, just a little different feeling, a little taken out of myself. I wheeled the table to where I could look into the next room. There were a series of connecting rooms with all the doors open, stretching the length of the building. All were dark but the one at the end. It was brilliant with light and there were white figures moving in it. It must be another operating room with an operation going on.

It was like a scene in a dream—the bright room so far away in the darkness, the silence complete, except for little hidden noises, the masked figures moving noiselessly about their business like puppets. Like a dream, far away, some other place, another world—hell, I felt all right. I stood up and put my clothes back on. I felt perfectly all right.

It was quiet and dark down in father's room; the shade was down on the window. He's sleeping, the nurse said.

I stood by the bed. No change. No change at all.

How do you feel? asked the nurse.

Oh, me—fine.

I know you helped him a lot. She had a nice voice, a little on the deep side. I liked her—a big, soft, copious, Italian-looking woman with very gentle eyes. God, I hope so.

Yes, I think he's resting better now, he's quieter. I think he'll be stronger in the morning.

I stood beside him for a moment; no thought came, no feeling. Strange, it might almost have been anyone now. I touched his forehead with my hand, stroked the hair back from the forehead—the way he used to stroke my forehead when I was little and sick with a headache, standing over my bed, putting me to sleep. That brought him back to me—suddenly he came back. This was he, this was my father, and he was sick and dying. Feeling came back to me, tears came—I threw my head down beside his on the pillow, my cheek against his cheek, and let the sobs burst inside me. But the nurse drew me away. You'll wake him, it's better for him to rest now.

I'm sorry—I don't know—

I know, she said, I know how you feel.

But I hadn't wakened him, he was sleeping deeply. I wiped my eyes. Good night, I said, you call me up again tonight about nine and tell me how he is.

All right, she said, good night. You'd better go to bed early.

I was almost all the way home in the car before I realized that I couldn't stand it. The aunts would be there, with their faces red and their handkerchiefs wet and their air of suffering. I looked at my watch—three-thirty. There would still be something doing at the mill. Go there. Not try to work but just see what was doing, whether they found the bad roll.

It was dark in the mill. The lights were on, a light here and there where somebody was working, and the rest black and tenebrous. I walked down to the roll-grinder; old MacCarthy runs it, an old Irishman way past the age limit but still strong and active.

Hi there Mac, did you find the bad one?

Yessir we did. This is the one was makin' the trouble.

The roll was mounted in the turner and revolving while a jet of water at the back played on it and polished in the pumice. MacCarthy sat beside it on a high stool, regulating the flow of water and feeling the roll now and again with his fingers to see how it was coming. The water flashed on the bright smooth shaft of steel as it spun in the light from above. MacCarthy was an artist at this sort of work; he'd been at it for years, maybe forty years or more. He'd gone to work in the mill as a boy, in grandfather's day.

I guess you've been at the hospital?

Yeah.

How is he now, Mister Don, is he a bit better maybe?

It's hard to say, Mac, you can't tell at all what's going on inside him. He just lies there.

Does he know you still?

Oh yeah, he knows me all right.

Well that's some good news.

The roll turned steadily in the light. Quiet now in the mill. Nothing else doing. Just the two of us, shut in by the surrounding gloom.

Well sir, I guess I've known your father as long as any man in the city. Why I can even remember the night of his birth. We were building the Carrick works then and I was on the night gang, and you know your grandfather used to love to come down at night when things were goin' and have a look around. He would drive out to the mill in one of them two-wheeled buggies and maybe stay an hour or two. Well, this night your father was born he was out there because they weren't expectin' your father for a day or two, but he came all of a sudden and that old black your grandfather had workin' in the stable came a ridin' out here to tell him your father was born. We hadn't any telephones or anything like that then.

Those must have been the days, all right.

Well, they was better in some ways and worse in others.

Less damn running around.

Oh, sure. Then I remember when your father was a little boy in short pants. I was in the South Side then, and your grandmother would drive over there sometimes on a fine day and stop her carriage up along the road and just sit there under her parasol watching what was going on. Of course she couldn't come in the mill for the dirt, but your father would be out of the carriage right away and playing around and the first thing he would be down in the mill headed straight for trouble and the black after him to bring him back. Yes sir, I remember that well.

Well, Mac, I want you to know something—you're one of the best friends my father's got. I know that, I've heard him say it. He thinks the world of you.

And don't I know he does? Never a Christmas, Mister Don, never a one goes by that he isn't down here with a gift for me. Yes, they can say what they like, your father's a gentleman, he's a real gentleman and has always been, and that's something you don't see around here anymore and half of them don't even know what it is.

The roll spun on and on and we sat there by it, silently, watching it, fascinated by it, spinning, spinning, and the soft purr of the water on it and the trickle of the water running away in the drain.

Well, so long Mac, I guess I'll be going home now.

Good night to you then, Mister Don.

But I didn't go home even then, even though it was really evening now. Ought to go home and eat roast beef. But something held me, something moved me. I went down past the corner of the mill and then along the north wall that runs right down to the river. At the water's edge there is a raised embankment and there I stopped. You could see the water flowing below, going along slowly, just moving, full of the filth from all the mills, full of the coal-black and the dirty brown of iron. It wasn't so cold for the time of year. Nearly night now. Night coming on. Would he be any better? Would my blood bring him through? Nothing more I can do. Nothing I can do at all. Wait. Wait. Something floated by in the river. What was it? Hard to see in the darkness. A form. Gone now. A piece of wood probably. The way he grinned at me. The way he laughed at me when I was little. His love and the pain in his love because I never did things right. Never angry though. Just suggesting. "I want you to talk these things out with me son, maybe I can help." A light in the sky from the furnaces down the river. Most of them not running now, but one or two still working, casting their pulsing light on the night sky. In the old days the whole sky would be red, bright red, blood red, and beating with life. Like the aurora. Surging, pulsing, the flames storming the darkness. But now faint, very faint, just a tinge of light—like a bright cloud over a distant city—I felt the cold and turned away from the river to go home.

COLOPHON

The text of this book was set in Palatino, a typeface designed by Hermann Zapf (1918-   ). This face designed in the mid-Fifties was influenced by the classic Italian Renaissance types. The design of this book as well as RANDOM ESSAYS is fashioned after the design by Tree Swenson for POUND AS WUZ.

Composed by Books, Deatsville, Alabama.

The book was printed by Princeton University Press, Lawrenceville, New Jersey on acid free paper.